THE SPY
WHO LAID ME

Edited By

ERIC SUMMERS

Herndon, VA

ISBN 13: 978-1-61303-053-0

Published in the United States by STARbooks Press

PO Box 711612, Herndon, VA 20171

Many thanks to graphic artist John Nail for the cover design.
Mr. Nail may be reached at: tojonail@bellsouth.net.

STARbooks Press Titles Edited by Eric Summers

Contents

TAKING IT FOR MOTHER RUSSIA
By Donald Webb

Donald Webb resides in Victoria, BC. He has been published in numerous gay magazines and anthologies. Contact him at: andon402@shaw.ca.

It was going on 4:00 pm when Mikhail Kirov parked his rusty old Lada in the parking lot outside the offices of the General Staff building in downtown Moscow. He'd been summoned to a meeting with Oleg Ivanov, the Chief of the Intelligence Directorate. His mind was in a whirl. As far as he knew, he hadn't done anything wrong. *It must be something major though*, he thought, *or my immediate supervisor would've spoken to me.*

A blast of artic air hit him when he exited his car and rushed into the building. After a security guard checked his ID and did a body search on him, he passed through a metal detector. He waited in the lobby for about 15 minutes, before a young dark-haired hunk came and collected him, and led him to the office of the Chief of Intelligence. The hunk knocked on the door, then pushed it open and announced Mikhail.

Oleg Ivanov, hands behind his back, stood at a window overlooking the Meskva River. He turned and faced Mikhail. "Come on in, young man," he said.

Mikhail was surprised to see an auburn-haired, well-built man, in his mid-forties. He knew there had been many changes in the Directorate since the fall of the old Soviet Union, but he was still expecting to meet an old guard KGB.

Ivanov smiled when he saw the confused look on Mikhail's face. He raised his eyebrows. "Not what you were expecting?"

"Sorry, sir. I thought I would be meeting with Mr. Ivanov."

"Last time I looked in the mirror, I was still Ivanov."

Ivanov walked over to a corner of his vast office, where a sofa and a couple of easy chairs were arranged around a coffee table. He pointed at the sofa. "Have a seat, Kirov."

Mikhail took a seat and then expectantly waited for Ivanov to explain the purpose of his summons.

Ivanov opened a small refrigerator next to the sofa and removed a bottle of Stolichnaya Vodka. He poured a generous amount into two shot glasses and handed one to Mikhail. He raised his glass, clinked it against Mikhail's, and then said, *"Nastarovia."*

Mikhail said, *"Nastarovia,"* then downed the shot. He wasn't a drinker, so the Vodka, sent an immediate warm feeling down his gullet. This is strange, Mikhail was thinking. Why am I sitting here drinking with the Chief, when I thought I'd been called in to be reprimanded?

Ivanov locked his office door, walked over to his desk, pressed a button, and then announced to whoever answered, "I am not to be disturbed under any circumstances."

"Yes, sir," came the response.

On the way back to the sofa, Ivanov removed his jacket and tie and threw them on one of the easy chairs. He sat down next to Mikhail. "You're probably wondering what this is all about, no?" he said.

"Well, yes, sir. I am a bit confused."

Ivanov nodded. "What do you know about Sergei Primakov?"

Mikhail thought for a few moments. "I think he's someone important in the Kremlin, isn't he?"

Ivanov nodded again. "Yes, he is very important man. He's Deputy Director of the Arms Acquisitions Directorate."

Ivanov refilled the glasses with vodka and handed one to Mikhail. *"Nastarovia,"* he said.

Mikhail raised his glass and then downed the fiery liquid. He knew he shouldn't be drinking the second shot – he was already feeling light-headed, but how could he say no to the Chief of Intelligence? He'd be out on the street before he knew it.

A thick mat of salt and pepper hair popped into view when Ivanov opened a number of buttons on his starched white shirt. "It's hot in here," he said. "Take off your tie and jacket."

Mikhail blinked. *What's going on here? It sounds like an order. What should I do?*

Ivanov raised his eyebrows and stared at Mikhail, as though daring him to refuse.

Mikhail's head was spinning when he complied with the order. Ivanov's warm vodka laced breath sent a tingle down Mikhail's spine when he leaned over, undid the top three buttons on Mikhail's shirt, and said, "There, that feels better, no?"

Strange is more like it, Mikhail was thinking. *If I didn't know any better I'd think this guy was putting the make on me.* Mikhail's cock began to expand in his tight pants when he thought about having sex with the masculine Chief.

"Have you ever met Primakov?" Ivanov asked.

"No, sir. I don't even know what he looks like."

"Good. We're concerned about him and need a stranger who can investigate him."

"But, why me, sir? There are many senior agents with more experience?"

Ivanov smiled. "You might be right, but none of them have your special qualifications."

"What qualifications are you talking about, sir?"

3

Ivanov reached over and ran his fingers through Mikhail's hair. "He likes well-built young blonds."

Mikhail held his breath for a few moments. *God, how did they find out about me? I've been so careful? I'm going to end up in Siberia.*

Ivanov moved closer, opened the rest of the buttons on Mikhail's shirt, and then ran his hand over Mikhail's smooth chest. "Don't be alarmed, Kirov, we're in the same situation." He placed his hand behind Mikhail's head and drew the young agent's mouth to his. Mikhail relaxed and opened his mouth to Ivanov's probing tongue. He slipped his hand into Ivanov's shirt and ran his hand over Ivanov's muscular chest. They kissed for a long moment, and then Ivanov broke contact, checked his watch, and said. "Take off your clothes. I have important meeting in an hour, so I don't have much time."

When they were both naked, Ivanov pushed Mikhail back onto the sofa and knelt between his long muscular legs. He lifted Mikhail's dick and rubbed it across his face. "Nice," he said. "You're going to work out just fine." He sucked Mikhail's knob for a few seconds, then he let his lips slide all the way down Mikhail's eight inch boner, not stopping until his lips were buried in Mikhail's silky blond bush. He held still for a few moments, and then he slowly let the stiff shaft slide out of his mouth, took a deep breath, then deep-throated Mikhail again and again.

"Oh yes, sir ... suck my dick," Mikhail moaned. *Shit*, he immediately thought, *I hope it's okay to speak to the Chief in that way? I hope he doesn't take offense*. But he didn't take offense, and kept deep-throating Mikhail.

After a good five minutes of cocksucking, Ivanov sat back on the sofa, licked his lips, and said, "Your turn now. Prove to me you are worthy of assignment."

Mikhail took his place on the floor and stared at Ivanov's magnificent piece. It was thick and long, and tortuous veins entwined the circumference. His juicy skin had slipped back to expose his large knob. Precum oozed from the big hole. *No wonder he's the chief*, Mikhail thought as he took hold of the rod and sunk it into his mouth. Mikhail was an experienced cocksucker, but he could only ingest half the length of Ivanov's dick. He fondled the Chief's big nuts, bobbed his head up and down, and reached up and tweaked Ivanov's nipples.

"Oh, yeah," Ivanov moaned as he wiggled his ass on the sofa. "Squeeze my nuts." And then when Mikhail complied, "That's the way."

Mikhail wanted a taste of Ivanov's tail – he liked eating butch ass, so he pushed the Chief's legs up and buried his face in Ivanov's hairy perineum. The clean masculine aroma stimulated his senses, causing him to pig out on ass. His tongue circled the tasty hole and then slipped right in. He opened Ivanov's sphincter with his thumbs, then tongue-fucked the wide open hole for a few long moments. He slipped two fingers in and probed deeply, not stopping until he felt the Chief's prostate under his fingers. Ivanov's asshole pressed down, and he fucked himself on Mikhail's hand. Saying, "Ah, ah, ah," each time his prostate contacted Mikhail's hard fingers.

He could hardly believe his ears when Ivanov suddenly said. "Fuck me. Shove that big dick up my ass."

Mikhail sat back on his haunches and stared at the lust crazed Kremlin boss. *Thank God, he wants me to fuck him. If he tries to fuck me with his huge rammer I'll walk out of his office regardless of the consequences – no one's getting into my butt.* Ivanov smiled and said, "There's grease in the top right hand drawer of my desk. Mikhail, hoping Ivanov wouldn't change his mind, hurried over to the desk and found the stuff. When Mikhail got back to the sofa, Ivanov held his legs against his chest and spread his cheeks.

After pouring grease onto his fingers, he shoved two of them up Ivanov's widely dilated chute. Ivanov's mouth opened in a wide groan as Mikhail twirled his fingers around and around. "Now! Now!" the Kremlin boss shouted, "Fuck me, quick. I want your big dick inside me."

Mikhail placed the head of his dick at the entrance to Ivanov's chute, then with one mighty thrust, he was buried balls deep in Ivanov's hot silky channel. Ivanov's eyes rolled back, and his mouth opened in a silent scream. Mikhail grabbed his ankles and deep poled him, giving him what he craved. Ivanov grabbed his own dick and jacked off in time to Mikhail's pounding ramrod. "I come, I come," he yelled after they'd been at it for a while, and then salvo after salvo of hot cream erupted from his massive organ. Mikhail's climax soon followed.

He slowly withdrew his slimy dick and then collapsed on the sofa. Now that he'd shot his load, he was scared of the consequences, but he relaxed when a smiling Ivanov said, "Very good fuck." He threw a towel at Mikhail, and used another one to clean himself. "We will do again sometime. Now we speak about business."

He explained that Mikhail was to get close to Primakov to determine if the Deputy Director was selling arms secrets to the Chechen rebels. Mikhail was to play the role of a rich playboy who was only interested in sex. As a cover, they would set Mikhail up in an expensive suite and provide him with an expense account and a BMW.

"You shouldn't have problem getting together with him ... he frequents an upscale bar off Gorky Park. He goes there after he finishes work, around six every day," Ivanov said.

While dressing, Mikhail asked, "What if he doesn't fall for me?"

Ivanov smiled. "He will ... have no doubt. You're his type. He was close to a man who looked very much like you. We have put that man in isolation until this exercise is complete."

"What if he wants to fuck me?"

"You have a problem with that?"

"Well, yeah. I'm strictly a top."

Ivanov shook his head and grimaced. "Smarten up! You're an agent, for fuck sake. You'll have to take it for Mother Russia. If you don't ... there's always ... Siberia." He handed Mikhail a thick envelope. "All the information you will need is in there, including a photograph of Primakov. Don't tell anyone else about this assignment. Contact me directly when you have information. My cell phone number is in envelope."

Mikhail tucked the envelope under his arm and left the Chief's office. As he approached the hunk behind the desk in the reception area, he could hear Ivanov's voice. The guy quickly silenced the voice. Mikhail's face became hot when the guy winked at him, and said, "Hope you enjoyed it. Been there, done that – my hair's the wrong color ... I'll show you out."

# # # # #

Over the next few days, Mikhail moved into the new suite, spent a vast amount of money on new clothes, and studied the contents of the envelope. The photograph of Primakov showed a middle aged man with steel-grey hair. His sharp features gave him the look of a man who didn't tolerate insubordination. In his youth he'd been on the Soviet Union's Olympic gymnastics team and still maintained a trim muscular physique.

On Friday afternoon, Mikhail, dressed in his new finery, walked into the bar Primakov frequented. He immediately recognized Primakov sitting alone at the end of the counter. There were very few other people in the room. Mikhail took a seat at the counter.

"Afternoon, sir," the barman said. "What would you like to drink?"

"I'll have a bottle of Baltika and a shot of Stoli. While you're at it, please give the gentleman at the end of the counter a shot of Stoli."

The barman poured the Baltika into a chilled beer glass and placed it in front of Mikhail. He poured two shots of Stoli, placing one next to Mikhail's beer and one in front of Primakov. Primakov looked over at Mikhail, raised his shot and called out, *"Nastarovia"* and downed the Stoli.

Mikhail raised his shot and said, *"Nastarovia,"* downed his Stoli, then he took a long swig of his beer.

Primakov picked up his amber colored drink and then walked over and joined Mikhail. "Thanks for the drink," he said. Then he squared his shoulders as if he was on a reviewing stand and announced, "I'm Sergei Primakov," as though he expected Mikhail to salute.

Mikhail nodded and shook hands with Primakov. "I'm Mikhail Kirov."

"You know my name?" Primakov asked.

Mikhail shook his head. "No ... should I?"

Primakov smiled and said, "Good. We are equal here."

Over the next few hours they had three more drinks, talked about a number of issues; the Americans, hockey, the UN, and the Olympics. Eventually, the discussion went in the direction Mikhail desired. Primakov checked his watch, and then said, "I would like to take you home sometime, but not tonight. I have another arrangement."

"I'd like that ... I'm disappointed it won't be tonight."

Primakov said, "Good." Then, he handed Mikhail two of his business cards. "Write your name and phone number on the back of one."

Mikhail did as requested and then returned the card. Primakov placed the card in his jacket pocket, and then stood. "Can I give you a ride home?"

"That would be great, Sergei ... can I call you Sergei?"

Primakov smiled and nodded, "Yes you may, Mikhail."

Mikhail placed the business card in his pocket and followed Primakov out of the bar. As soon as they exited, a black Mercedes sedan pulled up at the curb. A young man, in a chauffeur's uniform, jumped out and held the back door open for them. When the driver was back in the car, Mikhail gave him his address.

When they arrived at Mikhail's building, Primakov said, "You live here?"

"Yes, my father bought me a suite in the building."

"Very nice."

Primakov held Mikhail's hand for a few moments, and then said, "I'll give you a call when I'm free."

"Good, I'm looking forward to that, Sergei."

Mikhail patted Primakov's hand then exited the car. The car was still at the curb when Mikhail passed the doorman and entered the elevator.

Mikhail immediately phoned Ivanov and filled him in. "He's going to check you out before making a move," Ivanov said. "Give it a few days and see what transpires. The horny old toad will not be able to resist you. Don't forget, you'll be taking it for Mother Russia. Keep me informed."

When the dial tone came over the air, Mikhail knew he'd been dismissed.

# # # # #

Two days passed before Mikhail heard from Primakov. He was relaxing in his living room when Primakov phoned and invited him over for drinks. Mikhail had a good idea of what "drinks" entailed. He was nervous, but at the same time, he was determined to show Ivanov that he was capable of the assignment. Primakov sent his driver to pick up Mikhail, who deposited him at an impressive townhouse, surrounded by a high steel security fence.

The driver used a remote device to open the gate for Mikhail. "Mr. Primakov will meet you at the door," he said as Mikhail exited the car.

Primakov, dressed in lounging pants and a silk robe, opened the door for Mikhail. "Welcome to my humble abode," he said with a sweeping gesture of his arm.

Very humble, Mikhail was thinking as he took in the richly furnished interior. "I've been looking forward to this, Sergei," he said.

Primakov hung Mikhail's coat in the hall closet and then led him into a solarium at the back of the house. Sweet smelling tropical plants surrounded the glass enclosure. Without asking, Primakov served Mikhail a cold Baltika and a shot of Stoli. They clinked glasses, said, "Nastarovia" and downed the vodka. As Primakov leaned back on the sofa, his silk robe opened wide, revealing his massive hairless chest. When he lifted his arm and placed it on the along the back of the sofa, muscles rippled over his six-pack abdomen.

He lifted a glass of amber liquid and took a sip. "That's good," he said, then, "Why don't you make yourself comfortable. I'd like to see that young body of yours."

Here we go, Mikhail thought, and then he stood and removed his shirt.

Primakov stood up and ran his hands over Mikhail's smooth chest and back. "Wonderful," he said. "Let's have a look at your legs."

Mikhail kicked off his loafers, then slowly undid his belt and opened his fly. His gray slacks slipped to the floor. Primakov knelt in front of Mikhail, removed Mikhail's pants and socks, and then ran his hands up and down Mikhail's hairy legs. "Beautiful, beautiful," he said. Mikhail's hard on bounced out of his briefs when Primakov slipped them down his legs. Primakov closed his eyes and rubbed his face in Mikhail's pubic bush. A long groan emanated from his mouth when he rolled Mikhail's nuts against his chin. He nuzzled Mikhail's moist nuts for a few moments, and then he stood up and stripped.

A gasp escaped from Mikhail when Primakov's dick came into view. The thick shaft, at least ten inches long, sprung from his groin and curved up to his navel. *Oh, God*, Mikhail was thinking, *is he actually going to shove that monster up my ass?*

Primakov smiled when he saw Mikhail's reaction to his dick. He took it in two hands and slowly thrust it back and forth through his fists. "You like?" he asked.

What could Mikhail say? He could hardly slip on his clothes and run out of the house. He didn't want to end up in Siberia. He nodded, "It's fantastic. I've never seen such a weapon." But he was also thinking, No wonder he's in charge of Arms Acquisitions.

With Mikhail on top, they lay on the floor in a sixty-nine position. He held Primakov's dick in his fist and tongued the broad head. Precum oozing from the hole, coated his hand. He tried valiantly to deep throat Primakov, but he could only get the head in his mouth, so he used his hand on the bottom half of the shaft. Primakov pulled Mikhail's ass to his face and rimmed his virgin orifice. Mikhail, thinking, maybe I can fuck him, raised Primakov's legs and tucked then under his arms. He stared at the surprisingly hairless valley for a short moment, and then he dropped his head and sucked on Primakov's asshole. The great man's sphincter slowly opened, allowing Mikhail's tongue entry. Mikhail rimmed him for a few minutes, and then he slowly pushed a finger in and probed deeply.

11

Meanwhile, Primakov was doing his own probing. Mikhail gasped aloud when two fingers slipped into his chute. Nothing foreign had ever been inside him. He lay dead still on top of Primakov, and tried to relax as the fingers in his ass probed deeper and deeper, eventually massaging his prostate. He couldn't believe how good it felt. He spread his legs further apart and pushed back on the fingers. "You like?" Primakov said as he pushed another finger in. Mikhail felt as though his ass was on fire, but he was enjoying every minute. It felt good to assume the passive role for a change.

Primakov rolled Mikhail onto his back on the rug then stood. "I'll be back," he said, then disappeared from the room. Now's when I take it for Mother Russia Mikhail was thinking when Primakov returned with a large towel in one hand and a bottle of oil in the other. He lifted Mikhail's legs to his chest, placed the towel under his hips, and then squirted a large amount of oil over Mikhail's hole. He crouched next to Mikhail's butt and ran his fingers back into Mikhail's virgin chute. Mikhail slowly ran his hand up and down his stiff pole as he watched Primakov violating his nether end. Primakov kept at it for a long time. Mikhail was amazed when four of Primakov's fingers were sliding in and out of his hole. He'd never thought he would like it, but he did. In fact the feeling was amazing.

Now on his knees between Mikhail's legs, Primakov oiled his huge boner. When he placed the head of his dick against Mikhail's opening, Mikhail said, "Please, take it easy ... I've never done this before." Primakov nodded, and then slowly, centimeter by centimeter, slid the head of his rod into Mikhail's chute. Mikhail was hyperventilating. He wanted to move away and yell, "No, I don't want it!" but he really did want to see what it would feel like to be fucked, so instead, he pushed down, then watched Primakov's shaft sink into his channel. He couldn't believe the erotic feeling. There was some pain at first, but then he only felt pleasure as his chute accommodated the massive intrusion.

Once his cock was fully buried, Primakov rested on his hands and toes, and slammed in and out of Mikhail, who could feel the monster deep inside of him, battering his prostate. Mikhail squealed like a pig when his untouched dick, suddenly and spontaneously erupted, shooting cum over his face and neck. He could feel Primakov's dick pulsing as he deposited his seed deep in his ravaged chute.

Afterward, when they were cleaned up and dressed, Primakov said, "I would like to see you again, are you willing?"

Mikhail nodded. "Yes, I want to see you again, Sergei."

"Good."

# # # # #

For the next two weeks, their affair continued, and Mikhail was getting accustomed to the daily pummeling. In fact, he couldn't get enough of Primakov's big dick and loved every minute of their sessions. He had never seen any evidence of Primakov's culpability and secretly hoped he never would. After they'd fucked on a Sunday night, and he was ready to leave, Primakov said, "I have to be at an early morning meeting tomorrow. Would you be able to drop something off for me and pick up a package in return?"

Oh. Fuck, Mikhail thought, *here we go*. "Sure, Sergei, I can do that."

Primakov gave him a thick envelope and instructions about where to deliver it. When they kissed at the door, Mikhail felt like Judas, but *what the fuck*, he thought, *suck it up, you're an agent*. When he arrived home, Mikhail phoned Ivanov. A team of agents accompanied Ivanov when he stepped into Mikhail's suite. They opened the envelope. Sure enough it contained state documents. Primakov's fingerprints were lifted from the documents, and a DNA sample was taken from the flap.

The next morning, Mikhail delivered a different envelope to the contact and received one in return. The contact was immediately arrested. Later that day, Ivanov phoned Mikhail, and said, "Primakov, of course, pleading his innocence, is locked up. The state thanks you."

"I enjoyed taking it for Mother Russia, sir," Mikhail said.

"Good. I want you to stay in that suite until further notice. I might need you for another assignment. I'll be over later to see how well you learned to take if for Mother Russia."

THROUGH THE WALL
By Kitty Key

Kitty Key shares a condo with two adorable rescue dogs. When she's not taking them for long walks on the beach, she works for an international marketing firm. Her short fiction has been previously published in the STARbooks collection *Rock & Roll Over*.

Ben knows little to nothing about Ford. He doesn't know his favorite food or color or what he likes on his pizza. He doesn't know if he was ever married or even his real name. The list of supposedly true known facts on one Michael Ford can be counted on one hand: he's married to his job; he enjoys hurting people in the name of his job; guns are his favored weapons on the job; he has a hard-on for vehicles typically driven by people who had his job in the Nixon-era; and he can converse entirely in grunts and facial expressions. All of these facts are related to Major Ford, the NSA Agent and not Michael, the gruff co-worker/neighbor who is supposed to be his friend. Well, at least in front of the rest of the world. They're undercover, after all.

At the moment, Ben's supposed to be hacking into their target's computer, but he can't really focus with Ford breathing down his neck. Finally, Ben gives up and turns in his seat to face Ford, who is leaning over the back of the couch and not-so-patiently waiting for Ben to do his thing.

"When you were a kid, what did you want to be when you grew up?"

Ford doesn't blink in surprise at the random question. He doesn't do much of anything other than continue to scowl. The scowl is pretty damn effective. Ben holds back the girlish "meep" sound that's creeping up his throat and goes back to staring at the computer screen in front of him. He tries not to think about how close Ford's lips are to his ear and how easy it would be to turn and kiss him.

# # # # #

They're on a stake-out in front of some alleged terrorist's house and nothing is going on. Ben wonders if stake-outs are always this boring. On TV and in movies, it seems like the cops are only there for a few minutes before they catch the bad guy red-handed. He and Ford have been sitting in the dark for an hour and not so much as a tree branch has moved. Ben didn't realize being a spy was going to be so boring when he signed up with the CIA.

"Can we turn on the radio?" Ben asks as he shifts in his seat to try and get comfortable.

Ford doesn't answer or even look his way.

"This is really boring," Ben continues.

Ford twists his neck a bit to glance into an alley next to the house.

"Do you even like music?"

Ford grunts slightly, which is at least some kind of response.

"I mean, you are human, right?"

Finally, Ford turns around to look at him with his ever-present scowl. "Shut up, kid."

The scowl is still intimidating, but not as much as in the beginning. Ben allows one corner of his mouth to turn up. Something that might be amusement flashes in Ford's eyes before he turns back to watching the house.

# # # # #

"Yes, I'm human," Ford says out of nowhere as they're walking into the courtyard of the apartment complex.

"Huh?"

Ben can't hear too well at this point. There had been many explosions and guns. He vaguely wonders if his health insurance covers hearing aids. Surely the government would want its assets to hear, right?

Ford does the scowl thing and then shakes his head. "C'mon, let's get you cleaned up."

There are thin lines of blood running down Ben's white shirt. He follows Ford because he doesn't know what else to do after seeing someone shot right in front of him. Not just right in front of him, but close enough to get sprayed with bodily fluids. Vaguely, he wonders if Ford happens to have a washer and dryer among all that spy equipment. Or at least bleach.

# # # # #

Ben is shaking like a leaf by the time he's given his shirt over to Ford. He buries his head in his hands and wonders not for the first time why he thought it was a good idea to sign on with the CIA. This is not something Ben ever pictured himself doing when he was a child. He is not James Bond or Jason Bourne or some other famous spy. All he ever wanted to do was write code for video games. Was that too much to ask?

"Here."

As Ben looks up, Ford throws a towel in his direction. Ben rubs it over his sweat-soaked face and then just holds it in his hands, twisting it back and forth. He's surprised when Ford settles down next to him.

"You've got some blood on your neck," Ford says casually without looking away from a pile of surveillance equipment.

Before Ben can move to find yet another splotch of some dead guy on his skin, Ford snatches the towel out of his hands and rubs at the spot gently. He's close enough that Ben can feel Ford's breath against his face.

17

"There," Ford says as he leans back again.

His voice sounds soft instead of gruff like it normally does. Ben turns his head to say thank you or something similar, but he gets caught up in this slow melt that Ford's eyes are going through. It seems as if he's watching glaciers turn to pools and Ford just lets him. It's an actual moment of human interaction that doesn't involve protecting the country or any of that shit.

In the back of his mind, Ben wonders if he should kiss Ford. Something about Ford makes him question everything about himself. He brushes his fingers against Ford's wrist just to test the waters. Ford freezes for just a second. Not long enough that any random stranger would notice, but long enough for Ben to sense it.

"I know you're human," Ben says softly.

That's when he leans in and kisses Ford. For a brief, glorious moment, Ford kisses him back with all the passion Ben suspected was lurking underneath the hard ass exterior. Strong hands grip Ben's shoulders and he slides closer, letting a leg hook over one of Ford's. His own hands press against Ford's waist, feeling the hard musculature there. He wants to move into Ford's lap, into Ford's very personal space, into his life until Ford is forced to acknowledge him as more than just a charge who can hack into any system imaginable, but as regular guy. A regular guy who really wants to stay right here pressed up against Ford's warmth for the rest of the night.

Of course, Ford pulls back before Ben can squirm any closer. He firmly pushes Ben away.

"You need to go home."

Ford's voice is low, gruff yet shaking just a bit. Ben is glad he doesn't say something cliché like "we can't do this," but he doesn't like this kind dismissal either.

"Ford ..."

The pools of warmth in Ford's eyes start to freeze up again. He stands up and walks to the far corner of the room.

"You're feeling vulnerable. It's natural to want to be close to someone." Ford makes a sound that's almost like a sigh. "But it can't be me."

Ben wants to argue against this faulty logic, but he knows doing so would be pointless. This is a man who follows orders and one of them is surely "don't fuck around with your charge."

# # # # #

"I know about the bug in here. I know you can hear me," Ben says to the ceiling once he's showered and retired to his room. "And you probably have to listen to me, so really you have no choice but to sit there and take this."

He takes a deep breath and tries to imagine what Ford's doing as he listens to this. Probably scowling.

"Maybe I was feeling vulnerable, but that isn't the first time I've wanted to kiss you. It won't be the last either. You do things to me that I don't even understand. Maybe if things were different. If I wasn't your charge. I don't know why, but I like you. It's completely counterintuitive all things considered. I guess office romance is a no-no in the spy business, but I wish it wasn't."

Ben lies back against the pillows and sighs. "I just thought you should know."

# # # # #

Awkward is definitely the word Ben is looking for to describe today. Every time he happens to run into Ford in the office, he stammers and blushes, and Ford scowls and then stomps off. Ben isn't even sure what he's trying to say through all that stammering. His mind kind of goes blank in Ford's presence, but he knows he should say something, so he tries to act normal, but normal is impossible now.

19

Besides his inability to speak around Ford, there's also the dozen times other co-workers have caught him daydreaming. Of course, they tease him for it, accuse him of falling asleep on the job, but the very thought that any of them could suspect he was really fantasizing about Ford causes a fit of babbling that has more than one co-worker walking away with their hands raised.

Eventually, Ben starts staring at his watch, counting down the hours, minutes, seconds until he can escape this extremely bad sitcom that has become his life at work. As soon as the clock ticks over to five, he's rushing into the locker room to grab his stuff and get out of there. Of course, Ford is waiting by the car because obviously life hates Ben.

"Ford."

The fact that Ben can even utter the other man's name is surprising at this point. Ford just grunts in return and pulls open the passenger door before walking around to the driver's side. Ben frowns, but slides into the car. Before he can finish buckling up, Ford has gotten in the car and started it up. He drives away from the office, but not in the normal direction.

"Where are we going?" Ben asks nervously.

Ford looks at him out of the corner of his eye and smirks a bit. That doesn't do much to reassure Ben. At all.

# # # # #

They wind up at a beach, which both of them are woefully overdressed for at the moment. Not that either of them have moved to get out of the car.

"So ..." Ben says in the hopes that Ford will start talking.

"This has to stop."

Ford looks at Ben with those steely eyes. His voice is firm. Obviously Ben is not only supposed to know what Ford is referring to, but he's supposed to agree.

"What?" Ben asks instead.

"If you keep ..." Ford wrinkles his nose a bit, "pining over me, you're going to compromise everything. They'll assign you to another agent."

"I'm not. I mean, I ..." Ben begins to babble as he desperately fights back a blush.

"You are."

Ben feels this bubble of anger rising up beneath his embarrassment. He turns his head and glares at Ford.

"Excuse me for being human."

Before Ford can say much of anything, Ben is out of the car, slamming the door behind him. He walks away, and Ford doesn't stop him.

# # # # #

For the next week, Ben finds himself snapping at everyone from his mother to little old ladies at the checkout lane. He avoids Ford like the plague and everyone else at work mysteriously finds something else to do any time he gets near them. At home, Ben sticks to his bedroom, where he searches for surveillance devices and abuses the hell out of the controllers to his game consoles.

The only person who doesn't seem to be afraid that Ben will go homicidal on him is his best friend, Matt, who tries to get Ben to open up and explain what's going on, but Ben doesn't respond. He hates himself for feeling anything toward Ford and he wants the NSA Agent and the CIA out of his life for good if this is what it's going to be like with them in it.

# # # # #

On Saturday, Ben is in a hardware store of all places when he spots one of the suspects he and Ford had been trailing weeks before. He really just wants to ignore what he sees, so he doesn't have to deal with Ford and/or the end of the world but winds up telling his handler about it anyway. There's a lot of planning and plotting after that with another agent, Lily, who is probably one of the most kick-ass women Ben's ever met. During which Ben sits on Ford's couch and stares blankly at the spot Ford had been sitting in when they kissed.

"Ben?" Lily shakes his shoulder lightly. "Do you agree with the plan?"

"Yeah, sure, whatever," Ben answers even though he hasn't been paying attention.

"Good." Lily nods in satisfaction. "Ford, you'll get him prepared then?"

Ford nods, and Lily heads out of the apartment. Probably to sharpen knives or plant bugs or whatever it is she does in her spare time.

"C'mon," Ford says gruffly before heading into the bedroom.

"Huh?" Ben blinks and then cautiously follows Ford.

Inside the room, Ford is in front of the closet, flipping through clothes. Considering that most often, Ben sees Ford in a suit or a tuxedo, he's surprised to see other forms of clothing in there. He's even more surprised when Ford starts pulling stuff off of hangers and tossing them at him. Somehow, he manages to catch all of the garments including a silky black thong.

"Umm, Ford?" Ben asks warily. "What is all of this for?"

"You."

A grinning Ford has always been a scary thing, but now Ben feels this little flutter in his stomach on top of the fear. It's quickly extinguished when Ford tosses a pair of combat boots at his stomach.

"Get dressed, Ben."

# # # # #

No one had ever told Ben that leather chafes, but it does. It's all he can seem to think about even though Lily has her hands all over him, attaching wires and straightening cuffs. When she's finally done, she hands him a wallet with an ID in it. Ben stares at it and wonders where he's supposed to put it.

"Your name for this mission is Viktor Gorsky. Your parents emigrated from Russia when you were a child if anyone asks," Lily explains as she shows Ben the ID before shoving the wallet in his boot.

"I don't speak Russian," Ben reminds her.

"I know," she responds in that I-have-seen-your-file-you-know tone of voice. "You won't be expected to speak it. The guy you're meeting is an American."

"Shouldn't Ford be doing this?" Ben asks with a frown.

"He doesn't fit the profile."

"What profile is that?" Ben swallows nervously.

"Weren't you paying attention?"

Ben can't tell her that he was too busy thinking about Ford to listen to spy-stuff, so he just nods.

# # # # #

The bar is kind of tasteful and innocuous if you ignore the fact that the flat screen TVs are showing gay porn and all the staff are wearing nothing but thongs. Ben tries not to feel nervous. He tries to be Viktor Gorsky, whoever that is, and keeps reminding himself that all he has to do is chat up the owner of the bar, so he's distracted enough to not notice Ford and Lily raiding his backroom, which is possibly the only part of the plan he managed to retain.

He finds the owner sitting in a booth in the corner with a laptop in front of him. On either side of him are half-naked guys that look remarkably like himself, which finally explains the whole fitting-the-profile part of the equation. After taking a deep breath to shore up his confidence, Ben does what he thinks is a pretty good imitation of a model's catwalk over to the booth.

"May I help you?" One of the naked guys asks in this kind of catty tone of voice.

"No," Ben answers as he looks to the owner.

The guy looks up from his laptop and gives Ben a very slow once over. "Who are you?"

Ben starts to say his own given name, but covers it up with a smirk. "Get rid of them and maybe you'll find out."

After a long staring contest with Ben, the guy dismisses his lackeys with a wave of his hand. They slide out of the circular booth, glaring at Ben the whole time.

"You have my undivided attention."

Without being asked, Ben slides into the booth and then palms the laptop closed before the guy can stop him. He's surprised by his boldness. Maybe Ford has rubbed off on him.

"Now I do."

"Who are you?" the guy asks again.

"Tell me your name first," Ben says. Mainly because he doesn't know the guy's name since he wasn't paying attention during most of the whole planning the operation thing.

There's another staring contest and then the guy finally says, "Adam."

"Well, Adam," Ben says as he slides even closer. "It's a pleasure to meet you."

Adam smirks a little. "I'm sure. Aren't you going to give me your name, sweetheart?"

"If you behave yourself," Ben finds himself saying. "For now, you can call me Eve."

That earns Ben another smirk, which he feels pretty proud about until Adam grabs him by the back of his neck and pulls him closer, almost into his lap.

"Where's your apple?" Adam murmurs as his hand slides up Ben's thigh into seriously dangerous territory.

Ben is pretty much thinking things like "holy shit" and "this is a bad guy so it shouldn't feel good, right?" and "is it against the spy code to get turned on during a mission?" at this point, but he tampers down the upcoming I'm-freaking-out moment and guides Adam's hand up even further. Adam's thumb brushes up against the laces on the front of Ben's pants, and Ben gasps. He exposes his neck a bit, and Adam takes the bait. His tongue snakes slowly up before his teeth nip at Ben's ear. Ben is panting pretty heavily at this point and he almost doesn't hear Lily over the tiny earpiece she hooked up along with everything else.

"Ben. Adam should have a jump drive on his laptop. Grab it and get out of there."

Out of the corner of his eye, Ben sees the device. He tilts Adam's head back up and ghosts his lips against the corner of his mouth. When he's sure he's got Adam's full attention, he gives right back with that staring contest thing while reaching for the device. He surprises himself when he manages to palm it without Adam noticing. Slowly, he slides toward the edge of the booth, dragging Adam by his tie as though he's going to take him to a back room or whatever someone else would do in this situation. When he's in a position to get out of the booth quickly, Ben yanks Adam closer by his tie and kisses him hard.

"It's Viktor," Ben says before standing up and walking away toward the exit.

He expects someone to stop him with a gun or perhaps a large fist, but that doesn't happen. Instead, when he

25

glances back, he sees Adam following him about twenty feet behind. Ben smirks and exits the building.

# # # # #

He nearly screams when someone grabs his arm and yanks him around the corner, but quickly calms down when he sees that it's just Lily.

"Good job, Ben." She smiles at him and holds out her hand. "Where's the drive?"

Ben places it in her palm and takes a deep breath. "Are we done?"

"You are. Ford's going to get you home safe. I need to get this data analyzed."

At that point, Ben notices Ford lurking further in the shadows. Ben swallows hard as he wonders if Ford saw what he did with Adam. "Okay."

Lily nods at Ford and then takes off. For the longest moment, Ben just stares at Ford. He figures Adam will find them like this, frozen in awkwardness, when Ford nods toward the car at the end of the alley.

# # # # #

Ben is still feeling an adrenaline rush coupled with shock that he actually managed to do some cool spy thing without messing it up when Ford pulls up to the apartment complex. For the entire ride from the bar to home, Ford had been silent. The kind of deadly silence that used to scare the shit out of Ben, but this time he had hardly noticed. As he follows Ford to his apartment to change back into his regular clothes, he stares at Ford's ass and wonders what it would be like if things were different.

Inside the apartment, Ben realizes that things are different. He's still dressed up as Viktor. Maybe if he could do the cool seduction thing on Ford like Viktor did on Adam, it would work.

"Take that stuff off," Ford barks at him. "Be careful with the wires."

Ford turns away, but Ben grabs his shoulder and is pretty surprised when he manages to shove Ford against the door. He curls his fingers into the lapels of Ford's shirt and looks at him through his lashes.

"Make me."

A strangled sound that might be a laugh escapes Ford's throat. "Very funny, Ben. I don't have time for this."

"It wasn't a joke, Michael," Ben murmurs. "And my name is Viktor. You'd do well to remember that."

Ford's eyes narrow slightly. He's probably wondering if Ben has been drugged or has turned to the other side or something. Maybe he's confused over the use of his first name. Either way, he doesn't push Ben away. Ben smirks and slides one hand down Ford's stomach to the waistband of his pants. He can feel the muscles tense under his touch and hear the slight hitch in Ford's breath. In a surprisingly deft manner, Ben manages to pull Ford's gun out of its holster. He tosses it aside and as it thumps on the floor, Ford tries to pull away from the door. Ben grabs him by his tie and pulls him close.

"Going somewhere?"

Before Ford can answer, Ben is kissing him. Not just a brush of the lips leading up to something passionate like their first kiss, but a full-on, full-throttle, biting, licking, penetrating I-want-to-fuck-your-brains-out kiss. He waits until Ford kisses him back with just as much pent up frustration before he pulls away, slowly dropping Ford's tie as he goes. As Ford stares at him slack-jawed, Ben turns around and walks toward the bedroom. At the door, he pauses and looks over his shoulder.

"Coming?"

There's a delay that's long enough for Ben to kick off his boots and start wondering (a) how he's managing to act so cool and (b) why Ford is going along with it, but then Ford is shoving him up against the wall and attacking his lips with hard bites and little licks and thinking is pretty much no longer an option. He tugs at Ford's clothes, tearing them off and pushing them aside to get to more skin until Ford is wearing nothing but his tie and a pair boxer shorts. Ben, meanwhile, still has the leather pants on.

He pushes Ford onto the bed and straddles his thighs while grabbing Ford's wrists and pinning them down at his sides. He leans in a bit to whisper in Ford's ear.

"You know you want this."

Ford groans in response. It's obvious that every physical pause in the action is making Ford mentally pause. Ben stares down in Ford's eyes.

"Admit it," Ben demands.

"Please," Ford whispers. It's so low that Ben almost misses it.

"Say it," Ben growls.

"I want you."

It's barely a murmur and the struggle behind the admission is clear, but Ben presses on. He knows it's only Ford's training that's talking. If Ben really was someone else, he's sure Ford wouldn't have an issue. So he gives Ford a triumphant smirk before ravishing his mouth again. This time, Ford melts right into it, and Ben loses his cool then, desperately grabbing for their remaining clothing, ripping at it until Ford's wearing just the tie and Ben's pants are halfway down his thighs. It's okay though, because Ford seems to lose control himself, easily flipping Ben onto his stomach.

"Ben," Ford says, voice gritty and desperate.

"Please," Ben begs. "Don't stop now."

To Ben's relief, Ford does anything but that. The leather pants are ripped off completely but instead of spreading Ben's legs, Ford pushes them together, tighter.

"I can't … I can't," Ford says.

Then his cock is sliding between Ben's ass cheeks, his thighs. It's not exactly what Ben is looking for, but he'll take a compromise, so he flexes, pulls his legs together even tighter, bending his knees just slightly. Ford fucks into the channel they've created and it's close, but not close enough. Ben's on the edge, the friction of the bed sheets against his cock not quite enough to send him over.

"Please," Ben groans. "Please."

Ford drags their right hands underneath Ben and then down to his cock, Ford's hand guiding Ben's as they both jerk him off.

It's so hot to be completely at Ford's mercy like this, to let Ford take the lead, just like he does in their working relationship. Ford's hips are moving faster against Ben, his mouth spilling nonsense about how hot Ben is and how he's Ford's. He bites hard at the nape of Ben's neck as he comes, and the feeling of it splashing against his lower back and thighs, marking him, pushes Ben over the edge. He comes with a loud cry, shaking so hard afterward that his knees give out, and he collapses back onto the bed sheets in a heap.

# # # # #

The next morning, Ben wakes up alone and disorientated. He stumbles around the room before realizing that he's stumbling around Ford's bedroom and naked, no less. Quickly, he throws on whatever clothes he can find and heads out into the living room. Ford isn't there either, but the clock says it's long past time to be at work. Ben groans and heads to the door. Maybe if he hurries, he can be one hour late instead of two, and his boss won't fire him.

On the door is a note, which is held in place by a knife. Ben gulps a bit and then tears the paper down to read it. In block letters, it reads:

NOTHING HAPPENED.

"Well, that's a total lie," Ben mutters to himself.

It's probably some spy-speak for "don't mention to Lily (or anyone else) that we had sex last night." Ben folds the paper in half and slips it into his pocket before hurrying off to his own apartment.

# # # # #

Somehow, Ben manages not to notice the marks on his body until Matt points them out, loudly.

"Dude, you really got into your role last night, huh?"

There's some winking and nudging that Ben ignores in favor of subtlety adjusting one of the webcams so that he can get a look at his neck. Sure enough, there are Ford-sized teeth marks on his collarbone, which Matt never would've seen had Ben actually bothered to button up his shirt all the way before entering the office.

"Ben."

Quickly buttoning his shirt up all the way to the neck, Ben turns to see Lily standing at there. Ben ignores Matt's catcalls and follows her over to a conference room.

"We've got a situation," Lily says under her breath as she closes the curtains.

"Yeah?"

Ben settles down and tries to prepare himself for whatever Lily is going to say. Of course, Ford showing up a few seconds later doesn't help with that much. Or at all.

"We're working on compiling the information we recovered from the mission last night and should have enough to bring Adam Shepard in soon, but ..." Lily sighs. "He's developed a bit of an infatuation with Viktor."

"And?" Ford shrugs.

"Well, we can't exactly have Shepard running into you only to find that Viktor," she pauses and looks pointedly at Ben, "is actually Ben."

"Okay, so can't you just, like, hide me or something until you nab him?" Ben asks, not really getting why this is such a huge issue.

Lily goes on for a long time about how many resources Adam Shepard has and how he's got a lot of his men looking for Viktor and if they can't find Viktor, it's going to look suspicious and that's going to compromise the mission. Her argument is followed by Ford's rather short one in which he talks about monitoring Shepard and not letting him get anywhere near the asset. The fact that Ford is calling him The Asset again instead of last night's "god fuck more Vitya" is disconcerting. Not that Vitya is Ben's name either, but rather Viktor's pet name. But it's something.

"No big deal," Ben finally interjects. "Viktor will just make another public appearance."

There's some grumbling from Ford, but it's not as if he would ever actually say to Lily, "over my dead body you're letting some guy grope Ben again," so he lets Lily lead Ben out the back way instead, which disappoints Ben on some level. Not that he really expects Ford to admit anything about them, ever.

# # # # #

"Viktor, what a surprise," Adam smiles as he embraces Ben.

"How could I pass this up?" Ben gestures at the party swirling around them.

The party is on the back lawn of Adam's huge mansion. Most of the guests are corporate titans and diplomats with a splash of trophy wives, gold-diggers, and celebrities. In other words, your typical high-powered Los

Angeles party. Not that Ben has ever been to one of those before now.

He lets Adam lead him around and introduce him to people. Through the whole thing, Ben tries to be in the mind frame of Viktor. So he flirts and teases all while maintaining this aura of "you wish, baby." Meanwhile, he's waiting for Lily's voice in his ear, telling them that they're coming in to grab whatever it is they're after and to arrest Adam.

Ford is lurking around as one of the wait staff, and Ben can feel his glare every time Adam touches him, even in the most innocent of manners. Those glares touch something inside Ben, something that makes him want to make Ford insanely jealous. Make Ford reconsider this whole "nothing happened" plan. So he leans and licks Adam's neck when Ford passes by and then smirks when mister super-spy drops an entire tray full of champagne glasses.

# # # # #

Hours later, when Ben is nearly drained from pretending to be something he's not, he finally gets the all-clear from Lily. He excuses himself from Adam under the guise of getting something to drink but instead heads up the lawn and through some bushes. Peering through the branches, he sees a squadron of agents descend on Adam, who surprisingly doesn't put up much of a fight. Probably because Ford knocked him down before he even had a chance.

# # # # #

After the debriefing, Lily pats Ben on the back and then takes off. Instead of going home, too, Ben stays planted on Ford's couch.

"Good job," Ford says gruffly.

His eyes betray his voice though. It's obvious to Ben that Ford never expected Ben to be good at this spy stuff. It's also obvious that it's somehow hurting Ford that he is.

"Thanks," Ben says quietly.

There's a very long, awkward pause, and then Ford sits down next to Ben on the couch.

"Did you really have to hang all over him like that?" Ford finally asks.

"No, but Viktor did."

Ford meets his eyes again and frowns slightly.

"Do you have a problem with that, Agent Ford?" Ben frowns back.

"No, but Michael does."

Ben blinks in surprise and that's when Ford kisses him. It's all passion and longing, caresses and nips, and it's a thousand times better than last night or even their first kiss because it's Michael kissing Ben and Ben kissing Michael back, as an equal.

SECRET AGENT MAN
By Rob Rosen

Rob Rosen (www.therobrosen.com), author of the novels *Sparkle: The Queerest Book You'll Ever Love*, *Divas Las Vegas*, *Hot Lava*, *Southern Fried*, and *Queerwolf*, has been published in more than 175 anthologies, with more than two dozen from STARbooks Press.

"Liar!" shouted the General as he slapped my face, the red instantly rising to the surface. "Liar!" he repeated, the hand making a pendulum swing back in the opposite direction.

"Pants on fire," I whispered, forcing the grin down as I said instead, "I'm telling you the truth. The man is dead. Tied to a boulder at the bottom of the Savannah River, just as you ordered. And if my bullet didn't kill him, then the pollution certainly will." All in all, it was a true statement. There would eventually be a man tied to a boulder, a bullet lodged somewhere between his left and right eyes. Only, of course, it wasn't the man he had in mind, the man he'd assigned me to exterminate. Still, far be it from me to inform him of that tiny, little detail.

"You were seen leaving with this man from your hotel" came the reply, along with another slap. Dude was in for some heavy reprimands from the Department of Labor. Or OSHA, seeing as the rusted chair had fairly ruined my suit. "You were not headed in the direction of the river. In fact, you were seen driving with this man in Atlanta later that night."

I gulped. Not because he'd obviously had me tailed so much as the rope around my neck was cutting through my tender flesh. "It was a mannequin," I calmly explained. "After I dumped the body, I drove to Atlanta with the mannequin in the passenger seat. It was wearing his clothes. That way, if someone spotted my car, they'd be looking for the guy up in Atlanta and not at the bottom of the river." Made sense. Not a lick of truth to it, but like the other body, it would hold water.

The General momentarily paused to stare deep into my eyes. "This man was a North Korean spy and dangerous," he said. "You were meant to make contact, to gain his trust, and then dispose of him. All in the name of your country." He yanked on the rope. "You understand?"

I grunted, choked, and then promptly coughed. "He is dead. The body is at the bottom of the Savannah River." Of course, dead is such a subjective term. To the U.S. Government, to the North Koreans, he was as good as dead right about then. Dead as the body that would soon replace him. "Check the river."

The General released the rope and shoved me in the chest instead. "We cannot do that, Agent Miller. It would call attention to us. Even an anonymous tip would get back to them. If they find a North Korean at the bottom of the river, they'd know we killed him. And if they don't find him, they'll know we tried to kill him."

Which, naturally, I already knew. Still, there would be a dead man down there, just in case. "He is dead, General," I repeated. "I was ordered to kill this man and that is just what I've done. He is not in Atlanta; he is in Savannah. Fish food." If there were any fish left, I mean. Because, like I'd said, the river was about as polluted as you could get.

The rope was removed as I rubbed my palm across my aching throat. "You're free to go, Agent Miller," said the General, a look of disdain washing across his withered face.

And that was that. I didn't ask any questions; I was free, and that was good enough for me. Besides, I really had done my duty, or at least eventually would, just not exactly in the way he'd intended. And so I left and made my way back home, no shortcuts, no weird turns. Straight home.

Well, not straight, exactly.

I pulled my car in the garage, closed the door behind me, and headed inside, smiling broadly as I spotted him on the couch, a cigar in one hand, his cock in the other.

"They believed you?" he asked, smiling up at me through the smoky haze.

"What choice did they have?" I replied, methodically removing my clothes. "I said you were dead, so you were dead. The other body, the one I've yet to dump, will take your place, but by then it won't be recognizable, save for my bullet. They'll know I did my job, and no one else will be the wiser." Heck, even the mannequin would be found at some point, once I bought it. It would be hidden, but not all that well. Word would get back. It always did. And my tracks would be covered.

"And what about me?" he asked, a lick of his tongue across his impossibly full lips as he stubbed out the cigar.

I joined him on the couch, my tongue replacing his. He moaned and grabbed for my arcing cock as I pulled an inch away. "You'll stay here for a few days. Let some of the heat die down. Then we'll drive you to safety. Just as planned."

Deftly, he stroked my dick, a slick bead of precum working its way over the throbbing head. My groan joined his moan. Again I kissed him, my hand caressing his smooth cheek. Though with this man, whatever his real name was, everything was smooth. Heck, a baby's bottom was hairy in comparison. And speaking of bottoms, his was face-level in no time flat.

I took a deep whiff. Even his hole smelled clean. Just a hint of musk and sweat. "Will you go home afterwards?" I asked as I licked his chute, round and round he goes.

Again he groaned and bucked his ass into my face. "I can't. You know that. Not now."

In fact, I did know that. "Your people will come looking for you. Just like I did."

He nodded and pushed his stellar prick between his legs; no other comment in that regard was made, at least not just yet. His piss slit winked up at me, while I, in turn, craned my neck down to warmly greet it. His spunk hit the back of my throat like a bullet. Figuratively speaking. And so I downed his cock while my free hand gently prodded at his spit-slick hole.

"In North Korea," he said, "men do not do this."

I chuckled, knowingly. Because men did this everywhere. "And live to tell about it," I replied, instead.

Then he chuckled. Funny how his accent was so thick, but the laugh sounded the same as mine, as anybody else's. "Trust me, no one tells about it. No one does it and admits to it. No one," he moaned. "No one."

Which is pretty much how we'd made contact. Why, in fact, I'd been chosen for this mission in the first place. Little was known about him. Little except that he liked the company of men. In truth, I doubted that even his own people knew this. Not even his family, his friends, his wife. But he'd been out of his own country before. He'd left a trail. Of condoms, that is.

I slid a finger deep inside of him, his hole clenching for the briefest of moments before it allowed the intrusion. Then allowed for a second and a third. All while I sucked his prick and stroked my own.

All while my eyes went from his ass to the briefcase to my right.

See, he'd paid me off. Paid me not to kill him, once I got to him before he could get to me. And then he used the gay card to further persuade me. In truth, it was the latter that got him his way, during that unscheduled trip to Atlanta, where we'd obviously been spotted.

"A million dollars," he'd said, the cold of my pistol pressed tight to his sweat-drenched temple, before our Atlanta trip, post-coming, naturally. Because you can call me a lot things, but stupid ain't one of them.

Had I not just come, in fact, I probably would've at the sound of those few words. "A million not to kill you?" I released my finger, but kept the gun where it was. "That all you got?" I was only semi-joking. Still, he was desperate, so why not at least ask?

I stared down at his handsome face, at his hairless cheeks and almond-shaped eyes of brown. He stared up and replied, "Your superiors hate you for being born the way you are." He had me there. "So why make them happy now?" And he had me there, too. Plus, a cool, hard million would go a long way to assuage my guilt at working for who he was referring to. "Just pretend to kill me," he added. "Then take the money."

"And what about you?" I couldn't help but ask. "If you go back, if your superiors ever hear word of you again, mine will know I was lying."

He nodded, his eyes still on mine. "There's more money where that came from, my friend," he told me. "I can just disappear with the remainder. They'll never find me, so they'll have nothing to pin on your government." He allowed himself the briefest of smiles. "It's a win/win, as I believe you call it. You'll be rich; I'll be free. In more ways than one."

The more ways he was referring to drew me back to the present, to his ass in my face, to the briefcase off to our side, now in Savannah, no longer in Atlanta, where it had been stored for safekeeping. At least here, I figured, or not back in North Korea, at any rate, this little face-to-ass action wouldn't get him in trouble. Or killed.

Like he said, he'd be free.

So, for the time being, I forgot the circumstances that drew us together and focused instead on that stunning rump of his, at his cock assailing my throat, at my own cock that was still throbbing in my grip. The briefcase could wait. Besides, I already knew where he'd come by it and what my next steps would be, again post-coming.

"Now you will fuck me?" he asked, drawing me out of my reverie.

I laughed and retracted my fingers from his hole, my face from his cock. "Your English is as perfect as your ass," I told him.

"Top in my class in English," he replied.

"Bottom of the class in fucking," I added.

He got the joke and quickly ran to the bedroom, sprawling out on the bed, cock ramrod stiff and aimed high for the ceiling. So much for the Asian dick stereotype. Anyway, in I walked, staring down at him, at his compact body, rife with dense, hard, smooth muscle, pink nipples jutting out, mouth in a pant as he lifted up his legs before spreading them wide. "Fuck me, Secret Agent Man."

Again I laughed as I retrieved a lube and a rubber. "You know the song?" I asked as I slid the rubber on, then slapped my cock head against his winking chute.

"No American television," he replied. "But old-timey radio you can get."

"Lucky you," I said, dripping the lube over my cock and down his crack.

"Lucky me," he agreed, moaning as he grabbed a hold of his stellar prick, his balls rising as he stroked and I entered him, slowly, evenly, gently, as a million volts of adrenaline shot up my spine and a trickle of sweat bee-lined down my face. "Lucky fucking me."

Inch by steely inch, I filled up that tight, little hole of his, until my balls were brushing up against his smooth, muscular ass. Then I swatted his hand away and took hold of his cock, which pulsed in my grip, the head already slick, the turtleneck it usually wore tightly stretched and all but vanished.

Out from his ass I retracted, his back arching as he grabbed a hold of his nipples for a tug and a tweak, my cock hovering in mid-air for the briefest of seconds before it was again slammed in. Out, in. Out in. Slow at first, but building up speed. Guy was tight as a drum, too, his hole clenched tight around my cock, my entire body on fire as I fucked the hell out of him.

"They teach you that at secret agent man school?" he panted, while I jacked his cock and pummeled his ass.

"Make the enemy happy," I replied, omitting the part where I then exterminate then. Because why, I figured, ruin such a delightful moment?

And so faster and faster I fucked him, pistoning his ass as I rapid-stroked his cock, both of us moaning up a storm as the sweat flicked off of us. The last moan of his was the loudest, as his cock erupted in my hand, come flying up before landing with a splat on his belly and thighs. And then my dick shot up his ass, filling that rubber with ounce after ounce of white-hot cum as my ass went into overdrive, bucking into him with lightning force.

When I popped my eyes open and stared down at him, he was smiling up at me. "Too bad our countries can't get along like this," he said.

"Come-rags instead of nuclear weapons," I replied, with a smile of my own. "And speaking of come-rags, I'll be right back."

Only, when I returned, it was a gun in my hand instead of a warm, wet towel. Needless to say, the post-coital bliss quickly went bust after that. "You said you weren't going to kill me," he managed, sliding back on the bed, his face growing as white as my sheets.

I nodded. "I said I wasn't going to kill you, right," I agreed. "Only, now I am. Now that I know where you got the money from. Because I know that your government doesn't have a million in U.S. currency lying around for its spies to use."

The dart hit his chest a second later. No blood. No fuss, no muss. Just the poison, which killed him in less than ten seconds flat. One less North Korean spy. Easy as that. And just like I'd mentioned before, I had completed my mission.

Almost.

Because I still had one more little thing to take care of. Apart from getting that million into a Swiss bank account. Again, as I said, I'm a lot of things, but stupid ain't one of them.

The body was stashed in my car's trunk. It'd be disposed of soon enough, and not at the bottom of the river. See, for one, my bullet wasn't lodged between his eyes, as promised, and, for two, it really wouldn't have been too smart to sink him down there, should he be discovered and his government find out.

Ironically, it was the river scenario that first clued me in that all was not as it appeared. The briefcase was the second tip-off. And both of these pointed back to the man I was headed toward.

I found him in bed after I broke into his house. For a General, he had strangely lax security. Or at least lax compared to my secret agent man training. "Rise and shine, sir," I said, conking him gently on the head with the end of the North Korean's gun. One that shot bullets instead of darts. Because this job required both muss and fuss.

"Agent Miller," he coughed out, eyes wide. "What the fuck?"

I backed up, gun aimed his way. "Fuck, yes. Apt word. I fucked the North Korean and then you were gonna fuck me."

He coughed again and pushed himself up on his elbows. "You're out of your mind."

I chuckled. "Not even close, General," I replied. "See, I thought it odd that you wanted me to dump the body in the river. No way would our government ever want that kind of publicity." I cocked the trigger. "Not unless you were hoping to bring me down for doing it. Because I'd surely get fired if I was found out. Fired or worse. Because the North Koreans don't take too kindly to that sort of thing."

"Get out of here at once," he hollered, his face terror-stricken.

I ignored the remark and continued. "Still, you hedged your bets, just in case the North Korean wasn't so easily killed. You bribed him to kill me, and with the money you gave him, he'd be able to disappear, never to darken our doorsteps again. Or his country's. Win, win, to quote a wise, though dead, man." I chuckled and aimed. "Tsk, tsk. Not too smart to use the same sort of briefcase that we agents use. Telltale, General. Made in America."

And then, pow, that bullet found its target, right between the eyes. Because it was him or me by then. And no way was it going to be me.

Oh yeah, there was a third clue, too, that ensured that it really wasn't going to be me. The one where the North Korean had said that my superiors hated me for being born like I was, namely gay. Only one way he could've known that for sure, and that was straight from the horse's mouth. And said mouth was hanging limp right then and there.

And, pretty soon, would be water-logged as well.

In the dead of night, I watched his body sink into the Savannah River. If they ever found him, they'd also find the

North Korean's bullet. But that was one big if. Only thing they'd know for certain at that very moment was that he was shot and presumably dead. And I'd get a new boss. Hopefully one not so fucking bigoted. Or dumb enough to bribe a North Korean spy. Or try and pull one over on yours truly.

Because this secret agent man is a lot of things, but ... well, you know the rest.

WASTED ON THE YOUNG
By Mark Apoapsis

Mark Apoapsis is the cover name of a writer who lives in an undisclosed location, employed in a plausible day job. Information on pets, significant others, and hobbies is classified.

Without stopping to put on any clothes, I padded over to my computer and logged in to work. I was barely awake enough to remember my four-digit memorized passcode after typing in the six digits from the ever-changing security tattoo on my wrist. But coffee could wait. I was eager to check on the results of my experiment.

The shiver that went through me when I saw the data collected automatically last night had nothing to do with the cool air against my bare skin. If the results were correct, I was halfway to helping a lot of people live longer lives. I'd have to go in and check my mice in person, but it looked like the gene I'd modified had caused seizures right on schedule, and two of the mice had died overnight. If I knew which genes to activate to cause the disease, I knew which ones to turn off to cure it.

I couldn't wait to get to the lab! I planned quickly: I could skip breakfast. I supposed that putting on some clothes would be a good idea. I'd already had a shower before going to bed, and slept in a fresh pair of shorts. I hadn't jerked off last night (I guess hitting forty has a few compensations), so I just pulled on some jeans over my shorts, and grabbed the first shirt I came to, a green T-shirt with a pocket.

I was halfway out the door when I remembered it was Saturday. I hadn't missed my weekly visit to my grandfather in years. If I went to the lab first, I'd be sure to lose track of time. Sighing, I pulled a long-sleeve shirt on over my T-shirt.

Not that my grandfather cared about formality, but I knew the tattoo bothered him because it reminded him of the one that his uncle had had to wear. One of those generational things.

# # # # #

It was a bright, sunny autumn day, just the kind Grandpa had always loved. On days like this, I normally used to find him on a bench somewhere on the nursing home's wooded grounds, enjoying the last of the warm weather. This past year or two, though, he'd been increasingly forced by illness to stay indoors, missing more and more days like this. It was sad. I could still remember when he was vigorous enough to carry me around on his shoulders and playfully toss me into a pile of bright leaves to land with a satisfying crunch. At his age and with his declining health, this could be his last autumn, and he might already have seen his last summer. I knew he used to love summers at the beach in his youth.

I didn't see him on the front lawn, so I checked my compass watch. I'd given him one of his own for his ninety-first birthday, so my watch automatically pointed to his location as I approached the building. He was upstairs in his room. I sighed, knowing that it meant he wasn't feeling well.

His door was open. He looked pleasantly surprised when I came in.

"Nick!" he greeted me warmly. "Is it Saturday already?"

"Yes, Grandpa. Didn't your watch tell you I was in the building?"

"I'll never learn how to work this fool thing. So, what's new?"

I sat down and told him excitedly about my experimental results.

He looked blank. "Why would you want to cure mice of seizures?"

I started to explain. Then I saw the twinkle in his eye and realized he was teasing me. He wasn't that far out of it.

"I hope you think about things besides work sometimes."

"Well, sometimes I think about a lot of things I don't get to do."

"Ah yes, that young fella at the lab. When are you going to ask him out? At least he's a nice Jewish boy; your mother will like that."

"Yeah, right!" I laughed, wishing she were half as open-minded as her own father. "Besides, I may have the Jewish part pegged right, but the gay part is probably wishful thinking."

"Couldn't hurt to ask," he said. "Not like the old days."

"Tyler's, like, half my age."

"Yes, you're such an old man," he scoffed. "You're how old now? Thirty-five?"

"I wish! I just turned forty. Remember, you all took me to dinner last month, and Mom asked if I'm ever getting married ..."

"Oh. Right. Anyway, let me show you something."

He rummaged around in a dresser drawer and found a photo album. The old-fashioned kind: an actual physical book with hardcopy pictures. The thing must have weighed as much as a hundred tablets and took up most of the drawer. He leafed through it and pointed to one faded picture. "Would you say I look older or younger than you here?"

Except for the old-fashioned clothes, it could almost have been a picture of me. "A little older, maybe."

47

"I was thirty-one when this was taken. So you're doing pretty well."

"Well, people in the twentieth century aged prematurely. They didn't know about nutrition and the sun ..."

"Not to mention all those new-fangled expensive medicines you take nowadays," Grandpa said dryly. "Not that I don't pop a dozen pills a day myself. If only they'd invented that stroke medication in time for your poor grandmother."

"If only she could have held on a few more years, lived a little healthier. Medical science is making amazing progress! By the time you're one-hundred ..."

"I should be so lucky! I'll be satisfied to enjoy my few remaining years ... It looks like a nice day outside. Why don't we take a walk?"

"Are you sure you feel up to it?"

"Truthfully, the doctor told me to stay in bed. But if I can't enjoy a beautiful Saturday morning with my grandson, what's the point of still being alive?"

"I told you. Hang on just a few more years ..."

But he was already out of his chair. Before he'd taken two steps, he suddenly collapsed. I leaped from my chair, but I can't move as fast as I used to. He fell to the carpeted floor.

I pushed the button to call the nurse. He arrived quickly. He was a new guy, dark and muscular. I almost suspected Grandpa of faking his seizure to give me a chance to meet this guy.

"He's had one of his atonic seizures," I explained, "triggered by orthostatic hypotension." I helped him pick the patient up. Grandpa's shoulders felt like sagging bags of kindling. Sad to think this was all that was left of those strong shoulders I used to ride on so often as a little boy.

"You sound like you know what you're talking about," said the nurse as we laid Grandpa on the bed. "You a doctor?"

"Not a medical doctor, no. Just a researcher at a biotech firm." More like a research assistant, but I was trying to impress him. "But I'm working on finding a cure for this very condition."

"That's great! It's probably the biggest cause of death for men over ninety."

"The biggest one left, yeah."

"Well, we'd better let him rest. He usually sleeps for hours after one of these drop attacks."

I leaned over my grandfather and said, "I'd better get to work now, Grandpa. Hang in there!"

# # # # #

"You have the lab almost to yourself this morning," the uniformed security guard, Steve, commented as I pressed my thumb on the reader and waited for the green light.

"Almost?" I asked, waiting for a new passcode to fade in on my wrist.

"That grad student is working this weekend. Tyler. Hard-working kid."

I hoped Steve didn't guess why it took me three tries to key in my passcode correctly.

# # # # #

My wristwatch compass showed me where Tyler was; I'd exchanged locator codes with all my coworkers. I made sure to pass by the door to the lab where he was. "Morning, Tyler" I said.

"Oh, hi, Dr. Rosenblum," he said with a friendly grin that made my heart pound.

"Hey, I told you! Call me Nick."

I'm a fool, I told myself as I let myself into the high-security lab. At best, he looks up to me. He's never going to see me as a buddy, an equal. Let alone what I want.

Speaking of cute young guys, the janitor, Juan, was changing the lining of my mouse cages. He looked to be midway between my age and Tyler's.

"*Dos murió,*" he reported sadly. He never seemed to understand that some of the experimental mice were supposed to die.

"*Es bueno,*" I assured him, taking off my outer shirt since it would be too damn hot for the lab coat.

I'd been on friendly terms with Juan since his first week here. Some lazy researcher had left confidential documents in the copy room for someone else to shred, and Juan had been about to cart them away with the ordinary recycling. I'd known just enough Spanish to explain his error, and he'd seemed delighted that I was trying to speak to him in his own language. He didn't seem to speak a word of English. Now he did most of our shredding for us and cleaned cages on top of his general cleaning duties.

# # # # #

Two hours later, dissection of the dead mice and a blood sample from the living ones had confirmed everything I'd hoped for. I hung up my lab coat and called Rick, the researcher I worked for. "Senior" researcher, though he was younger than me.

"That's fantastic," Rick said.

"You sound out of breath."

"Jogging."

When I'd described my findings, he sounded excited. "Do you think we can develop a drug stable enough to be delivered as an aerosol under battlefield conditions?"

"Huh?"

"It has to be practical for biowarfare applications."

"Warfare? I was hoping this would lead to a cure!"

"Oh, sure, I guess a medical application would be possible, too. But the company needs to bring a product to market now. You know how long clinical trials and FDA approval can take."

Biowarfare? I pictured hundreds of healthy young men in foreign military uniforms, all suddenly collapsing to lie helpless on the ground as our troops descended on them. If they followed the rules of war, they'd only take them prisoner, I told myself, staring at the bloody mess on the dissection table.

"Besides," he continued, "you're closer to a drug that can cause seizures than one that can cure them, right?"

"But ..."

"We'll talk more on Monday. Good work!"

I hurled my phone at the wall, but it was so lightweight, it stopped short and fluttered to the ground. Whatever happened to good solid receivers you could bang down, like in the old movies? To make up for it, I stormed out and slammed the lab door so hard behind me that it bounced.

After pacing aimlessly around the building awhile, I decided it might help to talk to someone. My compass showed Tyler was still in the low-security lab where I'd seen him.

But strangely, that room was empty. I found his compass-watch hidden in a drawer. Mystified, I headed back to retrieve my phone – and was dumbfounded to find Tyler in the high-security lab, rifling through the cabinet where we store small batches of prototype drugs that are ready to send to clinics for testing.

I tried to sneak up behind him. Stupid: I should have blocked the way out. I was halfway across the room when he whirled around, swore, and made a dash for the door, moving with the agility of youth and easily evading me.

I knelt awkwardly to pick up my phone and ran after him while voice-dialing the security desk. I was already out of breath by the time Steve answered, but I managed to gasp out "Tyler's stealing some pills!"

Tyler ran down a hall that would lead him to the fire exit. I used to be good at track in high school, but there was no way I could catch an athletic guy in his twenties anymore.

This was a modern building and didn't have an elevator. Well, I supposed there must be a freight elevator in the back near the loading docks, but not like those old buildings with elevators and ramps. But the only way to get from the lobby to the lab was to climb a showy spiral staircase made out of glittering crystal petals that looked too delicate to bear our weight. If you broke your leg, you needed to take a few sick days or telecommute. I keep myself in good shape for my age, but by the time we reached the top, I was winded. Why was it that buildings always had elevators back in my youth, when I didn't need them, and now that I did, they were gone? I suppose they'd been for the sake of wheelchairs, back when there were still incurable diseases and injuries that could irreversibly paralyze a person.

Then, as Tyler whipped around the corner, his feet flew out from under him. I skidded to a halt and damn near landed on my ass myself. The floor had just been mopped. What a stroke of luck!

Tyler tried to scramble to his feet, but winced and went down on one knee. I grabbed his arm. Steve, the burly guard, came trotting up behind me, breathing hard. I hauled Tyler to his feet.

"Ow! I sprained my ankle."

"You've got worse problems than that, punk!" Steve snarled.

We half-carried him down the hall, his arms over our shoulders, to an unused lab. Steve insisted on stretching him out on the table and tying his arms to the table legs. We used Steve's belt for one arm and Tyler's own belt for the other.

Steve reached into our captive's shirt pocket and pulled out a small plastic bag containing a few dozen pills. I recognized the color coding. "Those are our diabetes drug candidate, for next month's Phase I trial."

"What?" cried Tyler. "I thought they were hydrocodone. Fuck!"

"Vicodin," I translated for Steve.

"You were going to sell them on the street, weren't you?" Steve snarled. "Stupid kid!"

"I needed the money."

Steve examined the pills. "You're lying," he said.

"Yeah," I agreed, "why would he think we were stocking hydrocodone?"

"Not only that, the street price of nine pills has got to be less than he makes here in a week. But stealing our drug candidate for our competitors; now that would pay well."

"No! I swear!" Tyler looked very young and scared, lying there helpless.

Steve backhanded him. "Who hired you?"

"Hey!" I grabbed Steve's arm.

He shook me off. "Watch him. I'll see what I can dig up on him." He rolled the kid onto his side and took his wallet.

# # # # #

I got a wet paper towel and dabbed at the blood on Tyler's cheek. "Your lip was bleeding. But it's stopped."

"Thanks," he said, pathetically grateful.

53

"How's your ankle?"

"Not too bad."

"Let me check."

"No, leave it alone."

I gently removed his shoe and sock. "Strange. No sign of swelling. Is it the other one?" Ignoring his protests, I bared his other foot and carefully massaged both ankles. "Does this hurt?"

"Not much. Guess I just twisted it."

He looked at the door. "Is he going to come back?" he asked, sounding even younger than he was.

"I'll call Rick. Steve will listen to him."

But I immediately got forwarded to Rick's voice mail. I didn't feel comfortable describing the situation in a voice message, so I just asked him to come in as soon as he possibly could, explaining that we had an emergency to deal with.

Steve came storming back in. "OK, punk. Who are you?" He turned to me and explained, "His ID is a fake. His university never heard of him. There's no record he exists." He grabbed a handful of Tyler's thick hair and yanked his head back, exposing his throat. Then, to my horror, he pulled out a knife.

"What are you doing?" I cried.

"Relax. I just need a DNA sample. I should take it out of his hide, but ..." He cut off a lock of soft brown hair and handed it to me.

This lab didn't have any equipment, just a sink, a refrigerator, and a supply cabinet. I reluctantly left Tyler – or whatever the kid's name was – bound and helpless, in Steve's hands.

# # # # #

I did the DNA sequencing in fifteen minutes flat. And I was right to be uneasy about leaving them alone. By the time I brought the results to Steve on a data coin, he'd stripped the kid to the waist and was whipping him with a length of rubber lab tubing. Tyler's chest was crisscrossed with welts, angry red against otherwise perfect skin.

"What the fuck do you think you're doing? Leave him alone! I'll call the police!"

"Fine. Be sure to tell them he said he's a drug dealer. The local cops beat an accused drug dealer to death just last month."

He had a point. "Here's his DNA sequence," I said, just to get rid of him.

He handed me the rubber tubing. "See what you can get out of him."

# # # # #

The kid kept himself in great shape, I noted, feeling a twinge of envy tinged with desire. My grandfather always said that youth is wasted on the young. I exercised more than I ever did at Tyler's age, and I was still losing the battle.

He was breathing hard, and he looked at me as if terrified that I'd continue his beating. I tossed the tubing aside.

"Maybe I should put something on that," I said gently.

"No thanks."

I put my hand on his shoulder, feeling solid muscle under the supple skin. "Are you really a spy?"

"I'm just trying to make enough money to finish my degree, sir."

I hate it when young guys call me "sir."

# # # # #

Steve returned. "This doesn't make sense. His DNA matches Sidney Wolf, VP of Business Development at Spiagen Bionanomics."

"Isn't that the company that's trying to buy us out? Wait ... VP, at his age?"

He showed me the screen of his tablet, which was displaying a picture of a gray-haired, balding man with heavy jowls. "This is the most recent picture I could find, taken seven years ago. He'd be sixty-eight now."

"He's in pretty good shape for sixty-eight," I said facetiously, surveying Tyler's perfect, scarless body, still stretched out for my inspection. The lash marks were fading to pink, I noticed.

"Nick, please! Let me go, man!"

I wanted to. But the beefy security guard had his own ideas. "You're not going anywhere until you explain why your DNA says you're the fucking VP in charge of hostile takeovers at our biggest competitor."

"All right." He drew a shaky breath. "I'm Wolf's clone. He had ten of us created, so he could harvest spare parts when he needed them."

"My God!" I whispered.

"He's already taken a kidney from me. And killed my favorite brother for his heart."

The thought of a rich old man carving up this innocent young guy like a tender piece of meat, helping himself to his organs, was obscene.

"That can't be legal," Steve said.

"Rich and powerful men like him make their own laws," the kid said. "After I escaped, I tried to hide behind a new identity."

"We've got to help him, Steve!"

"You might have asked, kid. Instead of ripping us off."

"I thought you'd turn me over to him."

"Never!" I promised, patting his chest. "Only ..."

"What?" Steve asked.

I turned to him. "Only, he's too old. It's been, what, thirty-some years since Dolly the sheep was born? No one could have cloned a human being over twenty years ago."

"That's what they wanted you to think."

"He must be Wolf's clone," Steve said. "How else do you explain the matching DNA and fingerprints?"

A chill ran down my spine. "Fingerprints?"

"I compared our records to the DMV. They matched Wolf's fingerprints."

I forced the words out through a tightening throat. "Even identical twins don't have the same fingerprints. He must be ..."

It didn't seem possible. I stared at our captive, trying to imagine an advanced medical treatment that could restore wrinkled, sagging flesh to the supple, leanly muscular condition of the body now stretched out shirtless before me, glowing with youth. That firm square jaw, lightly covered with stubble, showed no trace of the jowls in the old picture. On the other hand, his chest showed no trace of the lash marks it'd had minutes ago, which would have taken days to completely heal on another man's body.

But what convinced me was the change in Tyler's expression when he saw he couldn't fool me any longer. His eyes were as clear as ever, his face just as unlined, but suddenly there was more cynicism behind those eyes than any man should be able to accumulate in only twenty-five years.

"You son of a bitch!" I said softly. "All that bullshit about the rich and powerful doing whatever they want, and it was you all along!"

"He's Sidney Wolf?"

"Yes," I admitted.

"What were you trying to do?" Steve demanded. "Sabotage us or steal our secrets?"

"Why not both?" our prisoner said with a smirk.

"You've found the fucking fountain of youth!" I said. "How long were you planning to keep it to yourself?"

"Whom do you expect me to share it with?" he asked mockingly.

"Everyone!"

"Don't be a fool! Do you have any idea what would happen if the whole world had access to longevity treatments? The overpopulation in this country alone ..."

"What gives you the right to decide that you deserve a long life and no one else does, you selfish bastard?"

He just smirked his superior smirk.

"We should call Rick," I told Steve.

"I already talked to him. He's on his way over."

"He may be able to reverse-engineer whatever they did to make him young. We could sell it." I started hunting through the supply cabinet. "I can run some basic tests on a blood sample to give him a head start."

"I have excellent patent attorneys," Tyler said smugly as my needle penetrated the skin of his arm.

"Possession is nine-tenths of the law in this business, pal," Steve reminded him.

# # # # #

I had just started some automated blood tests running when Rick arrived. His blond hair was damp, as if he'd taken a quick shower. He'd changed out of his jogging clothes, but in a hurry, apparently. He wasn't wearing his usual T-shirt under his button-down shirt.

"What the hell's going on?" he demanded when he saw Tyler bound and bare-chested.

"You're not going to believe this," Steve said. "First of all, it turns out Tyler is a spy. And his name isn't really Tyler. But it gets better. He's actually a VP of Spiagen Bionanomics."

"He looks a little young ..." Rick said uncertainly.

"That's the interesting part," I put in.

Steve showed him the picture. "This is what he looked like seven years ago."

"Whoa!" Rick exclaimed. "I'd heard they'd done some proprietary research in regenerative medicine. But this! Are you sure?"

"Could I borrow your knife, Steve?"

He looked surprised but handed it to me. I used it to cut a shallow slash across the naked chest of our prisoner, who just swallowed hard and glared at me.

I watched the blood trickle down his chest, tracing out the contours of his muscles. I wondered whether the treatments that had restored his youth had automatically given him that sculpted body, or if he was just more motivated to take care of it now that he had a fresh start and a reversal of what had happened to it the first time. Then I went to the sink and wet a paper towel with warm water. Once I had sponged him off, the only sign of the cut was a pink line where healthy new skin had sealed it. Rick was practically drooling. And unlike me, he didn't usually drool over the sight of bare-chested young men. I showed him the blood tests, and he eagerly disappeared with it into his private lab.

# # # # #

Steve seemed to have calmed down. After an uncomfortable silence, I said, "Maybe we should give him his shirt back."

59

"What for?"

"Why not?"

"We can't, anyway. I cut it off of him. Didn't want to untie him."

Half an hour later, Rick returned, talking excitedly about stem cells and drug molecules.

"Anything I can do to help?" I asked.

"Yes. What would really help is to see the breakdown products of these molecules I found circulating in his blood."

"So you want me to take a sample of ..."

"His urine. Yes." He went back to his lab, obviously eager to continue working.

I'd never taken a urine sample from another man before and certainly not from an unwilling shirtless hunk strapped to a table. But who was I to argue with the boss?

"You wouldn't dare," the prisoner said. I ignored him and got a cup.

Wordlessly, I unbuttoned his fly and reached in. His undershorts, hidden under his grungy, inexpensive grad-student clothing, felt like they were made of silk. Obviously he hadn't counted on being captured and having his underwear pawed through.

"You're enjoying this, aren't you, you fairy?" Some old attitudes should be allowed to die with the people who hold them.

I pulled his cock out through his fly. I made a minor discovery in the process. When I'd told my grandfather that Tyler was a nice young Jewish guy, I'd been wrong on three counts out of four.

We twisted him into a position that allowed me to hold his limp cock against the inside of the cup. Tyler held out for ten minutes before filling the cup. Then again, lots of guys would've had trouble urinating while tied up, with two men watching, one of them holding onto their cock.

"Back in a minute," I told Steve. "Keep your hands off him, okay?"

"I'd sooner have your goon beat me to a pulp than have your filthy hands on me again, faggot."

"Don't make me make you drink this," I said cheerfully.

Rick was too wrapped up in work to do more than mumble an acknowledgement. I hurried back, passing the young janitor, Juan, going about his business. I wondered if he'd seen or heard anything, and what he made of it. I didn't know enough Spanish to explain something this delicate, so I just exchanged a smile with him as I passed.

# # # # #

I was getting just about impatient enough to check on Rick when I glanced at my compass and saw that he was heading back to the room where we were. He burst in, saying, "I think I'm on to something! There are signs of genetic manipulation. If only we had a close relative, so I could get a baseline genome!"

"Look," I said, "if you're talking about kidnapping his family members, that's where I draw the line."

"No need. There's another way. I'm betting they would only have modified his somatic cells. If I could compare them to his germ cells, I could look through the differences and figure out what they did."

"Makes sense," I said neutrally. "One sperm sample, coming right up."

# # # # #

Somehow, whenever I'd visualized what it would be like to pull Tyler's pants down around his ankles and give him a hand job, I'd always imagined it being under friendlier circumstances. I'd never pictured holding down

61

his struggling, naked torso with my free arm while a burly, uniformed straight guy pinned his hairy thighs to the table.

Well, okay, maybe that's not entirely true.

"This isn't going to work, faggot!" he screamed yet again. "I'll never come with a filthy pervert groping me."

"We'll see about that," I said, cupping his balls lightly while stroking the underside of his cock with my thumb. Despite his protests, his cock had already hardened.

"How can you help that fag do this to me?" he appealed again to Steve.

"Shut up!" Steve told him.

"Look!" I said, exhausted, "I didn't ask for this. I'm not doing this because it turns me on." Even if it did, a little.

"Liar!"

"Fine. Steve, you're straight, right? Switch places with me."

"Uh ... you're doing just fine."

"He'd rather have another straight guy do it to him."

Eventually, Steve agreed. We switched places. Tyler's thigh muscles felt very solid in my grip, but his struggles had gotten weaker.

"That's it," I said encouragingly, watching Steve uncertainly take the prisoner's cock in his fist and begin sliding his hand up and down the shaft. "Pump him for information. Milk him of every secret he owns."

Steve grinned fiercely. He seemed to be getting off on this, in his own way. I think he secretly enjoyed having control over another man's pleasure. As for me, the sight of a beefy straight guy jerking off another straight guy, stretched out naked and helpless between us, was almost enough to make me contribute my own involuntary sperm sample.

"Almost there!" I said, keeping up the infield chatter. "He's going to shoot whether he likes it or not!"

Our prisoner's twenty-five-year-old body was on the verge of betraying him, but he'd apparently learned a lot in his long life about delaying ejaculation. In the end, I had to help. As his straight captor continued to tease his cock and play with his balls, I moved to his side, putting most of his naked body within my reach. Tyler twisted around desperately, trying to escape my questing fingers, but that only gave me access to fresh territory. Suddenly, he moaned in despair as his fluids gushed out in spasms, bearing the genetic secrets he'd tried to deny us.

"It's all over his chest," Steve observed. "None of it got in the cup."

"Guess we'll have to start again," I said, provoking a whimper from our vanquished prisoner. But I took the cup and scraped the hard-won fluid from his chest and belly. He offered no further resistance.

As I was pulling his pants back up, I noticed something in his pocket. Loose capsules, color-coded purple and turquoise. I showed them to Steve. "These are our other drug candidate. Sort of a super adrenaline booster." I slipped them into my T-shirt pocket.

"We should have searched him." Steve ran his hands along Tyler's legs, then stopped and pulled his pants down again. "A secret pocket!"

The inner pocket proved to contain a pipette with a blood sample. "Is this from my mice?" I asked.

"That does it!" Steve said, taking out his knife. "I'm going over every seam in these."

I left him industriously slicing Tyler's pants to ribbons. I wondered what we'd do when we finally let him go.

# # # # #

Rick's response when I brought him the sperm sample was, "Never mind that! Take a look at this!" He steered me over to the microscope. "Nanomachines, programmed to repair damaged cells! I'm sure of it!"

Eagerly, I took a look. And for the next hour, I worked with Rick, forgetting everything else in the world – even visions of nearly naked young bodies stretched out helplessly on tables at the mercy of sadistic security guards.

Eventually, I had to excuse myself to urinate. Then, on the way back from the men's room, I made a detour to check on our prisoner.

He was gone! In his place, Steve was stretched out unconscious on the table, wearing only dark green boxer shorts. There was no sign of Steve's uniform, but his shoes and socks were on the floor, along with the shreds he'd made of Tyler's clothing. Tyler's shoes were gone.

I touched Steve's sinewy neck and felt a strong pulse. His well-muscled, hairy chest was rising and falling slowly. Having now seen both men in their shorts, it was hard to picture Tyler overpowering him. He must have taken Steve by surprise. And apparently drugged him: I couldn't wake him up by shaking his shoulders, or even by slapping a wet towel on his face and chest. He didn't stir even when I stuck an ice cube in his armpit.

I thought about alerting the police to look for a male in his mid-twenties, wearing a security uniform much too big for him, but decided to consult Rick first.

But Rick wasn't in the lab. I almost panicked, and thought about running to ask Juan if he'd seen him. I'd passed the janitor a minute ago, wheeling a huge garbage can full of shredded paper. Then I calmed down enough to remember that there were better ways to track people nowadays.

My wristwatch compass led me to the kitchenette. I felt silly. Rick was probably having a cup of coffee, or an instant meal.

But Rick wasn't in the kitchenette. Only his shoes and socks. Bending over, I found his watch stuck inside one shoe. Then I heard the door shut behind me. I whirled around. There was a pair of dark green boxer shorts hanging on the doorknob. I picked them up. They were soaked in something. I sniffed them, trying to identify the medicinal odor.

The last thing I remember was my vision blurring as I fumbled for the doorknob.

# # # # #

I woke up in a basement. Shredded paper clinging to my clothes and a freight elevator nearby gave me a good clue of how I'd gotten there.

I was strung up by the wrists, tied with strips of some guy's shirt to a pipe running overhead. My feet were bare, and my ankles tightly bound together. Rick, Steve, and Tyler were strung up from another pipe, facing me. Rick was barefoot but still dressed, while Tyler was clad only in his silk boxer shorts, and the muscular security guard was completely naked. His hairy chest had been shaved smooth. His pecs looked even more impressive laid bare like that, with no hair to soften the chiseled lines.

A man was standing with his back to me, with the logo of the janitorial service across his back. "Oh, you'll tell me, all right," he was saying to Rick. "I broke your musclebound security goon; I can break you." Steve just hung there like a side of beef, looking utterly defeated.

I recognized our captor, even from the rear, as Juan. Speaking perfect English.

He grabbed the front of Rick's button-down shirt, ripped it open, and began attaching electrodes at various points, even over his small pink nipples. It was state-of-the-art equipment; the wires trailing across Rick's pale chest looked as wispy as his nearly invisible chest hairs. They led to a small handheld controller. Once the electrodes were in place, Juan pressed a button, and Rick gasped, writhing as if in pain. Obviously, the electrodes weren't just passive sensors.

"Again: What's your passcode?"

"Oh, my god," Rick said softly several times, with his eyes squeezed shut. He moaned, writhing helplessly. "Oh, god!"

"The passcode?"

Rick shook his head, then grimaced. Then whimpered.

"OK!" Rick cried out. "2570."

Juan glanced at his controller. "That registered as a lie." He pushed a button, and Rick moaned.

As I watched helplessly, Juan forced the correct passcode out of Rick. Then he grabbed his prisoner's bound wrist to read what his tattoo currently displayed. He sat down cross-legged on the ground and picked up a tablet computer. "*Bueno*. Let's see what you've got."

He tapped away intently for a long time. Finally, he said, "So that's what your other drug candidate is. A super-soldier pill. No wonder Wolf wanted to steal it." He glanced at the nearly naked intern, whom I still had trouble thinking of as a powerful old man. He looked young and helpless at the moment.

"That's not exactly what it is," Rick said hoarsely.

Juan consulted his hand-held display. "You're lying," he said matter-of-factly, "which means that's exactly what it is."

He paged through more material. "Ah! These must be the tests you did today on your, ah, 'intern.' Interesting.

Evidence of genetic therapy, maybe even nanotech." He read silently for a long time.

"Sperm sample. That would explain some of the noises!" he chuckled. "And blood work." He was silent for a long time. Then he stood up and examined his youngest-looking prisoner. "It's true, then. I didn't believe it, until I saw the DNA match and the blood work." He ran his finger down the perfect skin of his captive's chest and belly. "It's one thing to slow down the aging process. But to actually reverse it!"

Tyler shivered at the touch, but kept his mouth shut.

"You've done a very thorough job on him for one day, Rick. I'll keep Wolf to experiment on, but you've saved me lots of work." Giving Tyler's bare chest one last proprietary thump, he returned to his laptop. "And your assistant has made a breakthrough on a drop-attack drug, I see." He glanced back at me. "Oh good. He's awake. I may need his password to delete his data. Your account only seems to have read access."

He stood up and stepped over to Steve. As Juan reached out to him, the naked man whimpered. "15921592159215921592 ..." he mumbled.

"Pobrecito!" Juan said in mock tenderness. "Don't worry; I just need to check your tattoo again." Juan twisted his prisoner's wrist to get a better view and returned to his laptop to type it in.

"No luck." He got up again and advanced on me. "Sorry, Nick, I need your password to delete your data."

"Please!" I begged. "It took me years ..."

"Que lastima," he said sarcastically. He yanked my T-shirt out of my pants and began pulling it up. Reflexively, I glanced down at my exposed belly – and noticed a flash of purple and turquoise in my shirt pocket. The super-adrenalin boosters Tyler had tried to steal! I'd forgotten I had them. As my shirt came up over my head, I quickly

ducked my head down and thrust my tongue into the pocket. Somehow, I managed to suck a few of the experimental pills into my mouth during the brief moment when my face was hidden inside my inside-out shirt. I swallowed them dry while Juan was stretching the shirt out of the way behind my neck. He stepped back, as if to admire his fourth shirtless captive. At forty, I wasn't the oldest of us, but I was acutely conscious of the fact that I was the most aged as I gazed wistfully at Tyler's perfect body.

I watched helplessly as Juan removed the electrodes from my boss's bare chest and transferred them to my own. "You don't understand," I pleaded. "My seizure work's not meant to be a weapon."

"It should bring in a lot of revenue, however it's marketed," Juan said, pressing the last two electrodes firmly in place over my nipples.

"Please! I'm only hoping to find a cure for my ailing grandfather!"

"Yeah, right! Couldn't you come up with something more orig ... Huh ..." He was staring at his hand-held device. "¡Hostia! That's actually true?" Juan's brown eyes were filled with what seemed to be genuine sympathy. "Sorry, man. But it's not like I'm destroying your work. I've got a copy. In five years, you can buy the treatment from my company, ¿no?"

"But you don't have the expertise. I do."

"Tell me your password, and I'll hire you."

"Go to hell!"

"All right. We'll do this the hard way." He pressed a button.

I steeled myself for an electric shock. But it was nothing so crude as that. It felt like someone was applying crushed ice all over my chest.

Then it ended abruptly. "The password?"

"Never," I gasped. If I could just hold out until the pills took effect!

This time it was fire instead of ice. Somehow he was able to stimulate my nerves however he pleased.

He stopped the torment and asked again. I managed to remain silent.

This time my body was wracked by intense pleasure, more unbearable than pain. Worse than if he'd been playing with the head of my cock right after an orgasm.

"Tell you what. Just tell me the first digit. I can't do anything without the other three."

I shook my head. When he pressed the button again, it felt as if there were dozen mouths all over my chest, nibbling gently. Then not so gently. Then it started to hurt.

"Six!" I shouted. The pain vanished. Juan looked at his read-out and nodded. "Good. Now the second number."

"You said only one," I protested stupidly. I felt a wonderfully warm sensation enveloping my chest, like a warm bath. Then a hot bath. Then scalding.

He got two more digits out of me. Then he gently wiped the sweat and tears off my face with a paper towel and squeezed my bare shoulder. "I get five wrong entries before it locks me out. That gives me a fifty-fifty chance of simply guessing the last digit. Why not make it easy on yourself and just tell me?"

I was breathing so hard, I could barely speak, and my heart was pounding. I told him.

Now that my ordeal was over, I felt as if a great weight were lifted. The other defeated men still hung limply, but I felt full of energy. I felt as if I could ... Hmm.

As Juan turned his back on me, I bent my arms, levering my body up, and kicked out at him with my bound feet. He stumbled and whirled around. I kicked him in the belly, barefoot, and he doubled over. The bonds on my feet had ripped loose. I pulled myself up to where my teeth could reach the cloth strips tying my wrists, and was free before he could get up. I grabbed my erstwhile tormentor by his shirtfront and hoisted him off his feet. His flailing foot kicked me in the gut, but I barely felt it.

"What did you do, get ahold of some super-soldier pills?" Rick asked. "Hurry, untie us! We don't know how long they last in humans."

"In a minute." I found that Juan's thick uniform shirt tore easily in my hands. I ripped it into strips and used them to string him up beside Tyler. I had no trouble dangling him over my head with one hand while tightening a knot with the other. Then I pulled my own T-shirt back on, being very careful not to damage the fabric or my ears by not knowing my own strength.

"I meant what I said," my captive panted. "I'll hire you to find a cure for drop attack syndrome. Rick just wants to sell it as a weapon."

"Don't believe him!" Rick said.

"Shut up," I told Juan. "I should gag you." I grabbed his undershirt. It shredded like so much tissue paper.

"I'll give you anything you want, man!"

The thing I most wanted wasn't his to give: Tyler's perfect young body, strung up helplessly in easy reach. But leaving that aside: "I don't believe you."

"I swear!"

Was he lying? It occurred to me that I had a way of telling. Thoughtfully, I began peeling electrodes off my skin and sticking them to Juan's smooth brown chest.

Five Years Later

As I ran effortlessly along the wet sand, I could tell from all the admiring glances that I must look as good as I felt.

It's true: youth is wasted on the young. I'd never kept myself in such good shape the first time around.

Nevertheless, I was getting left behind. The footprints I was following were already getting eroded by the surf, and their owner was nearly out of range of my compass.

I passed a toddler finishing a sand castle with his middle-aged grandfather. I smiled nostalgically. That part of my life was over. I glanced back once to see the man lifting the boy onto his shoulders.

It was exhilarating to be able to run for miles, feeling the warm sun on my bare skin. I slowed down only to admire a pair of athletic college-age guys dunking each other in the breakers.

The faded footprints seemed to veer off. My compass agreed, pointing away from the ocean. I navigated through the sea of beach blankets and umbrellas and found myself at a small shack at the edge of the sand. He was in there. The door was ajar, so I walked in.

It seemed to be a storage shed used by lifeguards for stashing equipment. The blond man on his knees looked young and well-built enough to be a lifeguard – both guys did – but what he was performing was definitely not mouth-to-mouth, involving, as it did, only one mouth.

"Hey!" the standing man complained good-naturedly. "Nick! Didn't your mother ever teach you to knock?"

"Don't you know you're supposed to turn off your locator watch if you want privacy?" I retorted.

"Someday you'll have to teach me how to work the fool thing."

The lifeguard was looking me over, in a way I was still getting used to. "Whoa. Are you guys, like, twins?"

Even the cock that had been in his mouth looked just like mine – or like mine used to, before I'd let my foreskin grow back. "Close relatives," I admitted.

"You know what would be hot? If you guys could stand close together, I could alternate ..."

"Um, sorry," said his original object of desire. "I'm a little old-fashioned that way." I wondered if I was blushing as much as he was.

"Whatever," the lifeguard said and went back to what I'd interrupted.

"I'll wait outside," I said uncomfortably.

Ten minutes later, my "twin" came out, with his swim trunks back in place, looking smugly self-satisfied. "Race you to the surf!" he called, and I had to sprint after him.

When we were chest-deep in water, he playfully splashed me. I didn't splash back.

"What?" he teased. "Upset that I didn't share that fella with you?"

"What? No! A three-way with my 'twin brother'? Ewww!" I splashed him just for mentioning it. "It's just ... I thought you were straight!"

"Truthfully, this wasn't my first time. My best friend in college ... Well, back in those days, we were expected to get married and go our separate ways. So we did." He looked wistful. "If things had been like they are today ... You don't know how lucky you are, kiddo."

"OK, here comes another lecture about the bad old days," I chuckled, though my mind was still reeling.

"No, I mean you're lucky that I didn't stay with my friend. Then I would never have married your grandmother." He brightened. "Hey! Betcha you can't carry me ashore on your shoulders!"

So I dove between his muscular legs and picked him up, and started walking to shore. I relished having a back strong enough to support another man, even once his full weight had returned.

Whooping, he yelled, "You owe me about a hundred of these rides, you know! Plus forty years of interest."

STRIPPING THE COVERS
By Mark Apoapsis

"I'm picturing this big brawny body of yours sprawled limp and naked across my bed after I'm done with you," the hot stranger shouted intimately into my ear. Probably no one else heard him, with the possible exception of the buddy I'd come in with. The stranger had wedged himself in sideways between our barstools, his back pressing familiarly against my friend's shoulder at the same time as he played with my chest hair. This was probably the closest I'd ever come to being in a three-way with my all-too-vanilla friend. My shirt had started with two fewer buttons fastened than I'd have chosen to keep buttoned in class or on the street, at least without a T-shirt underneath. The guy had undone a third one for me several minutes earlier and occasionally toyed with the fourth.

"After you're done doing exactly what to me?" I shouted back, wanting details. The idea of a brawny body, my own or someone else's, sprawled limp and naked on a bed was enough to guarantee that any part of my body that had been limp before was now as hard and taut as the rest of me. The guy was a good five inches shorter than I, though promisingly muscular. This looked like an opportunity to realize my rarely-fulfilled fantasy of being dominated by a much smaller man.

"For starters, I'll go over every square inch of your body with my tongue. For six hours. Then once more with my fingertips for good measure."

That sounded promising at first. It took a few seconds for the wording to register. For once I didn't have to pretend to be the big dumb lunkhead I was often taken for; it came naturally, thanks to the rich mixture of alcohol and testosterone now flowing through my veins. It didn't help that most of my blood supply seemed to be diverted away from my brain and into one particular vein serving a certain external organ.

Then the phrases he had used finally penetrated my alcohol-hazed brain, which slowly worked out that it was probably going to be the only part of my body that was going to get penetrated tonight.

When I just stared at him stupidly, he prompted, "Unless you have an early class or something. You don't take classes on Sundays, do you?"

"Uh, yeah, as a matter of fact, I have a 10:35 class."

"Then we should get out of here now," he said smoothly, toying with the next button on my shirt.

I said goodnight to my friend, who nodded understandingly – at least, he thought he understood. It wasn't too unusual for one or the other of us to get lucky in this bar. Unfortunately for me, the last time I'd heard the combination of code phrases "every square inch," "six," and "good measure," it was a fellow student pretending to ask for my help looking for her lost phone, when really she was summoning me to three tedious hours of memorizing cyphers, encryption keys, and more code phrases.

At least this one was male, and in a gay bar, which was promising though not conclusive. Unlike my regular courses that involved grades, it wasn't clear that my covert extracurricular courses technically forbade instructors and students fooling around on the side. Certainly he acted interested enough as we made our way out of the bar with my arm around his meaty shoulders and his arm wrapped around my waist, thumb tucked familiarly under both the waistband of my pants and the boxers beneath. And he was a lot younger than most of my professors. Maybe I was getting laid tonight after all. My cock seemed to think so.

Once he got me into his car, I leaned toward him, but he pushed me gently away. "No need for that," he said with a laugh. "No one can see us anymore. We can drop the cover."

"I was afraid you'd say that. I'll bet you're not even gay."

"Oh. Sorry, man. You really are gay? I wouldn't have guessed. Here I was thinking it was an implausible cover, a big muscular guy like you."

"You can't tell by ..."

"Yeah, I should know better than to judge by appearances. That's probably why they don't let me do fieldwork."

"Is this going to take long? Is this a quick contact, so I can go back in there and try again?" I saw in his face that wasn't going to happen. "This is one of those hours-long training sessions, isn't it?"

"'Fraid so."

"So much for my hopes for tonight."

"Poor guy!" He ruffled my wavy black hair, almost affectionately. "What were you hoping for? The slap of flesh on flesh? A long night of half-naked bodies rolling around on the floor of my living room?"

"Pretty much. And I was hoping you'd make me ..." I stopped myself. It was none of his business what I was into.

"Make you what? Breakfast?"

I laughed. "No. And I'm not going to finish that sentence."

"Something about the way you were letting me fondle you makes me think you were hoping you'd enjoy being humiliated and forced into submissive poses."

"Good guess."

"Sweaty bodies pressed against each other? My hands all over you?"

"Hey! You can stop teasing me with things I can't have."

"But you can. I can offer you that much, anyway."

"What?! You just said ..."

"I'm one of your unarmed combat instructors. Wrestling is my specialty. And it's no lie that I enjoy making big guys like you submit to me. Over and over. Just as long as you understand that you're not going to wind up in my bed, and sweat is the only body fluid we're going to be mingling."

"Are you're actually taking me home, not to some secret facility with fluorescent lights and one-way mirrors?" Not that I was picky about ambience.

"Well, they fly me all around the country, and I think they rented my house on a month-to-month lease just before I moved in last week. But yeah. We're going to where I'm really living."

# # # # #

OK, sleepyhead, time to get up," he said the next morning, flinging off the blanket he'd covered me with on the couch while I was already half asleep. He'd let me crash there when I'd admitted he'd worn me out, and hinted that my roommate was used to me spending the night whenever I hooked up with someone. I was in my boxers, having put them back on after I removed the jockstrap and trunks he'd lent me for our wrestling practice. My instructor, who hadn't told me his name, was wearing a forest green terrycloth robe belted casually enough to reveal a large triangle of chest hair even denser than mine. Hair that my face had spent a lot of time involuntarily buried in last night; I knew it covered most of his chest and spilled down onto his rock-hard belly. "I made coffee and scrambled eggs. How do you feel?"

"Every muscle in my body is sore," I admitted. I stretched, then laced my hands behind my head and grinned up at him. "I couldn't be any more sore if you'd tied me up and spent the whole night actually fucking me," I said teasingly.

"Have I taught you nothing about leaving yourself open?" he said, reaching toward my wide-open armpit with intent to tickle. Last night he'd pinned my wrists and tickled me mercilessly a several times, using that as a novel submission technique in alternation with the more customary arm bars, leg bars, and sleeper holds.

I managed to get my hands out from behind my head and grab his wrist in one motion, striking with snakelike speed before his fingers could touch my armpit. He nodded in satisfaction. "You're learning."

I didn't let go of his wrist. "What are you wearing under that robe?" I asked.

He grinned. "Nothing. Think you can get it open, big guy?"

"I think I can get it all the way off you, you little shit," I said.

"I'd like to see you try."

In the end he made me agree to eat my cold scrambled eggs wearing my boxers as a bib in exchange for being allowed off the floor and for an end to the tickling.

All in all, probably my fourth or fifth hottest encounter since I'd entered college and certainly the hottest one in the line of duty.

# # # # #

If all my training had been like that, it would have been the best job ever, but most of my other clandestine training sessions had been pretty boring so far. Well, with the notable exception of Duct Tape and Handcuffs 101; I only wished I'd dared to take advantage of the cute instructor while he was letting me practice on him.

I certainly couldn't complain about my secret job. I probably averaged less than three hours a week of covert training, and in exchange for that, they paid my tuition, room and board and gave me a generous stipend. Most of the training was not in person but in the form of encrypted slide presentations and sometimes videos. I could safely watch those in my dorm room as long as I did it in my boxers with my blankets drawn up to my waist. My straight and definitely not curious roommate wouldn't dream of looking over my shoulder, since he assumed I was watching porn. One video practically was: it was designed to show me what to expect if I were ever captured and tortured for information. The edition I got was all-male, which made sense once I saw how much of the torture focused on weak points very specific to male psychology and anatomy. Most of the parts showing the simulated torture itself were a little intense for me to take much pleasure in, but the bondage and humiliation leading up to it was as arousing as any porn I'd ever rented and with much better acting. At least, I hoped it was acting.

Occasionally they would pull me in for some in-person instruction, usually less hot and sweaty than the wrestling lessons I'd just been treated to. Aside from that, I could live the life of a normal college student, except for some occasional pressure to take certain courses. I might have taken the biology courses anyway, but I would have chosen Spanish over French if it had been up to me. They say that women think French is romantic, but I've never given a damn what women think is romantic, and French doesn't seem to be such a common fetish among guys. I found Latinos hot and thought it might help if I could flirt with them in their mother tongue. I wondered if I was being groomed to be sent on some overseas mission in Paris. That would be sort of cool. I fantasized about climbing the Eiffel

Tower, trying to figure out which security guard was actually a terrorist dressed in the uniform of the unconscious guard I'd found gagged and bound to a girder in his shorts.

But I was given no hint of what my first assignment would be, or when, all through my freshman and sophomore years. They gave me very little further unarmed combat training, and I got just an hour of weapon instruction, on a firing range – less time than they spent teaching me how to survive by eating bugs if I had to. I had the feeling all of those were basic skills I was being taught for unexpected situations, and I was being groomed for an assignment involving little or no violence. That suited me; I couldn't imagine picking up a gun and killing a guy with it. I liked the idea of risking my life for my country, but if I were ever ordered to take no prisoners, I'd find it very difficult to obey.

For all I knew, I was already being given assignments that were part of some larger operation I wasn't privy to because they kept asking me to do little things that made no sense as training. Once they sent me a ticket to a student play and instructed me to strike up a friendly conversation with the red-haired woman who would be seated on my right. That was slightly uncomfortable; she seemed to be interested in me, and I got the feeling she was hoping I'd ask her out. Fortunately, I had no orders to arrange a date or acquire her phone number, so I didn't have to string her along beyond the final curtain. I don't know what they'd hoped to accomplish. The play was all right, but I probably wouldn't have bothered to go on my own time and my own dime. I was more into the home football games, if only because it was a better place to meet guys, even if almost all of them were straight.

# # # # #

Some of the things they made me do in person turned out to be more in the nature of tests than training. That had been happening more and more often in my junior year. Once they had me work for a night seating people in a restaurant, where some of the customers were ringers, including my former poisons and drugs instructor and my seatmate from the play. They'd graded me on whether an observer – the bartender, I later suspected – could detect a flash of recognition when I encountered another operative.

Then, a few weeks after the holidays, they texted me an address and a time and date: their most straightforward way of arranging a training session. They gave no details, always obsessed with secrecy despite the encrypted transmission and the simple cipher I had to decode in my head that would make it unreadable to anyone looking over my shoulder. When I got to the assigned location, which turned out to be a sound studio (presumably fake, but the soundproofing later proved to be real enough), I found another guy waiting in the tiny lobby. Most likely not my instructor, since he was my own age. I recognized him instantly: I'd met him in the stands at a football game the previous fall, and we'd really hit it off. We'd even gone out for a few beers afterward, and had talked for a long time. Long enough for me to figure out that he was straight, unfortunately, but I'd almost asked for his contact information anyway, so we could hang out again. He had seemed to enjoy my company, too. Now, I wondered if it had been an act, like me and the chick in the theater.

I thought I caught a flash of recognition and surprise in his face, immediately hidden. So, he was probably a trainee, too. I mumbled, noncommittally, "Hey. You here for a session, too? I wonder if they scheduled us both at the same time by mistake."

"I don't think they make mistakes."

Afraid he'd just blown it for us, I started to caution, "We should probably wait for ..."

The door into the studio opened, and a man a good bit older than we walked out. "Don't worry. This isn't that kind of test. You don't have to convince me you haven't met."

My fellow trainee and I exchanged relieved grins. "Good to see you again, man," he murmured to me.

"Yeah." I couldn't remember his name, if he'd even mentioned it. I tried to recall whether I'd given him my real first name or one of the aliases I used to keep my life compartmentalized, or no name at all.

"What kind of test is it?" he asked the man.

"You've both taken the video course on torture resistance techniques by now."

"Sure," I said, my face suddenly feeling a little hot.

"Sure," he said with a shudder.

"Well, this is the practicum."

"What?" I blurted before I could stop myself.

"'Practicum' means you get hands-on experience. Sort of a lab," the instructor explained. I didn't bother to tell him that I knew perfectly well what a practicum was, but he saw something in my face and added, "But you probably knew that. I've seen your test scores. Sorry, it's just that you look more like the type of guy we hire as muscle. I train those, too."

"He does, doesn't he?" my fellow trainee said, giving me a friendly punch on the arm. "But he's a pretty smart guy once you get to know him. What do we need to do?"

"Come on in and take off your coats ... for starters."

We followed him into the soundproof room, and he shut the padded door behind us.

"Don't worry. This is going to be very mild physical torture. We don't want to leave our promising young agents with scars – physical or otherwise."

"This is getting creepy," the other guy said.

"You can still back out. Plenty of trainees wind up doing very good work as analysts."

"But I really want to be a field operative," he said.

"So do I," I said.

"Good. Now, this involves a little role playing." He turned around to pick something up from the table. A water pistol? "This isn't a real gun, but pretend it is."

"OK," we said. My training partner and I were both starting to breathe hard. In his case, I think it was nervousness.

The instructor pointed the prop at me. "You! Stand right there and don't try anything." To my fellow trainee, he said, "This man turns out to be an American spy. We have to find out what he knows. Strip him to the waist and tie him to the chair with his belt."

"What?! I can't do that!"

"Then I suggest you reconsider that desk job."

"But ... Okay." He put his hand on my shoulder and gently pushed me into the chair. I was only too happy to play along. I wanted him to get a good grade, after all. Besides, I had a pretend gun aimed at me. I had to let him strip me.

"Sorry, man," he murmured as he began fumbling nervously with the buttons of my flannel shirt.

"No worries," I whispered.

"Anyone hearing you whisper to each other like that in the field is likely to suspect you're in league with each other. Do you want to wind up tied up right beside him?"

Damn, what a thing to say just when I was fending off a growing hard-on by sheer force of will. But he took the hint and was silent as he divested me of my shirt. I sucked in my gut involuntarily as his knuckles tickled the fine hairs running down my belly as he was unbuckling my belt. He got behind me and bound my wrists, pulling the belt just tight enough that I probably couldn't have gotten out, but not tight enough to be uncomfortable. I was more worried about the tightness in my pants.

"How'd I do?" he asked, turning to the instructor.

"Reasonably well, so far," he said. He held out a car battery and some wires ending in alligator clips. Not the big thick cables and clips you'd jump-start a car with. More like something you might clip to a man's nipples. Or ... worse.

"What, you want me – no way! I can't do it!"

"Why not?"

"Well, he's a nice guy. Anyway, I'm not looking for a job in counterintelligence. I won't ever be asked to interrogate anyone. I thought the idea was to see how well I can stand up to being tortured."

"That too. You'll get your turn."

"But – Why do I have to ...?" He looked back at me, clearly in anguish.

"Dude, it's all right," I assured him, my voice husky with what he probably took as fear.

The instructor asked him, "You know what you have to do if you're with a fellow agent and his cover is blown, right?"

"Get away as soon as possible and report in because he'll compromise me under torture sooner or later?"

"Before that."

"Pretend I had nothing to do with him? No matter how much I want to help him?"

"Precisely. You have to maintain your own cover, which might involve assisting the enemy in capturing the other agent if there's nothing you can do for him without compromising yourself. In some circumstances, you might even have to help interrogate your unfortunate colleague, depending on what your cover identity would be expected to do. It could get a little rough."

"I can't! I just can't torture this guy."

"Very well, then."

"No, wait." He paused, took a deep but shuddering breath, then came to a decision. "Give me that thing."

Avoiding looking me in the eye, he got as far as using the metal jaws of one clip to comb chest hair away from my nipple, but then he couldn't bring himself to let the jaws close on my nipple. Which would cause a trivial amount of pain, I was sure, compared to when he flipped the switch on and touched the other wire to my chest. But he'd barely touched the cold metal, jaws open, to the nipple he'd laid bare before snatching it away and turning back to the instructor. "Look, this isn't fair. Bad enough if it was a stranger, but I happen to know this guy, a little."

"In real life, if you're unfortunate enough to ever face this situation, the other agent could well be your own partner, someone you've worked with and trusted for years and grown a lot closer to than you are to this man."

"Dude, it's no coincidence we know each other," I told him. I took a ragged breath. "They set it up, so we'd meet. They had this planned all along."

The instructor gave me a startled looked I'd come to recognize – like someone impressed at seeing an unusually smart gorilla put together a five-piece jigsaw puzzle all by himself. Between enduring condescending reactions like that from intelligent people and alienating other brawny guys who really are brainless jocks but are fun to play with, I'd trained myself to let people accept me at face value.

I'd been living two lives long before I'd ever been recruited. Well, four lives until I came out, and even now I preferred to choose the moment when I'd come out to each new acquaintance. I currently played pickup basketball with guys who still thought I was a straight dumb jock, especially when I insisted I couldn't remember who was on my team unless we played shirts and skins. It was second nature to keep track of who knew me under which of my four identities. My covert employment just added two more identities. The guy who'd just been teasing my nipple, for example, thought I was an intelligent straight spy-to-be.

The instructor said, "Your training partner is correct. We in fact arranged for each of you to meet several other trainees with this session in mind. We paired you guys up because you seemed to hit it off especially well."

"Please, sir," my lab partner said. "Isn't there any other way."

"If you still want to try for a field position, you can take a make-up exam with one of the other trainees we put in your path. I think we have an opening in two weeks."

"Thank you, sir!"

"Most likely the fellow who helped you seduce that English Lit major last spring break."

"Oh, man!" he moaned.

"But only if you pass the second half of this exam today."

"What's that?"

"Dude!" I said impatiently. Wasn't it obvious? We both had to pass the same training. What else did he think "You'll get your turn" meant? I spelled it out for him: "He's going to make us switch places."

"That is correct. But not just yet. You don't get off so easily as that." The instructor approached and took the torture device out of my partner's unresisting hands and ran his eyes up and down my exposed torso, like a side of beef he was preparing to carve a choice cut. "You were given a three-digit number to memorize and not reveal to anyone. Do you remember it?"

"I don't know what you're talking about," I lied, squirming in anticipation, my chest already heaving. I didn't know how I would react to the pain, but the sense of vulnerability, of being at another man's mercy, had given me a raging hard-on when it had been my peer, the younger guy, doing it. I'd rather it had been him, especially since we liked each other. But now ... well, I wasn't getting any softer.

# # # # #

I finally received my first field assignment in the middle of spring break my junior year, which I'd chosen to spend on the beach with some friends from my dorm. I'd received no further in-person training since the mutual torture, just some more slide presentations about precautions to take when on a deep-cover mission. It's amazing how much more interesting those seemed now that I'd had a taste of what it felt like to be strapped shirtless to a chair and tortured for information.

I still felt a perverse admixture of guilt, arousal, and pride that after changing places and stripping my lab partner to the waist, I'd broken him in only minutes, at a much lower voltage than it had taken the instructor to get me to reveal my own secret number. I might have held out longer, but when the instructor ordered my lab partner to pull my pants down, I stopped insisting I'd forgotten the number. Although I believed he was bluffing and would have stopped before inflicting what I could only imagine would be unbearable pain, I wasn't so sure he was bluffing about the part where my training partner was going to be forced to strip me naked. If he'd complied with that, it would have ignominiously laid bare my erection, which had subsided when the instructor increased the voltage on my nipples a couple of steps, but had returned the minute my lab partner started fumbling very hesitantly with the button on my pants. I'd blurted the number just in time to save either myself or my buddy, depending on whether he'd been about to chicken out again.

My training partner had then earned what would have been called an Incomplete, as opposed to an F, had it been an ordinary class, by allowing me to tie him up, and by enduring several minutes of me caressing the creamy, sweaty skin of his bare chest, belly, and armpits with a bare metal clip, completing a circuit that ended with the metal teeth I had clipped to his small pink nipple. Over a stiff drink afterward, we'd concluded that it was a lesson more than a test; that everyone breaks sooner or later and gets a passing mark anyway. We figured that part of the point was to experience being tortured, and to see a colleague being broken, so we'd have no illusions that anyone could resist it. He wasn't looking forward to having to torture his onetime wingman. I pointed out that he had another problem to look forward to: his buddy would be required to torture someone in turn, so he'd better hope there was a third trainee with them or he'd have to retake both halves of the test.

Now, months later, I was relaxing on the beach, and currently playing volleyball with some of my friends, a game I've always enjoyed not so much for the workout or the technical aspects as for the chance to watch the bathing-suit-clad bodies of some of my hunkier male friends reaching for the sky with armpits exposed, or leaping straight up to put their muscles behind a powerful spike, or diving heroically after a ball and rolling to their feet with sand coating their sweaty chests.

At one point, I chased after a stray ball, not because I was closest but because it was heading right for a trio of brawny guys, and I wanted a closer look. I was careful not to catch up to the ball before it reached them. The biggest of them, an impressively muscled blond who was, if anything, larger than I, picked it up.

"Thanks, man," I said.

"Who says I'm giving it back?" he said, grinning mischievously.

"Come on, man," I said, reaching for it, but he tossed it over my head to one of his buddies, a tall lean Asian wearing a bathing suit much skimpier than mine or even the blond's. I whirled and stepped toward the second man, but before I could reach him, he threw it back to the blond, again arching it over my head. As I whirled, the first guy tossed it to his other friend, a Latino whose brown chest and arms bulged with muscles that rivaled his blond buddy's. I took a step toward the Latino, and he tossed it back to the original guy. I resisted the temptation to tackle the handsome Latino anyway and turned back to the blond. I wondered how long I could keep them going, if I played dumb. This was even more fun than the volleyball, especially since it was all male and all hot.

The one who'd originally stopped the rolling ball now held it high over his head, making as though to throw it again if I came any closer. For a blond guy, he had suspiciously dark, thick hair sticking out of his armpits, the part of me trained to detect altered appearances noted automatically.

One of my friends trotted up, sand still clinging to his chest hairs from diving after my last spike. I resisted the urge to brush it off and instead drew him into a sort of two-man huddle. "Get ready to grab it when I distract him," I whispered. I closed in on the ball thief, reaching high over my head as if to take the ball or block a throw, then suddenly lowered my hands and dug my fingers into his exposed armpits. This worked better than I expected: He instantly doubled up in laughter, dropping the ball. My friend kicked it away and ran after it. I covered his escape by wrestling my foe to the ground and straddling his chest. After a few seconds of tickling his ribs to soften him up, I clamped my left hand around his meaty biceps and pinned his arm to the sand, taking away his ability to defend his armpit. I stroked the surprisingly ticklish smooth skin just below his armpit and worked my way into the silky black hairs at my leisure. I ignored his two big buddies. I'd just have to take the risk that they would grab me by my arms and legs, lift me bodily off their friend, and stretch me out spread-eagle in the sun while the blond decided what he wanted to do with me. But they stood back, laughing at their friend's plight.

"You bastard!" he said between giggles. "I'll get you for this."

My mission accomplished, I climbed off him and ran away. Not back toward the volleyball game – it would have been cowardly to lead the enemy to my friends – but toward the water. Laughing, he chased me into the surf. I dove into a wave. This was the most fun I'd had all break, especially when he finally caught up to me and grappled with me. I'd made it just far out enough that when we stood up and anchored our feet in the sand, the crests of the waves were lapping at our nipples and the troughs periodically exposing our navels. He didn't let me stand up very long; he grabbed my head and dunked me under the water. He crouched down holding my head trapped against his chest, which felt very warm in contrast with the water. I briefly considered and discarded the half a dozen lethal and nonlethal forms of defense I'd theoretically been trained in but wasn't very good at. He held me under for only a second or two, long enough to demonstrate his power over me but not long enough for me to panic. Then he let me surface, giving me a chance to draw a breath, only to playfully splash water in my face. I splashed back, then grabbed for him and knocked him down. We wrestled underwater for a moment and came up for air together, legs still tangled together, his arms wrapped around me from behind. I struggled to free one of the arms pinned to my side.

"When I get done with you," he said, "you're going to have bruises over every square inch of your body. I've got your measure, pal."

I stopped struggling, and he took advantage of that to crush my head against his chest again and lock it there in the crook of his elbow, while trapping my arm between our bodies. "That's right. No sense fighting it. I'm going to kick your ass six ways from Sunday." A wave washed over my head, and he muscled me a few steps closer to the beach, so he could keep my head out of the water. "What time is it?" he asked suddenly.

Neither of us was wearing a watch, and I couldn't have looked at mine if I had one, but I guessed it was well after noon. "Ten thirty-five," I said, resignedly giving the counter-sign.

"Perfect."

I felt something tickling the inside my ear, the one that wasn't pressed against his smooth tanned chest hearing nothing but his pounding heartbeat. I realized what his free hand was doing: inserting something into my ear. It felt like some kind of filament a few times thicker than a human hair. After first lightly tracing the spiral of my outer ear with it, he used it to probe deep into the even more sensitive ear canal. I couldn't do much about this intimate invasion, since he had my head completely immobilized.

He brought his lips close to my ear, the same ear he'd just had his way with. I felt his hot breath as he said softly, "Leave the recorder at the bottom of the ocean when you're done listening to the message. It's weighted, and its electronics will fry themselves automatically after you play it."

"What recorder?" I asked, but he was busy working loose the knot in my bathing suit's drawstring one-handed, the warm knuckle of his thumb grinding into my belly. In a moment he got it untied, and I felt his thick fingers slipping inside it. Metal and plastic brushed against my crotch as he stuffed a slim rectangular object in, sort of tucking it between my balls and thigh. His fingers made a lot of contact with my crotch in the process, even briefly brushing my genitals. Probably by accident: his hand was very big, maybe even bigger than mine, and even with the string undone, there wasn't much room left over in there for foreign body parts with all the space my own were taking up at the moment, and it was getting more crowded by the second. Having done what he wanted, he left his hand inside but let me out of the headlock. When I straightened up and tried to step away, he caught my throat in the crook of his elbow and pulled me backward, my back slapping against his chest and my feet scrabbling in the sand. Until I recovered my balance, I was supported mostly by his arm around my throat. If he had tightened his biceps and taken his other hand out of my bathing suit to reinforce his grip, he could have made me fall asleep in his arms. That should have been a frightening idea, but I knew I could trust him.

In this position, standing up and leaning back against him, I felt something trailing lightly down my chest. I peered over his biceps and saw a thin black wire that disappeared into my trunks, presumably connecting the earpiece to the recorder. It was well hidden where it passed through my chest hair where it ran alongside the trail down my belly. No one could have seen it from the shore, even with binoculars, even though he was presenting me to his watching buddies like a proud fisherman posing with the big one that didn't get away. The water was still deep enough that his watching buddies probably couldn't tell his hand was inside my trunks. I saw that my own friends had paused in their game to watch, too. Maybe they were concerned that I was in the power of a stranger who could drown me if he wanted, but more likely they just found my humiliating defeat entertaining.

"The earpiece will go down with it," he added. "It's attached, see?" While we were momentarily in the trough of a wave that hid most of our bodies from shore, his fingers lightly traced its path through my pubic hair, then emerged from my trunks to follow it up the trail of hair on my belly.

"Yeah, I noticed."

"I noticed something, too. What would your friends say if they knew you got a hard-on from roughhousing with some random asshole on the beach?"

"Most of them would be surprised if I didn't get one."

"Great. So it'll look perfectly reasonable for you to linger out here by yourself for awhile while you're listening to the message. They'll think you're waiting for it to go down."

"Are they finally giving me a mission?" I asked eagerly.

"If you're still clueless enough to think I have any idea what's on that thing, then I sure hope not, dumb ass." He dunked my into the water one more time, this time holding me down for a few seconds. When I came up, sputtering, he was already several body lengths away, swimming to shore. I wistfully watched the water sheeting off his bronzed muscular back with each powerful stroke. I'd have liked to have gone after him and invited him to have a beer or something. Better yet, both a beer and then "something." I reminded myself that he was probably straight, most likely not even as aggressive as his cover identity. If it hadn't been for our jobs he'd never have initiated that interlude of pleasurable horseplay, let alone touched my dick.

94

The message started by itself as I was retying my swimming trunks. Either I'd inadvertently put pressure on the switch with a finger – or other appendage – or my contact had hit the "on" switch for me, possibly while he was fumbling around inside my trunks. Or maybe he'd turned it on by accident while turning me on by accident.

Breathlessly, I waited to see if my first assignment would be something boring and mundane or the dangerous deep-cover mission I hoped for, maybe on the other side of the ocean I was standing in, or the ocean on the other side of the country. Then again, any assignment was potentially interesting. The blond agent who'd delivered the device had had an interesting assignment of his own that wasn't the least bit dangerous. After all, what's the worst I would have done to him, if I'd been a little stronger and gotten the upper hand? Maybe there were fulfilling career paths I'd never considered. I'd be totally convincing as a beach bully. I don't especially like humiliating smaller weaker guys, which most of my contacts were likely to be, but hey, anything to serve my country.

The recording gave me some very specific instructions about how I'd be spending my summer vacation, and no time on the beach was mentioned. It ended with a summary of some details I'd have to commit to memory. A lot about my general destination and the elaborate things I'd need to do to reach it, nothing about what to do when I got there, except to make contact and request further instructions. Then it replayed once more from the start, as if they'd worried it would take some time to get my mind focused on business again. It ended with a reminder to dispose of the device – how dumb did it think I was? – and went silent.

It was a good thing I was out to my friends, sexuality wise, because when I rejoined them no one thought it was strange that I looked so pleased with myself after getting my ass kicked. Later, two of my buddies got me drunk and got the story out of me. A carefully censored version, of course. Just the part about the guy's hand in my trunks.

# # # # #

I tried not to be too obvious about checking out the guy stripping beside me. I'd been lifting weights, having gained entry with the membership card I'd found under a bush exactly a hundred yards away from the Seattle bus station, and he'd arrived half an hour later, within minutes of the time I expected, wearing a short-sleeved red bicycle jersey. He looked like the guy whose half-naked pictures had been sent to my new cell phone: big brawny build similar to mine, swarthy complexion, thick dark hair, longer and straighter than mine. So I followed him into the locker room, noticing the tattoo on his forearm. As I opened my locker and knelt to untie my shoes, I discreetly watched him strip off his sweaty jersey to reveal a nearly hairless, nicely muscled chest with another tattoo on one of his pecs, and a few small moles just large enough to have been visible in one of the close-ups he'd posed for. I was sure it was the same guy, even without putting the battery back in my phone to double-check the photos.

The tattoos were probably temporary, and for all I knew some of the moles were, too. He didn't even glance in my direction as he stripped down to his briefs. I'd been told that real cyclists don't wear underwear under their bike clothes, but I doubt either of the two other guys changing in the room thought there was anything strange about that, and I was just as happy he was wearing something underneath. I forced myself to look away as he began to take them off. I'd seen enough. Since the pictures I'd received weren't totally nude, that meant I had no need-to-know what he looked like naked, and I didn't want the other guys to notice me checking him out longer than necessary.

I did watch out of the corner of my eye as he took a towel and a padlock out of his gym bag, stuffed everything into a locker, opened the lock while hiding the combination with his naked body, put the lock on and spun the dial, and headed for the showers. By this time, I was bare-chested and barefoot myself, having been slowly stripping off my gym clothes all the while. I was putting everything into my locker, naked, as the second bystander finished buttoning his shirt and left. If he'd hung around any longer, I'd have had to get into the shower myself, but I was glad not to have to stay naked longer than necessary. Normally, stripping to the buff in locker rooms is something I don't think twice about. Today, beginning my first assignment and hundreds of miles from home, I was acutely conscious of my nakedness, convinced that the other guys were studying me out of the corner of their eyes, even wondering if there were tiny spy cameras peering at me through the slats in one of these lockers, in which case I would be totally screwed. It was very unlikely, but not impossible, and I'd never felt so exposed.

During the few minutes I was alone and apparently unobserved, I dialed the combination on the cyclist's padlock. It opened on the first try, and I removed his bicycling clothes and put them on. They didn't feel quite as sweaty as ordinary clothes might have, and the guy's sweat had already half evaporated. They felt not so much clammy as pleasantly cool against my naked body after my workout. Another guy entered before I'd even finished pulling the pants over my genitals, but I relaxed when I saw he wasn't one of the ones who'd just left coming back for a forgotten water bottle or something; he had no way of knowing this was not my locker.

I found a windbreaker and some sweat pants in the gym bag, and put them on in case someone was observant enough to notice that a different guy was leaving in the same clothes. His shoes fit me perfectly. I left him nothing but the skimpy shorts and tank top I found in the bag, and a loose car key that I hoped fit a car parked somewhere within easy jogging distance for a barefoot man. Its only other contents was a fanny pack; I glanced inside and saw a wallet, and put it on. I replaced the nearly empty bag in the guy's locker, closed the lock and spun the dial, and left, nodding casually to the other occupant, who'd claimed a nearby locker and was now down to his boxer-briefs. It was a busy locker room; on my way out, I brushed past a guy coming in who I'd seen running on a treadmill, whose gray sweatshirt was darkened halfway down his chest with sweat. He'd probably be joining the cyclist in the shower. I was careful not to glance back at the original padlocked locker in which I'd abandoned my clothes.

There were two bikes parked outside. One matched the cleanest of the pictures I'd received, which had shown the guy who was now showering posing beside it, fully dressed in the very clothes I was now wearing. It was secured with a cable lock, which I opened using the same combination that had worked on the padlock. I assumed the cyclist, whom I was sure had been well paid, had been told to expect his clothes and bike to be missing, if only because it was important for him to act like nothing was wrong and certainly not report it. Probably he was a full-fledged operative, and probably the bike and clothes had not been his. It still felt weird to have taken them while he was in the shower.

I put on his helmet, took a sip from his nearly full water bottle, and mounted his bike. As I rode north along a memorized route, I tried to suppress the feeling I'd left something behind because of course I had: every stitch of clothing I'd been wearing, my new phone, the picture id I'd used to buy the bus ticket to Seattle, and the credit card I'd used to buy food along the way. I knew someone else would take care of destroying those, maybe just some local college student earning some money without even knowing whom he was working for. I imagined a student opening my locker, stripping and changing into my clothes, but then who would collect his clothes? More likely they'd just tell him walk out with my stuff in his gym bag.

# # # # #

It was a grueling ride for someone who wasn't really an avid cyclist, but I was in good shape, and I'd been training with longer and longer bike rides all spring. Some of the route was trails, many of which were very nice, almost what I might have chosen to do if I really were on summer vacation, had I known how scenic they were. Especially the scenery that kept jogging past me without shirts. Still, by the end of the second day, it was with great pleasure that I threw the bike into a ditch just out of sight of the trail, stripped off the bike clothes, and got into the clothes I found in a hiker's backpack that had been hidden behind a tree. There was plenty of cover in this forested region, and I'd checked carefully to make sure no one could see me, and not just because I was stripping naked outdoors; modesty or getting arrested for indecency were the least of my worries. I made particularly sure I was under the canopy and not visible from space.

I wadded up the bike clothes and put them in the backpack. It felt sort of good to be hiking. I using a somewhat different set of muscles, and the feeling was beginning to come back to my butt and my balls.

A GPS device I found in the backpack guided me to a campsite deep in the woods, already set up for me, just like the one where I'd spent the first night of my two-day ride, except I'd actually need to strike this tent and take it with me. I made a fire and, with great delight, burned the bike clothes I now associated with my aching muscles and numb nuts.

A few days later, I was thoroughly sick of hiking, too, and of having only two changes of clothes and having to do laundry in the stream. I was still nowhere near civilization, but according to the GPS, I'd managed to cross the border.

The first person I met on Canadian soil was another lone hiker. I'd been nervous, hearing him crashing through the woods, especially when I caught a flash of red. I was half expecting him to be a Mountie who would handcuff me and take me in for interrogation. But it was just a red flannel shirt, not too different from my green one and my blue one. Neither of which I was wearing at the moment, now that the day had warmed up.

"Hey there," he greeted me. Something about his features made me think he had some non-European ancestry somewhere; although his skin was as light as mine, he reminded me a little of my Latino friends and lovers. Up here, that was more likely to mean First Nations.

"How's it going?" I said.

"I hope you've put bug spray on every square centimeter of exposed skin, or you'll get bitten for sure."

"I've already been bitten like six times," I lied.

"I'd have thought more like ten."

"All right. Thirty-five times. By some measure."

Somewhat to my surprise, he quickly began unbuttoning his own shirt. He was fairly muscular, built a lot like me, with plenty of dark chest hair, mostly on his pecs like mine. I had better abs, but his weren't bad.

"Um," I said as he shrugged out of the red shirt entirely, "They didn't tell exactly what ..."

"Take off those jeans," he said, "and put on these cargo pants." He began unbuttoning them.

"Is this how you do things in Canada?"

"I was born in Texas, eh? You have something in common with my grandfather now: he sneaked in across our southern border." He removed his shoes and slid his cargo pants down his hairy legs. He was wearing blue boxer shorts.

"Nice to get one last look at a fellow American." Very nice.

"Switch backpacks with me. You've got a shirt in there, right?"

"Two." I undid my pants. "Neither one is clean, sorry."

He grinned ruefully and tossed me his pants. "I didn't expect them to be. You know, on my application they asked me to rank twenty things in order of disgustingness. I put 'wearing another guy's sweaty clothes' as number nine, but this is like the fifth time they've made me do it."

"I put it down as number seventeen," I admitted. "Sorry if it bothers you." Nine was a fairly high ranking, considering that crawling through sewers, eating bugs, and looting corpses were all on the list. "Seems like overkill; no one has even seen me in these clothes."

"That's what you think. At some point we were each observed through binoculars or satellite imagery, heading toward the border. This way it will look like we each doubled back." He had the same dark curly hair as me, and we both had a few days of beard growth. No one would mistake us for each other close up, but from a distance, we'd be impossible to tell apart.

"How do we know they can't see us now, meeting up, taking off our clothes?"

"It's a calculated risk," he said, folding his arms across his bare chest. He was standing barefoot in the pine needles in his boxers now, and so was I, with a cool breeze playing over our bodies. It felt liberating and intimate. "If you want to be really professional about it, we should have a cover motive. Unfortunately, there are no bodies of water around here large enough for skinny-dipping."

"No one would hike for days and arrange a clandestine meeting in the woods just to skinny-dip with his buddy anyway."

"True. There's a more plausible cover, if you're willing."

"What?"

"Well, this is totally optional, but ... well, see, I listed 'pretending to have sex with another man' way down as number twelve."

"I listed it as number twenty."

"You're kidding!"

"Nope. 'Pretending to have sex with women' was my number four." Admittedly I'd since had second thoughts, and if they asked me to update my rankings now, I might not put it in the number-four spot anymore. I'd been young and inexperienced, and had not yet given bugs a fair chance.

"I was going to suggest pretending to have sex with you, but now you've got me feeling nervous, to be honest."

"Don't worry, I'll pretend to be very gentle."

He grinned. "Want to pretend to just give me a blow job?"

"Sure. I'll make it look really, really convincing if you want."

"Just in case they have high-resolution imaging," he agreed, slipping off his boxers.

I knelt in front of him, saying, "Dude, you're doing an excellent job of pretending to be getting a hard-on."

# # # # #

I'm in position, I typed. I was sitting in a coffee shop, part of a huge chain called Tim Horton's, enjoying with newfound appreciation a lot of things I'd taken for granted all my life: a roof over my head, air conditioning, freshly made food and coffee, and free WiFi. The message was, of course, not sent through public cell phone text protocols, but Internet instant messaging, and my new phone heavily encrypted it before sending it over the airwaves to the coffee shop's router and then through the Internet. If they were being especially careful, they might have embedded the encrypted data in something innocent-looking, like the low-order bits of an image, instead of obviously encrypted traffic. To anyone snooping on the network, it might have looked like I was downloading pornography instead of receiving the reply: Ready for mission briefing?

I was hoping you'd say that, I typed. Can't wait to find out what all this cloak and dagger is for.

It's standard practice not to brief operatives before they're in the field. What you didn't know, you couldn't reveal if captured and tortured.

Fair enough. I'd cracked under much milder torture than a foreign government would have subjected me.

You will pose as a farmhand and infiltrate a farm. Obtain samples of soil, plant parts, and animal products for analysis. You will be contacted by an operative to arrange pickup of samples. Logistical details follow.

# # # # #

"My buddy's had a few too many," I explained to the bouncer as I edged out the door with a man my own age slung across my back, careful not to bang his head on the doorframe or crush his limply dangling arm against it.

"I can see that," he said, looking slightly amused but a little bored as if he saw men carrying the unconscious bodies of their buddies out of the bar every day.

In reality, the guy had only had one too many: the one I'd emptied the packet of powder into. All the other beers

I'd bought him would not have been enough to knock out a man of his size; he should have been able to walk all the way back to his nearby motel without my help. He was a big man. Same height as I; his driver's license, I knew, said 189 cm and mine said 6'2" – my real one, the one I'd filed away before my trip. Back in the bar I'd have guessed we were roughly the same weight, although right now I'd have sworn he weighed about five hundred pounds. His driver's license called him Brown, James. His friends called him Jamie, including the new friend he'd just met in the bar. We'd had a deep meaningful conversation ranging from hockey to pro wrestling (which both of us gave every appearance of believing was a serious sport), to how many kilos we could bench-press to cars to how many meters we could spit. We'd played a video game in the bar. We'd talked about where we'd purportedly grown up and about every clever thing, every dog we'd ever owned, and about awesome stunts that you shouldn't try at home but each of us had seen a buddy in high school attempt to reenact, in Jamie's case his best friend. We'd each told a story about the most embarrassing thing that had ever happened to us. I genuinely liked the guy, as long as it was a one-night thing; if I had to hang out with him on a daily or even weekly basis, it would get old fast.

The packets of powder had been one of the many useful supplies I'd found in the backpack my contact in the forest had given me. He had joked that it was more cost-effective to obtain the drug on the Canadian side, where he could get it for free. Not only did it knock a man out cold without any side effects beyond making his hangover worse, but also it interfered with short term memory. Jaime might vaguely remember meeting me and having a good time – part of me hoped he did – but he wouldn't remember feeling drowsy and gradually slumping against my shoulder. He wouldn't remember how I'd fished around in his pocket to find his motel key while he was still awake enough to mumble a protest.

Thankfully, the motel named on the key tag was the one where I'd been assuming he was staying, only two blocks away. We knew he'd reserved a room there online, but our analysts had no access to the actual check-in records of this small regional motel chain. It was only three stories, and there was probably an elevator somewhere inside, but I realized I'd gotten lucky in the bar when my hand came out of his pocket clutching a key tag for room number 125 – and not, say, 301. So it really wasn't as tough as I'd been afraid it'd be. When I'd seen what a big strapping fellow he was, I'd decided to first try to get him drunk in hopes he'd invite me to his room. Preferably for sex, but it hadn't taken me long to realize there was not enough alcohol in the whole bar to make that happen. I've had settled for cards or video games. Heck, by the time I'd reached the door with him on my back, sweating in the summer evening air, I'd have settled for pretending to watch straight porn with him. But no, he had to make me do this the hard way. I unlocked the door with his key, pushed it open with his butt, and flopped him unceremoniously down on the bed with a grateful sigh. I paused for a couple of seconds while he stopped bouncing and I caught my breath. Then I closed the door and stripped him.

One of the first things I noticed was that he was a boxers man, like me. But then, I already knew that. It had come up in conversation. After Jamie had told me his embarrassing story in the bar and demanded to hear mine, I'd been ready with a fabricated story featuring me waking up at 5:00 a.m. after a party at my (non-existent) house and going downstairs for a midnight snack only to find the buddies I shared it with – and worse, about a dozen guests – still talking in the kitchen when I walked in wearing nothing but my boxers. That had prompted Jamie to mention that he also slept in nothing but his boxers. Therefore, after I unbuttoned his denim shirt and tugged it out from under him, I also peeled off the T-shirt he was wearing under it, but I left his boxers on. Nicely defined pecs; he probably hadn't exaggerated much about how much he could bench-press. Dark armpit hair, bushy enough for a tuft to be visible under the arm I'd placed at his side, and fully exposed under his other arm, which I'd left flung above his head when I pulled his undershirt off. Curly chest hair running between his pecs and continuing down his belly into his boxers. Belly already going just a little soft to the touch even though he was only seven weeks and four days older than I, but a summer on a farm might fix that. Solid, hairy legs. Big feet, stubby toes. I tore my gaze away and got to work. I went through his pants, opened his wallet and set it on the desk, then picked up his denim shirt. In his shirt pocket was a slip of paper with the address and phone number of the farm where he'd landed a job. I sat down at the desk, got out the collection of pens and pencils I'd bought that morning, and selected a blue pen that matched the ink he'd used, along with some matching paper, which I crumpled slightly. I'd been given some basic lessons in forgery, and his almost childish block lettering was easy enough to emulate. I wrote down the address of a farm twenty miles from his original destination that our analysts had applied to under his name. Then I rifled through his wallet. I found nothing I particularly needed. The wallet I'd taken from the cyclist in Seattle while he was in the shower had contained a duplicate of Jamie's Social Insurance Number card. Social Insurance is just like our Social Security in that it started as a public pension account number and wound up being a required document to obtain a job. The two copies looked indistinguishable to me, but I swapped them anyway just to be sure. The cyclist's wallet had contained a driver's license purportedly from Jamie's home province bearing Jamie's name and date of birth and my photo, as well as a

Washington driver's license that I'd burned in a campfire as soon as I was sure I wouldn't need it. I'd also been given a supply of absurdly colorful foreign currency. My largest bill was a brown one with a design on the back that flaunted Canada's interest in DNA and drug development research, a possible clue as to why I was here in this motel room going through the pants of a man I'd just literally hauled off to bed. Even after buying all those drinks, I still had more cash than Jamie. I was tempted to transfer most of my smaller bills to Jamie's wallet so he'd have some spending money this summer, but it wasn't worth the tiny risk he'd notice. I put it back into his pants pocket without adding any money.

There was almost no risk he'd memorized any part of the farm's address or phone number. I took another look at Jamie's brawny half-naked form sprawled unconscious on top of the covers. The video game in the bar had fortuitously involved memory as well as other mental skills, and when I'd challenged him to a game after only two beers, it confirmed my impression and the assessment in his dossier: The guy was as much of a muscle-bound lunkhead as I'd ever pretended to be. If he did suspect anything, he could double-check the original message in his email. By the time he woke up, it would have been altered to match what I'd written on the scrap of paper. If our analysts hadn't already succeeded in breaking into his account knowing only his date and place of birth and his mother's maiden name, they'd have no trouble at all once I'd provided them with the names of his first pet, the street he grew up on, his high school, his best friend in high school, his favorite movie and sport, and the make of his first car. By dawn, all of Jamie's personal records would be laid just as bare to our analysts for probing as his body was to me right now. If they wanted to, they could check the size of his bank account as easily as I could check the size of his equipment, and he'd never know. But we were the good guys; we'd wouldn't violate even a foreign citizen's privacy any more than we needed to. Damn, but I wished the dude were in the habit of sleeping in pajama bottoms instead of his boxers!

I tucked the paper back into the pocket of the denim shirt, picked up his pants from where I'd tossed them and put the hotel key back in the pocket I'd fished them out of, then left his clothes strewn carefully around the floor on a path from the door to the bed in the order I imagined him taking them off.

Finally, I rolled him onto his side, tugged the covers out from under him, rolled him back into a supine position, and tucked him in to sleep off the drug. Come to think of it, I'd arranged the covers more neatly than he could have managed in his supposed drunken stupor. I yanked the covers loose and artfully uncovered one shoulder down to the nipple, and one large foot and hairy shin, before letting myself out.

# # # # #

By the time I'd worked on the farm for a month or so, I could go for whole days almost thinking it was an actual summer job and hardly remember that I was on an undercover mission. Answering casual questions with my cover identity's history became automatic, and anyway my cover identity was a big lug who wasn't expected to talk much. The real Jamie had been very talkative once I got a few drinks in him, but I'd decided I'd play him as the strong silent type who'd rather keep his mouth shut and be thought a fool than speak up and remove all doubt. Simpler for me, and true to the real Jamie for all I knew. He'd also been a rather friendly drunk, and I decided to be that way all the time: shy but friendly. Although really the only people I had to socialize with were my employers and their one other farmhand. The family seemed nice enough, for people probably covering up a top-secret government project. Pierre, the other farmhand, was a sturdy and good-looking fellow not much older than I, and very likable. He went out of his way to talk about his girlfriends, as straight guys sometimes do when they sense I'm attracted to them, so I figured he was onto my least important secret.

The farmer and his wife, on the other hand, seemed to watch me very carefully when I was anywhere near their daughter; I don't think it occurred to them that a big dumb farmhand might be gay. That might work to my advantage. I decided not to come out to any of them. If Pierre sensed I was hiding something about my past and watching what I said carefully, he could put it down to me being closeted. His suspicions didn't seem to keep him from wanting to roughhouse with me on occasion, which was easily the best entertainment I got, since I had no Internet access and couldn't be seen reading for pleasure.

I'd been provided with a couple of shirts with a camera hidden in the third button, which I wore whenever the summer heat didn't make a button-down shirt suspicious. We were far enough north that there were some days cool enough for that, at least when dressing for supper. Depending on the temperature and how strenuous and dirty the work was, I wore just about every combination of the shirt, a white T-shirt, and overalls. That made eight possible combinations (not that Jamie could count up to two to the third power) including going bare-chested on two particularly hot afternoons, following Pierre's lead. But whenever I wore the shirt without overalls on top, mostly at dinner, I collected footage.

My belt buckle was an audio recorder. And in a month I'd collected enough clues, from little slips made in dinner conversations and from overheard telephone conversations, to convince me that there was more going on on this farm than met the eye. Breakfast was even more revealing. Like any farm that raised pigs and chickens, we ate a lot of bacon and eggs. The bacon was produced in-house; there was a smokehouse on site. But why was it that I'd never once, in all this time, been asked to carry a basket of eggs into the kitchen from the chicken coop? I'd packaged up plenty of eggs to be sent to market. Several times, when taking out the trash, which had been carefully bagged and tied, I felt what I was sure were egg cartons from the store. I was certain that if our laboratories could get their hands on one of the freshly laid eggs and analyze it, they'd find high amounts of some kind of drug. I'd learned in biology class, not in spy class, that the technology existed to genetically engineer goats to produce useful drugs like human insulin in their milk, and that the annual flu vaccine was made from viruses grown in chicken eggs. It wasn't much of a leap to conclude the Canadian government was conducting biotech research, maybe for biowarfare.

We had no cell phone coverage way out here, and the farmhouse may have had an Internet line but didn't have WiFi, so I'd been told to just wait to be contacted. I did have a signaling device built into the waistband of three of my pairs of boxers that could punch a message up to a satellite, but that was for dire emergencies, since Canadian counterintelligence could easily detect an unexpected radio transmission even if they couldn't decode it. I was surprised they'd hidden it in my boxers, but I guess the theory was that a ring or a watch would be too obvious whereas no one checks a man's underwear. Or maybe the elastic was an easy place to hide a long antenna. But there's a reason rings are more traditional: you can wear the same one every day. When Pierre noticed how often I did laundry, he insisted on driving me to town, so I could buy a week's worth of boxers at the drugstore. Unless I could predict when I would need to send an emergency signal and dressed accordingly, I was going to have to get to my bedroom to use the pair I now kept in reserve at the top of my underwear drawer.

# # # # #

One day I was shoveling manure out of the pig pen when the farmer led a sharply dressed man into the barn, with Pierre tagging along behind. "Let me show you what we're dealing with here," the farmer was saying as they entered. "I can't believe that little thing could vacuum up pig shit. Dirt tracked into the house is one thing, and our regular vacuum does a fine job with that. Moist animal byproducts need a shovel, eh? That's what I hired Jamie here for."

The salesman, a handsome man of around thirty, with carefully styled straight brown hair, was impeccably dressed in a tailored shirt, tie, and dress pants. He looked as if he had never worked on a farm in his life. "Trust me," he said with a slight French accent similar to Pierre's. "This device is guaranteed to get every square centimeter of your barn clean of manure in six minutes or less. And if you buy today, I'll throw in a spare battery pack for good measure, a ten dollar value."

Finally! My contact! Saying exactly the right code words to make me trust him, whether the farmer did or not.

I was ordered out of the pen to let him demonstrate the vacuum. I stretched, holding all my fingers extended. When I saw the traveling salesman glance at me, I scratched my cheek with three fingers, and finally massaged my outer thigh with five fingers, hoping it all looked natural. Not that the farmer and Pierre were paying any attention.

The handheld vacuum turned out to suck at sucking up pig shit; the stuff tended to accumulate all around the intake. He turned it off, scowling, then said brightly, "What do you think, sir?"

"I think Pierre is going to help you load your equally impractical mulching machine back onto your truck while Jaime cleans your vacuum out, so you can pack it up and go. When you're done, don't forget you left your jacket in my office."

"I see. Well, thank you for your time, sir." He did a pretty convincing job of hiding the fact that he was not struggling to hide disappointment. He followed the other men out of the barn, leaving his sample case and vacuum with me.

I dampened the last rag I had handy and used it to wipe off the outside of the vacuum. I very specifically neglected to empty it. Then, making sure I wasn't observed, I stripped off the top of my overalls, leaving them hanging around my waist, and quickly peeled off the sweaty white T-shirt that was all I had on underneath. It was almost too hot today for the extra layer while I was working, so no one was likely to think there was anything odd about my shoulders being bare for the rest of the afternoon. I was glad I'd had it on; it made handy padding for the freshly laid egg I stole and placed in the sample case.

"I was hoping my contact would be the farmer's daughter, not a big hairy-chested farmhand," a voice drawled in some kind of Southern accent. I whirled around to see the traveling salesman leaning against the door frame.

"You're making a joke, right?" I said, shrugging back into my top.

"Bien sûr."

"You're not really from Quebec, are you?"

"Quebec, Kentucky, what's the difference? Look, we only have a few minutes. Once your boss notices that the other farmhand and I are done loading my truck, he's going to be suspicious if I take more than a minute to pick up my case."

"Understood."

"What do I need to know? I have some plant parts in the mulching machine and some soil and pig manure in the vacuum. Unless you cleaned it out?"

"What, do you think I'm – No. I just wiped it off."

"Good. They put you here to gather inside intelligence about anything I might have missed. Is there anything else you recommend I collect?"

"Yes. I put an egg in your case."

"Is that what you did with the T-shirt you were wearing? Used it for padding? Good thinking."

"Thanks."

"An egg is going to be harder and riskier to smuggle than everything else. Any particular reason for suspecting it?"

"They buy eggs from the store instead of eating what their own chickens produce, so I'm thinking the chickens are transgenic and produce something in their eggs, like maybe a drug or a virus. Do you think the Canadians are doing biowarfare research?"

"Either that, or they're secretly developing a lifesaving super-drug that they'll distribute for free to their populace while withholding it from rich Americans," he said dryly. "Either way, we need it. Good work, kid. Has anyone ever told you you're smarter than you look?"

"Frequently."

"And I'm told this is your first mission."

He, on the other hand, obviously had experience. He had to be at least thirty, and now that he'd dropped the smarmy salesman act, he radiated worldly self-confidence. "Yes. I take it you're a more seasoned operative."

"You could say that," he said smugly.

I looked wistfully around the barn. "This seems like a dangerous enough mission to me, but I guess you've been in a lot more danger in much more exotic locales." I imagined him in Paris, reviving an unconscious security guard by emptying a chilled bottle of the finest Sauvignon blanc onto the man's naked chest.

"I can't talk about past assignments, of course. Let's just say that I'm used to being more than a courier, and even as a courier job, this one is a milk run for me. Well, milk and eggs now."

"Hey, I just realized something. They don't have any goats or cows on this farm, but pigs are mammals, too."

He gave me that familiar smart-gorilla look, as though impressed that I knew pigs are mammals. "Hmm. Worth checking."

"Unfortunately the piglets are all weaned, so I can't get you a sample of the milk."

"That's all right. I'll take a skin sample."

"Oh, I see. Any genes that can be expressed in the milk glands would have to be in every cell of the body, just deactivated."

"Right," he said, giving me that unexpectedly-impressed look again. "The pig shit I collected might be good enough, but I don't want to count on that, now that I know that transgenic animals are more than a long shot."

"Yeah, fresh skin cells will be a hell of a lot easier to sequence than degraded DNA from shed epithelial cells." God, it felt so nice to cut loose and be myself! My friendship with Pierre was mostly nonverbal and consisted largely of roughhousing, which was great, but several weeks of that it was a treat to be able to have a technical conversation. "Not to mention it being mixed in with DNA from the slop and the intestinal fauna."

He'd paused in the act of opening his case and was staring at me open-mouthed. "Damn, boy! You really do know your shit." He got out what I assumed was a skin punch and closed the case. "Keep a lookout." Flipping his tie over his shoulder, he knelt down beside the sow. The pig moved out of the way, and he scrambled after it, still on his knees.

"Don't you want to take off your shirt so you don't get it dirty? Not to mention the knees of your pants?"

He gave me a look that suggested it was undignified enough that he'd had to leave his jacket in the house. "It's fine. I have a fabric brush in my case that really works like magic, unlike any of the products I'm pretending to sell. No untrained observer is going to notice anything in the few minutes it will take for me to reclaim my jacket and get out." He grabbed again for the pig, who squirmed out of his grasp.

I was about to suggest that I might be better at handling the pig, when I heard a noise outside. "Someone's coming!" I hissed, hurrying over to the kneeling fake salesman. I thought about giving him a boost into the loft, but I wasn't sure how agile he was, and there was no time; whoever it was would walk through the open door in seconds. Thinking quickly, I grabbed the operative's head, thrust it against my crotch, and stripped the overalls off my shoulders for the second time in fifteen minutes. The operative didn't object; in fact, he immediately dropped the sampling device into his shirt pocket and in the same motion peeled my overalls down further, so that from the knees up I was clad only in boxer shorts. Then, with a barely detectable grimace, he unbuttoned the fly on my boxers and reached in to fish around for my cock. As if aware of the urgency of the situation, it was already getting larger as fast as it could, making it much easier for his fingers to find that it would have been a moment before.

I heard a disbelieving curse in French and turned my head to see Pierre standing in the doorway, staring at my dick in the kneeling salesman's hand. He said, "I'll ... give you guys some privacy," and withdrew quickly.

The second were were unobserved, the operative dropped my dick like a hot frankfurter. "Sorry, man," he said softly. "I had to sell it."

"No worries."

"That was quick thinking. Most guys on their first field assignment wouldn't have been able to bring themselves to do that at all, let alone without hesitation. Very professional."

"Thanks. I picked up a little experience while crossing the border."

"I'll make sure no one else comes in," Pierre called loudly from just out of sight.

"Thanks, buddy," I called back. "I owe you one."

"Buy me a drink sometime."

"He really is a good friend," I muttered fondly. I told the operative, "We can trust him not to look in on us."

"Yeah, there isn't even a word for 'voyeur' in his native language. By the way, you can put that thing away now. We won't be needing it anymore."

"You got it out," I grumbled.

He was nonplussed but recovered quickly. "You're going to have to take care of that yourself, buddy. I've got work to do. Let's see if this time I can collect enough cells for the lab to grow a silk purse."

"I'll hold the pig for you," I said, stuffing my shrinking cock back through my fly and buttoning it in. I was wearing locally-bought boxers today, I noticed; no chance of sending the wrong signal while I was handling my cock. I covered up my chest with the overalls and helped him chase the pig.

We had more success with me holding the pig. The squeal of surprise and pain she let out in response to involuntarily getting her ear pierced was enough to make Pierre call out, "What the hell are you guys doing in there?"

He added a short question in French, just a couple of words, but words they'd never taught me in class.

The operative shouted back a denial in the same language, something about kicking the pig accidentally while we were in the throes of passion.

"What did he say?" I asked.

"You don't even want to know what he thought we were up to," he said quietly to me as he put the tool and the sample away in his case.

Looking at the pig glaring at us from the corner of the pen, I said, "There's a word for that in French?"

"For two guys and a pig? Several, depending on the exact positions and techniques and the gender of the pig," he answered instantly, completely deadpan. "Hey, muss up my hair a little, okay?" He quickly pulled his tie askew, tucked the tip between the buttons of his shirt as if he'd had to hastily button it up, and untucked one side of his shirttails from his pants, while I tousled his brown hair. He'd used too much hair spray for my taste.

When he was satisfied he was properly unpresentable, he said, "It was good for me, and I hope it was good for you. Thank you for a very pleasurable thirty seconds, sir." He shook my hand with grave formality. Turning to the indignant pig and bowing politely, he murmured, "*Mademoiselle.*" Then he picked up his sample case and strode out of the barn. I felt a small pang of regret. I hoped our work would throw us together again. Maybe I'd get to know him well enough to tell when he was pulling my leg. Maybe it would even be in a situation where our covers required him to touch my dick again, or even carry out what we'd pretended to do. He was sort of cute, for a guy in his early thirties. At the very least he was fun to talk to. But realistically, I expected that was the last I'd see of him.

As it turned out, I saw more of him, a lot more, over the next hour. Barely ten minutes after he'd walked out, the farmer called me and Pierre into the house. The salesman was on his knees – where, come to think of it, he'd spent most of our brief acquaintance one way or another – and this time his hands were not on my dick but clasped together on top of his head. At some point, he'd tucked his shirt back in and straightened his tie, as though to hide the evidence of what we'd supposedly been doing in the barn from the farmer once Pierre had seen what he expected.

The farmer had his shotgun aimed at the man's heart. The sample case was on the desk, wide open, and the egg I'd stolen was sitting in plain view, nestled in my T-shirt. I was suddenly very conscious of my bare shoulders, convinced that the boss and Pierre must surely have noticed I'd been wearing a T-shirt an hour before. I almost blurted something like "So that's what happened to my T-shirt," which would have been believable to Pierre, at least, who knew I'd had it off in the salesman's presence. But I held back, reminding myself that they were less likely than I was to notice a little exposed male flesh, being neither spies nor gay.

The salesman looked relatively calm for a man on his knees with a gun trained on him, but that's not saying much. I think it's fair to say that he was no longer radiating self-confidence.

The farmer was talking to someone on his land line, cradling the receiver between his shoulder and ear. "I've got my farmhands here. They can do it. How much should they ... OK. Will do." He hung up. "Pierre, Jamie, this is no salesman. This is an American spy."

"Huh?" I said. I tried to look baffled, and for Pierre's benefit, also betrayed.

"Who's he spying on?" Pierre asked incredulously. He gestured at the egg. "The chickens?"

"Trust me, he's a spy," the farmer said. "Counterintelligence Canada is sending some agents, but they say we need to take everything off him, anything that could be a communications device or a camera."

"We'll frisk him," Pierre said, hauling the man to his feet with one meaty hand.

"Not good enough. They say that spy equipment can be miniaturized so much these days that they could be hidden anywhere in his clothing. He might also have a cyanide pill."

"My government doesn't provide those," the operative said in his Kentucky accent. "We have to pay for them ourselves if we want them." I admired him for being able to joke under the circumstances. Then again, our training taught us that humor was as good a coping mechanism as any, and he was obviously using every bit of training he had to keep from giving his captors the satisfaction of seeing him break down.

"So when you say 'take everything off'..." Pierre said slowly.

"They want us to strip him."

Pierre raised his eyebrows. "OK. I'll hold his arms while you unbutton his shirt, Jamie."

I was glad I'd had a little training in this. I hesitated only for a second, as surely any decent man would have. I began by reaching for his throat, trying not to look apologetic, and unknotting his tie. I pulled it off and was about to toss it on the floor when the boss said, "They want it all bagged for analysis." He help up a garbage bag that already had something in it – a suit jacket, I saw when I added the tie.

Merely opening the collar of his shirt instantly stripped my fellow operative of his façade of calmness. He was doing a good job of keeping his face impassive, but with his throat exposed, I could see his prominent Adam's apple bob every time he swallowed hard. Which he did several times as I continued unbuttoning his dress shirt, even though I had one more layer to go before I uncovered much bare skin. When I untucked the shirttails from his pants, and Pierre shifted his grip to help me rip the shirt from his back, he started struggling, but he didn't stand a chance. Either one of us could easily have subdued him single-handedly, as became even more obvious once his arms and shoulders were bare and his chest covered only by a thin tight undershirt. In all fairness, there were hints of wiry biceps that had been hidden under the clothing, as if he at least worked out on occasion. Probably inside a gym; his shoulders were so pale I doubted he ever took his shirt off outside, and even his forearms were only slightly tanned. All in all, his bare arms looked like sticks next to Pierre's, and the contrast between his pale scrawny shoulders and Pierre's meaty, suntanned hands clamped on them made him look even more vulnerable. I could have tried to help him – I could probably have knocked the shotgun away and knocked my boss out since I had the element of surprise, and my training might give me just enough of an edge over Pierre to take him out – but we'd have never made it out of the country. I knew very well what the protocol was in situations like this, and I knew this poor bastard did, too.

I unbuckled his belt, wondering if our earlier conversation was now stored in the buckle and whether the Canadians would be able to crack the layers of security. There was no particular reason they'd have issued a courier a recorder, but if he had any electronics, they were most likely in his belt or his watch. I pulled off his belt, unstrapped his watch, and they both went into the garbage bag.

"Don't forget his undershirt," the farmer said.

"He can't be hiding anything under here," Pierre objected, running his hand over the prisoner's chest and flank.

"Do it anyway."

120

I tugged the front of his undershirt free of his pants and began pulling it up, exposing a concave navel above a trail of silky hair that disappeared down into his pants. I grabbed the hem with both hands and peeled it up as far as the bottom of his ribcage. Pierre and I were used to coordinating our work, so I said, "On three, lift his arms. One, two, three." I had a fleeting glimpse of bushy armpits as I yanked the undershirt over his head, and as soon as it was completely off, Pierre quickly pinned his arms behind him again. Once the undershirt had joined the outer shirt in the garbage bag, the farmer sent me out for baling twine to bind our shirtless captive's hands. That was what I'd have done at this point, too. I'd once dated a cute math geek, even scrawnier than the salesman, who had explained to me the theory behind what I knew from experience: that when you're planning to strip a man, you should wait until after you've got him bare to the waist before you bind his wrists. Then you can take his pants off at your leisure. I'd been playing the big dumb jock for him and suspected he didn't believe I'd understood his lecture, but the truth was that after literally hanging on his every word for an hour, I found the topic so fascinating that I took a course in topology the next semester just for the fun of it. Turned out it's a lot drier without the hands-on demonstrations involving handcuffs, sturdy water pipes, scissors, and expendable T-shirts.

The captured operative was still struggling uselessly in Pierre's arms when I got back with the roll of baling twine. There was a sheen of sweat on his pale torso, which was hairless from the belly button up, except for a tuft just below his throat, a few hairs around each of his small dark nipples, and a sparse curly patch between his underdeveloped pecs. The farmer had obviously assessed his unimpressive musculature and seemed unconcerned he'd break free; he didn't bother to demand the prisoner hold still even though he had a shotgun aimed casually at his bare chest. A black belt could have broken away from Pierre and rolled toward the farmer's legs in the same motion, but like me the captured operative had probably had all of three hours of instruction in martial arts as part of his basic spy training.

Pierre held the prisoner's wrists together and watched me bind them with twine, making any hope of escape even more remote. Then he wrapped his strong arms around the shirtless man's torso and lifted him off his feet. I caught one of his kicking legs and untied his polished shoe, tugged it off, and tossed it into the bag on top of his undershirt, then peeled off the black sock. Once we had him barefoot, I roughly yanked his pants down and pulled them off, with Pierre again holding him off the ground. This left him clad only in white briefs, breathing hard, now very obviously marshaling all his training to try to suppress his terror.

This had been the hardest thing I'd ever done in my short career. I'd thought it had been hard delivering shocks to a bound and helpless fellow trainee who I'd bonded with over rooting for the same football team. Now I had to turn my back on an actual comrade, someone who'd been working with me to protect our nation's interests. Not to mention the fact that I tend to quickly bond with any guy who's held my dick in his hand. I wished there was something I could do for him without compromising the mission, but there wasn't. Not only couldn't I help him, I'd had to help the enemy by divesting the guy of every means of escape. This really sucked. I'd thought this would be a way of helping my country without the part where I had shoot people, but at least in the military a man's allowed to openly help a comrade in trouble.

"I see Jamie has noticed the same thing about his pants as I noticed about his jacket," the farmer said, and I realized I was standing clutching his open pants in my hands with my head bowed. Now I really looked at them, but I saw nothing strange about the pants. Surely if some detail got by me, it would get by my cover identity. I looked up with my best big dumb grin (Who, me? Notice something?) and he prompted, "What does the tag inside the leg say?"

I read aloud, "'Dry clean only.'" I scratched my head theatrically to buy a few seconds, then got it just in time to keep it from being told. "Hey, wait a minute! Where's the French? There's always French."

"Not where he comes from. That's why I made him open his case. I wondered where someone who told me he only travels domestically could have bought clothes with English-only labels. And sure enough, he was trying to smuggle out an egg. Even the T-shirt he wrapped it in has an English-only tag."

I silently put the pants in the garbage bag, willing my hand not to shake. Good thing I'd suppressed my first impulse to admit I recognized the T-shirt. At least my overalls were locally purchased. So were boxers I was wearing today, if for some reason the boss had Pierre strip me and check. But I had two dresser drawers full of incriminating evidence: three of my pairs of boxers and two of my other T-shirts. Possibly not the jeans and shirt my contact in the forest had carried from Canada by wearing them, but both of my other button-down shirts with the built-in cameras. And how many times had I deliberately left the tag sticking out the back of my T-shirt in an attempt to look more careless than I was, and so that Pierre would tuck it in for me? His fingers on the back of my neck was the only man-to-man contact I got on this assignment, except once in a while when he was in a boisterous and playful mood. It was sheer luck that I hadn't been the one caught, instead of the experienced operative I'd just helped to strip to his shorts. I forced myself to pick up the roll of baling twine and kneel at his bare feet.

"No, you idiot," the farmer said. "Don't tie his ankles yet."

"Hey, is he supposed to read your mind?" Pierre said hotly. He always loyally defended me. But I didn't mind the farmer calling me an idiot. He was the one stupid enough to aim at a captured spy's heart and not his legs.

"How are you going to get his underwear off with his ankles tied?"

"What do they think he has hidden in his underwear?" Pierre protested, laughing incredulously. I laughed along with him. I managed to make it not sound forced by thinking of something legitimately funny: What did the farmer say to the traveling salesman he was aiming a shotgun at? Answer: "And don't even think about going for a cyanide pill, or I'll kill you."

Our boss said, "They were very clear about that. They want him naked."

The prisoner gulped visibly as I loomed over him again. Clearly this wasn't the kind of debriefing he was accustomed to being put through when a mission came to an end. And how could I bring myself to act like I was glad to take away his last scrap of clothing? I didn't think I could do Outraged Patriot very convincingly at the moment, but I knew I could totally pull off Sadistic Fraternity Jock Bully anytime. I hooked a forefinger into the elastic of his briefs, smirking, and pulled it toward me until it was stretched to its limit. I made a show of peering inside and inspecting his genitals, to buy myself a moment to think. I wished I had time to feel around for the button I suspected was hidden in the waistband that would send a distress call. If Counterintelligence Canada detected a transmission – and they'd be monitoring the farmhouse now for sure – would they ever believe I had pressed the button by accident? Probably not; once their analysts had their hands on his shorts and examined them closely, they'd see the button was designed to be impossible to press by accident. It was too risky, and besides, what did I think my side would do? Send a chopper full of Marines across the border? So I let the elastic snap back cruelly, then yanked the briefs past his small limp penis, his rather heavy ball sac, down his pale and somewhat hairy legs, and finally over his bare feet, leaving him naked in Pierre's arms, head slumped toward his chest in shame. Or despair. Or to avoid meeting my eyes. Or in a futile attempt to hide his blush.

"Should we find out what he knows?" Pierre asked, releasing the bound and naked man to unbuckle his belt. The leather suddenly looked very rough to me, and the operative's exposed skin very tender.

"I'm not afraid of you," the naked man said bravely, although his balls belied this by shriveling before our eyes and trying to crawl up into his groin. Why are our bodies always instinctively worried about our balls before anything else? Pierre, now circling him, was in fact eyeing his vulnerable chest and belly, his scrawny shoulders and back, and his butt, which I assumed was as milky white as his crotch before me and would show any lash marks nicely.

Less nervously than I would have, sounding resigned to his fate, the operative added, "Professional interrogators will probably break me once they've had me for a day or two, but a little belt whipping isn't going to make me give up any information." He was glaring defiantly at Pierre, but I realized it was a warning aimed at me. Sooner or later, he was going to finger me. And not in a good way, like earlier.

"No," the farmer said. "Leave the questioning to Counterintelligence. Go outside and drain the rain barrel and turn it on its side and chock it. We'll drape him over the barrel until the agents arrive. It'll make it easier for them to search him."

# # # # #

"Good work, boys," the farmer said as we watched the captured operative dragged off in handcuffs and forced into an unmarked black sedan, clad only in a scratchy-looking blanket wrapped around his waist, which they'd brought with them. I had offered to lend him some clothes, at least a pair of boxers, if only for the sake of public decency, but the farmer pointed out the barrel was out of sight of the road and of the bedroom where he'd ordered his family to watch a DVD with the shades drawn. He'd been given explicit instructions that to leave him naked for some reason. Seemed like a paranoid policy to me: What did they think, that there was a second spy who could pass him equipment hidden in this underwear or something?

My contact been outwardly stoic to the end, but I could feel him trembling when Pierre and I had carried him outside by the ankles and armpits. I wondered how much time I really had before they wrung every last secret out of him.

"Why would an American spy be snooping around here, anyway?" Pierre asked our boss as the car drove away and a tow truck pulled up.

"It's better if you don't know. Let's just say we served our country very well today."

"If we're done being heroes for now, can I get back to shoveling pig shit?" I asked.

"Why don't you boys take the rest of the day off? You deserve it. There are only a couple more hours of daylight anyway. In fact, you can skip your morning chores tomorrow. By rights we should all get medals, but I can do that much for you. Just remember what they told us: don't talk to anyone about this."

"Let's celebrate being heroes," Pierre told me as we went outside to put the equipment away. He slapped me on my bare shoulder. "How about a drink?"

"That would be great!" I said. "You did say you owe me a drink anyway."

"The hell I did! I said you owe me a drink. We ought to drive into town. You're buying, at least the first two or three rounds."

"Why is that?" I reached up and hung up the last of my tools on a nail in the wall.

"Because I covered for you, you numbskull!" He poked me playfully in my exposed armpit, causing me to instinctively double up in defense. "I guarded the door while you were getting that blow job. How does it feel to have been sucked off by a genuine foreign spy?"

I'd have been happy to help him find out for himself, if only to keep his mind off things like the fact I'd started the day with a white T-shirt under my coverall and that a white T-shirt had been used as packing material. I reminded myself again that Pierre was probably much less observant than I, and definitely less focused on the accessibility of other men's armpits. Although, surprisingly, not by much. We'd had some good times this summer. And now, partly because I knew it was the last chance we'd get, and partly because the more closely he bonded with me the more he'd trust me this evening, I tickled him back, greatly handicapped by the fact he was wearing a thick shirt. That was all the excuse he needed to continue attacking me.

"Did you come in his mouth?" he asked.

"Cut it out! I'm not telling you anything."

He wrestled me to the ground, straddled me, and pinned one arm above my head, leaving my armpit wide open. Now he had another foreign spy completely at his mercy, the second in one hour, if he only knew. My laughter wasn't feigned. Or even voluntary.

# # # # #

The nearest town was big enough to rate not only a few small bars and a few fleabag motels but one nice hotel, a property owned by one of the big international chains based in the United States. More to the point, it was tied in with the chain's central computer system for managing reservations and room status, and for processing credit cards. Feeling conspicuous in a shirt that was now so sweaty that no one would guess I'd showered and changed just a few hours before, I entered the lobby and checked in with one of the several credit cards that had been in the wallet the guy in Seattle had left in the locker for me. I hadn't used this one before; it was reserved for emergencies like this.

I rode the elevator up and took the risk of leaving my backpack locked in the room. It was probably safer there than it had been in the locked cab of Pierre's pickup truck outside the bar, and I needed my shoulders free. The one thing I removed was a small toolkit. I took that with me down the stairs in case the exit on the first floor had an alarm I needed to disconnect.

I'd picked the correct corner of the hotel. The stairwell let out right next to the loading dock where I'd parked Pierre's truck. The hotel offered valet parking, but I couldn't very well have taken advantage of it. It had gotten dark while we were in the bar, so probably no one saw me drag Pierre's limp body out of the cab by the armpits and lift it onto my shoulders.

I kicked the truck's door shut and reentered the stairwell through the fire door I'd propped open. Wishing I'd accepted that fifth-floor room they'd offered, I began trudging up the stairs. The eighth-floor room I'd held out for not only had the nicer view I'd demanded, which I had duly admired for a few seconds while yanking the curtains shut, it happened to be only three doors from the stairs. Once I'd finally reached my floor with my heavy burden and gotten through the door without damaging either of us, I was acutely aware that every door I walked past with my human burden was equipped with a spy hole.

I stretched Pierre out on the room's one king-sized bed. I wasn't too concerned about his shoes dirtying the bedspread; these were his dress shoes he almost never wore. If he'd worn his work shoes with dried pig shit in every crevice, I'd have taken them off – and bagged them and tried to transport them back to the United States for DNA analysis. The pillow I dug out from beneath the spread and placed under his head felt invitingly cool and soft, and there were more than enough of them for the both of us. I had to resist the overwhelming urge to stretch out beside him. He was a solidly-built guy, and I was exhausted from carrying him. At least Jamie had had a first-floor room. Pierre's disheveled shirt – a very nice one, I was guessing his only nice one, given that he'd worn it to town three times before, on dates with three separate women – was soaked with sweat, and probably not his own. Still, I knew I couldn't rest here. Pierre might sleep until morning, but the captured operative who could compromise me wasn't going to be sleeping at all tonight. I had to get as far away from here as possible. I picked up the telephone and dialed the non-existent room 1306. If the computer backdoor had worked the way it should, it would route the call to ... well, I didn't know where, exactly; somewhere in the United States I assumed.

"Housekeeping," a voice answered.

"This is Room 1035," I said warily, giving the code.

"We cleaned your room at six, sir. Every square centimeter of it."

Relief washed over me. "I've been compromised. My contact was captured a few hours ago."

"Before or after he made contact with you?"

"After, unfortunately."

"Will anyone report you missing?"

"A Canadian national – my coworker, the other farmhand – drove me into town for drinks. I gave him my last three knockout drops." I studied Pierre's big body appraisingly. Maybe under 200 pounds, although he'd felt like he weighed about half a ton for those last few flights of stairs. "He should be out for five to ten hours, depending on his metabolism."

"Hold on, here's my superior."

A much deeper voice said, "The computer briefed me on your mission when you used your credit card. The authorization password it gave me is golf bravo foxtrot indigo romeo."

"Acknowledged." That meant I could tell him anything and should follow his orders.

"The operative who was captured was the one posing as a salesman, I take it?"

"Yes. I didn't say anything or do to compromise him, I swear!"

"Don't worry about that. Right now all we care about is getting you to safety. Someone will debrief you afterwards."

Speaking of briefs ... "You should know that it was the labels on his clothes that tipped them off. You need to start issuing our agents in Canada clothes that have bilingual labels."

"Of all the stupid-- Some idiot's going to loose their job over this. We're so careful about that in Europe and Asia. Meanwhile, let's get you out right away, since your mission is blown."

I cradled the receiver against my shoulder and sat down on the foot of the bed, aware that I might be ordered down to the lobby any second if they had an agent available to extract me. I wanted to leave Pierre as comfortable as possible, and his comfort wouldn't be on their priority list. I untied his shoes as I spoke. "Actually, I managed to grab a sample: a transgenic egg."

"Excellent! I'll have to ask you to transport it across the border yourself. I can't risk another operative at the moment."

"I understand." But that didn't remove the time pressure; he might have a local driver who could be bribed to whisk me to a safe house. I had Pierre's shoes off by this time. I scooted further onto the bed to feel around in his pockets for hard objects that might press against his balls as he slept. I was going to leave his pants on. There was nothing I could do to fool him into thinking he'd blown his paycheck on an expensive hotel room, gone to bed, and forgotten he'd ever checked in. Not after just a few drinks spread out over happy hour. All undressing him would accomplish would be to cause him unnecessarily humiliation when he woke up and realized another man must have taken his pants off as he lay there helpless. I don't like to humiliate my friends. Not unless they ask for it. I found nothing in his pockets. I'd half expected keys, but then I remembered I'd appropriated his keyring.

"We can provide transportation once you get far enough away. And we can buy you some extra time. We've rerouted the room phone, so it won't let him call out, and the Front Desk and Guest Services and other buttons will route him to impostors here who can string him along." He paused. "I know this is your first field assignment. Did you remember to remove the battery from his cell phone?"

"Of course. I did that before leaving the bar, about five miles from here." No one would be tracking him that way. The phone and battery were in my backpack; I'd been hoping they'd tell me I could leave them on the nightstand for him. Maybe his phone without the battery, I thought now.

"Good work."

I rolled Pierre onto his belly and removed his wallet so it wouldn't stamp its image into his butt overnight. I leaned over him to put it on the nightstand where he'd find it. I noticed that the nice material of his favorite shirt was dry in back; clearly all the sweat making it stick to his chest was mine.

"We've flagged the room as vacant, so it won't be cleaned in the morning, but also as unavailable for assigning to new guests. Take his cash and credit cards and ID with you when you go."

"Done," I said, reluctantly reclaiming his wallet from the nightstand and sticking it into my left back pocket.

"Dispose of his phone and his clothes."

"All right," I said regretfully. I rolled Pierre onto his back again and began to unbutton his shirt, the only nice one he seemed to own. Curly chest hair spilled out along the lengthening opening. Then I realized I was wasting precious time, unbuttoning a shirt I was about to throw away. I ripped it wide open, revealing his muscular chest and impressive abs. This wasn't the first chance I'd had to admire his torso, just the first chance I'd had to stare at it up close without him being able to object. His chest hair looked and felt surprisingly feathery; until now I'd always seen it matted down with sweat. Right now it was dry, only damp in the places where my own sweat had soaked through his shirt.

"Will the hotel dumpster be good enough?" I asked.

"That will do fine. It will be on a garbage truck by 5:00 am and no one will think to look for it before then. Also, if you can sneak a large bundle out without anyone seeing you, take all the towels and bed linens, too."

I paused in the act of unbuckling his belt. "Why ... Oh. I see. So he can't cover up with them. You want me to take everything, even his underwear."

"Correct. How long do you think it will take him to work up the courage to open the door and call for help if he's naked?"

"Hours, maybe a whole day," I said in a confident tone. I actually had no idea whatsoever, having only known Pierre for part of one summer and not having seen him in the kind of situation I was putting him in. But I was afraid if I said anything different I'd be ordered to leave him tied spread-eagle to the bed for days with no access to the bathroom, or hogtied in the hard cold bathtub with his own urine trickling down his ribs. And I couldn't do that to him. I felt bad enough for what I was doing already. He might be a Canadian, but he was a decent guy and had never been anything but friendly and kind to me. And here I was, not only setting him up for a humiliating situation, but robbing him of everything, including his best clothes. The pants I was pulling off his muscular but surprisingly pale legs were probably his only pair that weren't work clothes, just like his shirt.

My assessment of Pierre's modesty seemed to satisfy the man on the phone. We spent a few minutes working out the details of how I would make my way back to the border.

Then I stripped both Pierre and the mattress completely bare. The hall was empty and the housekeeping closet on this floor wasn't locked, which saved me a trip down that stairwell I'd developed an irrational dislike for. I only had to pass five closed doors with their unnerving spy holes, carrying an incriminating bundle of bedclothes wrapped around an inner bundle of man clothes. I stuffed the sheets, blanket, bedspread, and towels into a canvas bag I found hanging from a cart containing tiny soap bars, shampoo bottles, a vacuum, and cleaning fluids. For some reason, the feather duster sticking out of it made me think of Pierre lying naked, back in the room, with both arms flung out. I fed his pants, shirt, socks, and undershorts down the garbage chute, then sent his shoes, phone, and battery clunking after them. I had to make two more trips for the pillows alone, since the hotel provided a selection of soft, medium, firm, feather, and foam, with a hypoallergenic one on a shelf in the closet, plus a decorative cylindrical throw pillow that had no conceivable use whatsoever. Except maybe as a pillow-fight weapon, I supposed, should Pierre unexpectedly wake up and so that I needed to defend myself. Whoever was in charge of hotel pillows had no sympathy at all for spies who needed to strand a guy naked in a bare room with nothing to hold in front of his crotch. I bundled the pillows up in the shower curtain to tote down the hall, feeling a little like the title character of Psycho, especially when I had to pull out my knife and slit them open for fear they'd clog the chute.

I decided to risk a fourth trip for the phone book, tourist guide, ice bucket, trash cans, and a few other items I could picture him holding in front of his crotch when he eventually worked up enough courage to venture out in the hallway naked and let the door close behind him. He might hesitate a couple of extra hours if he didn't even have that much to cover himself with. Not that he had anything to be ashamed of; he was rather well-endowed. My own was capable of attaining a very respectable length, but in its limp state – the one it would be in if, say, you laid us out unconscious on a bed side by side, or lined the two of us up in a fancy hotel lobby begging someone to call the police – mine shrinks down to almost nothing, and looks even smaller in proportion to my large frame. It would have looked pathetic compared to Pierre's.

He hadn't budged since I'd laid him down; if I stared at his torso long enough I could see him breathing slowly, but had to reassure myself by pressing my ear to his chest. That was an expected effect of the drug, but he was going to be stiff for days from lying in one position. I straightened out his limbs as best I could and squeezed his muscles all the way down each arm and leg, wishing I had time to give him a more thorough massage with the little bottle of lotion in the bathroom.

I looked around the room for anything I'd think of covering myself with if I woke up naked in a hotel room. Oh, right! Here I'd been worried he'd be willing to take the elevator to the lobby wrapped in a translucent shower curtain, and I'd overlooked something much better: the window curtains. Not so much the sheer ones, – if he was anything like me, he'd walk out naked before he'd clothe himself in something filmy that looked like a tutu – but certainly the thick blackout curtains. But I didn't take the curtains down; the hotel staff might notice from outside, coming in to work. I found I could barely reach the curtain hooks, and I was an inch taller than Pierre and was wearing shoes, but it was still the best option I'd left him with. I was about to decide I needed to tie him up after all when I got an idea. The bathroom was equipped with glass drinking glasses and a glass coffee carafe. I smashed them all to splinters on the marble desk with the bronze desk lamp base and used one of the rags from my backpack that the egg was padded in, which I could easily replace with with a discarded hand towel on my way out, to sprinkle the shards below the window, just where Pierre would have to stand barefoot to reach the curtain hooks. I sprinkled more on the armchair in the corner so Pierre wouldn't be able to grab it and drag it over, or stand on it if he did. The only other chair in the room had a wicker seat and wooden legs that screwed on. I removed one leg and leaned it against my backpack to take with me. Then I unscrewed a couple of light bulbs and shattered them near the door in hopes of discouraging Pierre from banging on it or cowering behind it while someone handed in articles of loaner clothing. That reminded me to also get rid of the lampshades.

Finally my work here was done. I found a pen and paper in the desk drawer and scrawled a note: "Sorry!! Really, REALLY sorry." I left it on his peacefully rising and falling chest, picked it up again and appended "P.S. Watch your feet on the broken glass," and put it back on his chest. I was careful to pocket the pen and pad of paper so he couldn't slip any notes under the door even if he could reach it. I took a final look at the poor bastard I was abandoning naked and exposed on an equally bare mattress. His scrotum and nipples had shriveled noticeably in the time it had taken me to throw his clothes away and prepare the room. I went to the thermostat and held a button down for a long time and watched the numbers slowly change until they reached 32. Naturally I was trained well enough to do the translation with my head without bothering to flip the switch to "F" (and back to "C" to cover my tracks!). I'd set the temperature for what I thought of as the high 80s. I heard the heater switch on. I gathered my stuff and crunched out of the room.

# # # # #

I drove poor Pierre's truck for two hours on two different highways, then ten miles down a back road where I abandoned it behind some bushes. I hiked three hours to another highway. All this driving and hiking, unfortunately, left my mind free to worry. I knew I'd be no problem for any competent professional to track. Maybe even for the local police. I wondered if the Canadians had a thermal infrared spy satellite in the sky at the moment. It was all too easy to imagine myself strung up next to the erstwhile salesman by morning, as naked and totally helpless as I'd rendered him. Actually, the part about being strung up naked didn't sound so bad to me, but I'd rather wait until I got back to the United States to do that sort of thing, where I could choose my captor. And where there'd be no torture devices in sight. Well, maybe some feathers or ice cubes. And we'd arrange a safe word just in case.

But I kept reminding myself that the danger of being caught had dropped dramatically when we'd left the bar and had been dropping exponentially from the moment I'd driven Pierre's truck away from the hotel. Pierre would still be out cold. Our boss had relieved us of morning chores. He knew we'd gone to town and expected us to be hung over and to sleep in. I figured when we didn't come to breakfast and weren't in our beds, he'd assume we picked up a couple of girls and rented a room in one of the cheap motels. Maybe even two rooms, which, come to think of it, might have made an equally effective escape plan – and a hell of a lot easier on my back and Pierre's dignity. I felt like slapping my forehead when I thought of that, halfway through the hike. In all fairness, though, it had been the first time I'd had to improvise a plan on my own, so maybe I could be forgiven for, as my math professors would have said, "reducing it to a problem we've already solved."

As I hiked, I kept adding up the times for the worst-case scenario, not counting the one where the salesman had greatly overestimated how long it would take them to break him. I imagined Pierre metabolizing the drug freakishly fast. How long would it take him to decide the front desk had not really called the police and wasn't really looking for clothes and shoes to lend him? How long before he'd tell them, "Look, if there isn't a bellman at my door with clothes for me in another ten minutes, I'm walking out of here naked and looking for a pay phone"? Once that finally happened, the authorities would start searching for me in a slowly expanding spiral from the hotel. I'd driven over a hundred miles away, and by the time they found where I'd hidden Pierre's truck in that 700-square-mile circle, I'd be far away, maybe across the border. A smarter thing for them to do would be to focus their search on roads going south, in which case I was fine, since I was a hundred miles to the east-northeast.

I reached the highway where someone was supposed to pick me up and settled down behind a tree near the road to wait. I kept imagining what they were doing to my captured colleague right now.

Right on schedule, just as it was getting light, a red pickup truck approached, flashing its high beams once. I ran out and it slowed down just enough for me to verify its license plate, run after it, and vault into the bed. I lay down as the truck smoothly accelerated. I'd been instructed not to talk to the driver, who knew no more than he needed to know.

# # # # #

Days later, I stopped by a tiny stream in the woods, somewhere near the border, and stripped off my sweat-soaked T-shirt, dunking it into the cool fresh water along with the outer shirt I'd doffed hours before. Neither shirt's label suggested this laundry method, in any language. I tied the damp T-shirt around my head after wringing it out and hung the outer shirt up to dry; I had no intention of putting it on before evening. I don't care how far north I was, it was still the middle of summer, and it didn't help that I'd been carrying a mini-refrigerator in my backpack, its coils sticking out of the pack and radiating heat right into the back of my neck as it pumped it out of the box to keep the precious cargo fresh. I took the box out now and set the solar panel in the sun to recharge the battery while I rested and refilled my canteen and ate a handful from my dwindling supply of trail mix. Funny how we always crave what we can't have: every time I closed my eyes, I saw omelets. Hard-boiled eggs. Scrambled eggs. Poached eggs. Eggs over easy. Eggs sunny-side up. Pierre face up, on a bare mattress, completely naked and utterly at my mercy. I promised myself that minute I made it to civilization I was going to treat myself to all six of the first things on my list, and once I was home and debriefed I'd find myself the closest willing approximation to the seventh.

"Thanks for washing the shirt for me this time," a voice said behind me. I whirled around and saw a familiar face grinning at me. "Although I have to say, you smell better than a lot of guys whose shirts I've worn." He was wearing a brown shirt this time, which he was in the middle of unbuttoning, revealing a hairy chest I'd seen once before.

"Nice to see a familiar face," I said. The last friendly face that had grinned at me like that was drinking a beer I'd bought for him and drugged.

"Thanks for giving me a paid vacation to play tourist all over my own country."

I rose to shake the hand of the man who'd switched clothes with me on my way into Canada. The last time I'd touched someone who was on the same side as me, I'd been stripping his briefs off and draping him over a barrel to wait for the Canadian counterintelligence agents. By now the poor bastard had surely told them everything he knew. The Canadians were better than most, and the American spies they captured usually came out of it alive and were eventually used for a prisoner exchange.

"Dude, don't just shake my hand!" He glanced skyward. "People may be watching."

I grabbed my countryman in a hug and pressed my lips against his, keeping my mouth primly closed. He caressed my naked back, sending chills all the way down to the base of my spine. I squeezed his solid biceps with my left hand and slipped my right hand into his open shirt, reaching around to explore the small of his back.

"That's better," he said when the simulated kiss was over.

I didn't release him, but held as on tightly as I could, which is pretty damn tight.

"Enough!"

I buried my head between his neck and shoulder. I liked the way he smelled, too. And I was afraid for him. He was obviously planning to head right back into the country I'd just escaped from, wearing the clothes a fugitive was last seen in – clothes with English-only tags, if anyone thought to turn them inside out.

"Dude! Enough!" With difficulty, he pushed me away and held me at arm's length.

"Sorry, man, I ..."

"Shut up and get those pants off."

I grinned and obeyed. I loved being ordered to strip. At least by the right guy.

"Hey, what's that you've got here, dude? A fridge? I don't suppose you've got beer in it."

"You know I can't tell you what's in it," I said, tossing him my pants.

"Fortunately," he said, lifting an identical unit out of his own backpack, "I brought enough beer for both of us. This will be almost enjoyable if I have a couple of beers in me." He began unbuttoning his pants.

THE TRAIN TO MOMBASA
By Jay Starre

Residing on English Bay in Vancouver, Canada, Jay Starre has pumped out steamy gay fiction for dozens of anthologies and has written two gay erotic novels. Contact Jay Starre on Facebook.

Darren Mason could hear a lion roar in the distance. The isolated farmhouse was far enough outside of Nairobi to be on the edge of a wildlife reserve – a park where lions roamed free!

An attempt at escape did not seem alluring. The lion let out another blood-curdling roar, this time closer, and he had to admit he was more afraid of that beast than the half dozen human beasts guarding him just outside his door.

He wasn't quite sure what they wanted from him. He was a scientist, not a reporter or a politician or anyone rich and famous. They had snatched him off the train to Mombasa when it stopped in a dusty little town early that evening and hauled him here.

They hadn't asked him anything. They spoke in Swahili, which he didn't understand. They pretended not to understand his English, but he sensed they did. Four were black Africans, and three looked like Arabs, although one of those was red-headed and could possibly be European. Yet even he spoke Swahili.

There was only one thing about himself that he guessed might be of interest. He was on the United Nations Atomic Energy Discovery Committee. He knew a heck of a lot about atomic energy – and about atomic bombs.

One of the Africans came in and deposited a plate of steaming vegetables and meat on the table. An assault

141

rifle was draped across his chest, as if Darren was any kind of physical threat to them!

It wasn't that he was a wimp or anything. He worked out regularly and actually was a regional tennis champion back in Massachusetts. But he had never fired a gun in his life, and the last time he actually got in a fist fight was when he was twelve.

That damn lion roared, almost outside the window. He was so agitated he dropped his fork and cursed. That's when the bedroom door opened again, and the red-headed one entered. The look of frightened anger on Darren's face was plain as day.

Grey eyes bored into his, and he was shocked to see almost the same look on his captor's face. What did he have to be angry about, or frightened of?

There was a moment of strange suspense as they stared at each other without speaking. Darren, scared out of his wits, was fully focused as he looked closely at his captor.

He was a big man, tall and broad-shouldered, but he held himself entirely poised. He looked as if he could leap into action at a moment's notice. His red hair was long and shaggy and held back by a kerchief tied like a headband across his forehead. He had a closely-clipped red beard and sharp features. His freckled complexion was tanned quite dark while his eyes were a soft brown under arched reddish brows. He was handsome, no doubt about it.

He wore heavy jean shorts cut off just above the knee and well-worn hiking boots. His button-up shirt was heavy khaki. He looked prepared to hike through the African wilderness if need be. An assault rifle was strapped across his chest just like the others.

It was his mouth that gave him away. Full and pink, and although set in a frown at the moment, it seemed all too lush and inviting to belong to a murdering terrorist.

Darren was certainly clutching at straws, but it seemed this particular kidnapper might be more friend than foe.

There was more. Those golden eyes swept over him in a calculating manner, no doubt judging him in some way or another, but they also lingered longer than necessary. They met his, dropped to roam over his seated body again then came back up to meet his eyes again.

Darren had been cruised many, many times by other men. With thick black hair and deep brown eyes, a round face and almost elfin features, he was deliciously good-looking and appeared much younger than his thirty years. His muscular body, trim waist, and round ass had other gay dudes dying to fuck him senseless.

That was exactly the look his captor was giving him. Darren had a hunch the man wanted to grab him, toss him on the nearby bed, yank down his shorts, shove his stiff prick deep into his butt-hole and plow his ass until they both shot their loads. Of course Darren was half out of his mind with worry, so any conclusions he was forming might be the product of fear-induced fantasy.

But he didn't think so.

Their gaze finally broke as the red-head stepped forward. The first thing he did was place a small radio on the table and turn it on. Music filled the silence, though not very loudly. Then, he leaned over and put his hand down flat on the table. He pulled it away. A small scrap of paper was left behind.

Darren peered down at it. He was stunned at what he read scrawled on it in rather poor penmanship. "Keep your mouth shut and follow my lead. I am on your side, and we're getting out of here."

He looked up to see the red-head down on his hands and knees beside the head of the bed and reaching underneath. He seemed to be working at dislodging something, his beefy ass wriggling in the air. Staring at that

143

solid butt all at once got his cock hard. How weird was that? His kidnapper was turning him on! Well, maybe he was going to be his rescuer, so that would make it all right. Maybe.

He seemed to have what he needed and pulled out a rather large pack. He got up and slung it over his shoulder. With his finger to his lips to indicate silence and still not speaking himself, he gestured for Darren to follow him.

The young scientist got up from the table and as quietly as possible did as he was told. The red-head went to the closet door at the foot of the bed and opened it. Darren had already checked it out earlier, hoping to find something in there useful, like a big machete or a spare assault rifle, but it was only full of clothes.

If he had pushed those clothes aside, he would have found the secret door behind them. The red-head had a key and unlocked it, then ducked to enter. He crowded in behind and leaned in close to hold on to the big man in the darkness. While enjoying a feel of his muscular back and even a few unintended bumps against his ass, Darren followed down stairs until they halted at a second locked door.

Once past that, they ascended, again in darkness with Darren clinging to the red-head's waist, which he didn't seem to mind. It seemed like a long way until an overhead trap door opened to the steamy African night.

After he bent down to close the door, he turned to Darren. It wasn't totally dark with the stars and a sliver moon, so he could see the tall man looming over him. His rescuer leaned in and whispered in his ear. The hot breath sent a shiver up and down his spine.

"Put these on. We have to hike a little ways in the dark. Stay very close to me. You never know what's out here."

"No worries! I'll stay real close," he promised as he took the object thrust into his hands and tried to figure out what it was.

Some kind of goggles. He slipped them over his head and eyes. He could see, sort of. He'd been handed night vision goggles, and amazingly good ones, too. Like a kid with a toy, he looked around in awe, spotting the farm house a few hundred yards back through a scattering of acacia trees. The trap door had been covered with brush, which fell aside when they exited. The red-head kicked it back over the door then turned and began to head off.

Darren scurried behind him, looking down at the ground and back up as he tried to get accustomed to the greenish glow offered by the goggles. "Do you mind if I hold onto you?" he called out as quietly as possible.

"Good idea. Grab hold of my belt from behind."

He reached out and grabbed, getting a good handful of solid butt before he slid his hand upward and hooked his fingers into the wide leather belt at his rescuer's waist.

"I said my belt, not my ass," he hissed.

"Sorry," he whispered back.

Now that the red-head had finally spoken, it was apparent from his accent he was a fellow American, which was extremely comforting. Why was he with the kidnappers, though? He was dying to ask, but silence obviously was more important for the moment.

The terrain was flat enough, and the forest was somewhat open with shrubs and acacia dotting the grassy terrain. It wasn't too hard to walk with the aid of the night vision, and they strode ahead briskly, which was fine with Darren. He wanted to get as far from that farmhouse as possible, as quickly as possible.

But where were they headed? His rescuer held some kind of small device in his hand, which appeared to be a GPS when Darren got a peek at it over his shoulder. He could tell they were moving south, which was toward the coast and Mombasa, where his train had been headed when he was kidnapped. Were they going to walk all the way? That was almost three hundred miles.

They had made good progress, and the farm house had to be at least several miles back when the night was suddenly disturbed by the most blood-curdling sounds. Yips, moans, and warbling chatter surrounded them.

"What the hell is that?" Darren hissed as he leaped ahead to pull himself practically on top of his rescuer.

"Goddamn hyenas. Don't worry. I've got something for them."

He pulled a pistol from its sheath in his belt and fired four shots in a wide circle around them. The shots were muffled somehow and sounded like mere pops. Little puffs of eerie greenish smoke rose up from where they hit the dirt. A moment later, the yips turned into startled whines and then nasty howls that retreated from them in a mad rush.

A moment after that, the most atrocious stink rose up around them. "Good god! That's rank," he hissed.

"It drives the hyenas crazy. They'll be in a bad mood all night now," he whispered back.

They continued on quickly, as much to leave that awful stench behind as to get away from the bad guys at the farm house. Darren was feeling marginally safer now that his rescuer had demonstrated his ability to deal with the scary African environment, when a lion's roar echoed through the night.

He had to ask."Will those stink bombs work against that?"

"Not as well, I'm afraid. But not to worry. Here we are."

They halted in the midst of a small copse of acacia. A four-wheeled, all terrain vehicle was stashed there under a pile of brush. "You seem to have planned this escape beforehand."

"Yes. I was the one who rented the farmhouse, and the only one who knows about the closet exit. I was pretty sure I might need out someday soon. I was right. By the way, my name is Troy."

He went on to explain he'd been planted with the terrorist group for almost a year. Now it was all spoiled since they had captured Darren. He couldn't leave the obviously helpless young American to their brutal mercy. He made no apologies about telling Darren he was pissed off at him for being so stupid and getting kidnapped.

The young scientist couldn't think of an appropriate answer to that. Instead, he asked the obvious. "How long do you think before they come after us?"

"At least a couple of hours, and I'm hoping we have until morning."

"How come? What do they think we're doing?"

"I told them to give me a few hours to fuck your hot ass. They agreed, as long as they got sloppy seconds in the morning."

Even though it seemed like bullshit, Darren believed him.

"Now get on behind me and hold on fucking tight!"

There was a long padded seat much like one on a motorcycle. He jumped on behind Troy and wrapped his arms around his waist. He couldn't help squeezing up close, which had his crotch pressed against the spy's beefy butt. Troy made no complaint as he started it up and they headed out.

The vehicle was equipped with state-of-the art mufflers and an engine that made a barely audible ticking sound. Their bouncing and rocking passage over the bumpy terrain was practically the only noise they made.

He leaned in close to speak in Troy's ear. It seemed it was safe now to ask his questions.

"What kind of stuff are your bad-ass pals into? Kidnapping obviously. But what else?"

"Terrorism, arms dealing, and even poaching. The dudes in this network are into anything that will make them money or cause trouble for the West. They hide behind religion to justify most of their criminal behavior, although some of them really are religious in a bent kind of way. They are scary, very scary. And I don't intend on letting them catch us."

He sounded determined, but also a little frightened. A frightened spy? Weren't they all courageous with nerves of steel? Probably the dead ones were. They drove on in silence for another half hour. Darren held on tight, to prevent falling off the vehicle but also just to enjoy the feel of the muscular body in front of him. His knees pressed into the outside of Troy's, his hands clasped just above his belt on his firm, and warm belly, and his swollen cock rubbed continually against the solid cheeks of the spy's hefty ass.

The world around them glowed greenish through the goggles, which they had both left on. Troy drove without headlights and slow enough not to crash. Eventually though, their way was blocked by a small stream.

"Crocodiles in there, most likely," he commented. "I have crossed this ford before, so I know it's shallow enough We'll just sit here a spell and watch before we attempt it."

That's what they did, sit in the silence and watch the swirling water for signs of crocodiles for about five long minutes before Darren spoke up.

"Sorry I blew your cover. And I'm sorry if you have to get out of Africa now just because of me."

"Sorry? I'm not all that sorry. I am thoroughly sick of this shit-hole continent! Nothing but goddamn bloody wild beasts and bugs and hot fucking days and nights."

"Actually, I have found Africa to be quite stunning. Until this evening, of course."

"Are you a damn fool? We're on the run from a bunch of nasty-ass terrorists, and every damn predator in the area is salivating at the thought of sinking their teeth into us. Quite stunning, goddamn it. Quite fucking stunning!"

"What are you so mad at me about? I didn't do anything to you," Darren replied defensively.

"No. You're right. Sorry. It's just that sometimes you Americans are so damn naïve. It drives me bloody nuts."

"Uh, aren't you American, too?"

"I'm British, not American."

"You don't sound British. You sound American."

"I'm a spy. I'd be a pretty damn crummy one if I sounded like what I really was."

Darren wasn't an idiot. He knew all their bickering was half his fault. How could he not be angry at his circumstances? But blaming his rescuer was hardly right. And he couldn't blame Troy for taking out his frustration on him either.

It was time for a peace offering. He thought he knew exactly what would get Troy out of his foul mood. It was a gamble, but he felt he owed it to the man to show some gratitude.

He rose up from the seat he straddled and then knelt down on the floor beside Troy. Before the red-head could guess at what he was up to, he buried his head in his lap. At least he could suck Troy's cock. If the spy wanted more, Darren's bubble-butt would be his for the asking!

He snuffled around in the khaki shorts while tearing at the buttons of his fly at the same time. Troy's muted laughter from above and the hands he placed on the back of Darren's head told him all he wanted to know.

The fat tube he fished out told him more. It swelled up into his mouth as he swallowed up the plump knob at the end and a good portion of the veined shaft. What happened next was not exactly as he'd expected, but hardly unwelcome. Troy didn't just sit back and get his cock sucked. No, the red-headed spy took control and fucked Darren's face.

He held onto the back of his head along the straps of the goggles with both hands and plowed his mouth. It wasn't rough, exactly, but it was deep and thorough. He pumped in and out, sliding his knob over Darren's plump lips and twirling tongue, probing the back of his mouth and then when it opened for him, sliding deep into the warm gullet back there. He fed the kneeling scientist his cock like it was a feast for a starving man, and Darren swallowed it like it was the tastiest meal he'd ever had.

Still wearing the night goggles made everything even more surreal. The greenish glow to the world was like something out of a half-nightmare, half-fantasy.

It lasted for much longer than Darren expected it to. There they were, poised in the savannah moonlight on the verge of crossing a crocodile-infested stream, with lions and other blood-thirsty beasts prowling around them, and Troy fucked Darren's face slowly, steadily, and without respite for what seemed like a solid half hour. Finally, he groaned and jerked and spewed a sticky load all over Darren's smiling face.

Totally unashamed, Darren licked the cum off his lips, then wiped it off his chin and cheeks and nose and licked his fingers clean. Troy laughed above him and then bent down and kissed him.

"We've got to get across this stream. Mount up, Darren."

There was no thanks or any sweet promises, but it hardly mattered. The blow job had been given in the spirit of selflessness. He didn't want anything from Troy, other than not to abandon him until he was safe back on that train to Mombasa!

They raced across the shallows, bumping and splashing, but without mishap. Darren clung to Troy with all his might and didn't let up until they were miles away, and he stopped the vehicle again.

"We'll wait here until dawn. The train will come down from those hills. We'll see it in time and catch it over there."

They were parked on a little knoll under the protection of an acacia. Below, about fifty yards away, the train tracks ran beside another stream.

"What will we do in the meantime?" Darren asked.

He got the answer he hoped for. "We'll fuck."

Troy stood up in the vehicle and pulled down his shorts then stepped out of them. While he bent down and rummaged through his pack for something, probably lube, Darren remained where he was but also removed his shorts while still seated, lifting his boots and leaning back to pull them off. He fully expected Troy to push him back and raise his legs, then drill his ass with his cock like he'd drilled his mouth a little earlier. But that's not what happened.

Half naked now, Troy turned and fired off another four rounds of the stink-bombs. "The wind is blowing up from the valley below, so all that stink will stay away from us. And hopefully keep any prowling predators well away, too."

The tall red-head settled over the broad leather vehicle seat, facing Darren. Then, to Darren's total surprise, he mounted his lap and immediately proceeded to ride his cock with his warm, clinging asshole. He had found lube in that pack, a bottle of some kind of slippery lotion probably for soothing dry hands but great, too, for making a squishy slot out of the spy's snug asshole.

This time instead of fucking his face with his cock, the spy fucked Darren's cock with his ass. The scientist had never been fucked like that. It was amazing, and it was hardly what he expected from the burly spy.

Troy crammed Darren's stiff pole right up his ass and sat down on it. With a grunt, he took it all, right to the balls. Behind his goggles, Darren's eyes got big as saucers as he felt that heated hole envelop his throbbing cock. He gazed up at the spy and moaned as Troy began to hump the cock up his ass with deep and thorough greed.

Darren reached around his waist and grabbed hold of the beefy butt-cheeks as they rose and fell over his cock. They jiggled in his hands and tensed, then relaxed as the red-head arched his back and drove down over the lengthy pole he rode.

The scientist's fingers slid into the deep crack and found the hole, feeling his own cock being swallowed and disgorged, then gulped right back in again. The lube-leaking hole clung to his stiff meat, riding up and down the length of it in a slippery glide that grew steadily faster and faster.

Distant cries and howls punctuated the stillness of the late African night, but none sounded close by. Hopefully the stink kept anything away while they reveled in their intense fuck. And intense it was. Troy's hot hole gulped Darren's long rod down with a clamping rhythm that had him squirming all over the seat. He gripped the spy's smooth ass-cheeks and held on as his cock grew hotter and hotter.

"I can't hold back! I'm going to shoot!"

"Go ahead. Blow your load! Shoot it!"

Troy's own stiff cock reared up from his crotch as he bounced up and down over Darren's lap, and the scientist wondered if Troy was going to come, too, but he didn't this time. Instead, he squeezed his sphincter tight around Darren's cock and milked it relentlessly as he whimpered helplessly and released his spew.

He flopped on the seat and shot up Troy's steamy asshole. It felt absolutely unbelievable to let go like that. He surely needed the release, and as the spy bent down and wrapped his arms around him, then kissed him for the second time while slowly letting his cock slip from that clamping hole, he felt entirely safe and protected.

They put their shorts back on and huddled together on the vehicle while they waited for the morning and the train to Mombasa. A rosy African dawn finally flushed the eastern sky just as they spotted the train making its slow way down the winding track in the distance.

Troy quickly led him down to the tracks where they waited behind the screen of a stand of brush. The train chugged by at almost a walking distance as it navigated a steep curve and it wasn't all that difficult to hop aboard one of the crawling cars.

They climbed a ladder to the top of the open car and jumped down inside. It was half-full of large sacks. "Coffee beans," Troy said.

"Now what do we do?" Darren asked, hoping their might be more of what happened the night before.

Troy grinned. There was no need for words as he removed his clothes and created a make-shift bed atop the coffee bean sacks. Darren helped, his boner rearing up eager for more action, just like Troy's.

This time, without the goggles on, Troy kissed Darren while he fucked his ass. The spy lay behind him on his side and lifted Darren's leg as he slid his lubed up cock into his open crack. The slippery pole found the young scientist's hole and began to rub against the puckered entrance. Slowly, almost tenderly, it pressed against the defending ring as it rubbed back and forth over it. Then it settled and began to push.

Darren groaned, but Troy's kiss muffled his moans as he steadily pushed with his hips and forced his lotion-coated cock-head to slither beyond the sphincter and pop inside. Troy lifted and pulled farther back on Darren's bare thigh, opening up the crack and the hole at the same time. Cock burrowed deeper, and deeper.

With the blue African sky above and the rhythmic clacking of the rails beneath their car, they fucked and kissed for the next half hour. Troy buried his cock to the balls, pulled out and plunged back in, holding Darren's smooth tanned thigh up in the air while he shoved his pink cock into the hairless pink hole over and over.

Again, the young scientist felt totally safe and protected, even though they were still far from Mombasa. With that stiff cock pulsing inside his throbbing asshole, and Troy's tongue in his mouth, he allowed himself to forget everything but the moment.

This time it was Troy who came first. He pulled out and grunted as he sprayed Darren's creamy-white ass-crack with a sticky load of spunk, still kissing him. Feeling the muscular body writhe and jerk against him was almost enough to get him to come again himself, but he held back. Perhaps there would be another chance to blow in the next few hours before they reached the island port at the end of their train ride!

He was right. It was almost night by the time they reached Mombasa. No one disturbed them in their nest of coffee beans, and they fucked twice more. Darren was somehow disappointed when they pulled in to the station in Mombasa.

An hour later, he was about to board a boat headed for Cape Town and safety. Troy had quickly arranged it. "Will I see you again?"

The red-head smiled and winked. An overhead lamp on a pole offered a garish light to their parting. He reached out and clasped Darren's shoulder. "It might be a while, but I'll find you."

The rush of relief he felt was profound. Somehow, he couldn't imagine never seeing the beefy spy again! "Will you be OK?"

"I fucking hope so! Sure, I'm tough. See you soon."

Darren boarded and looked back just in time to see Troy waving from the dock, then disappearing into the African night. It was as if he'd just woken from a dream, a frightening one, but also a thrilling one.

Yet, he was certain Troy would keep his promise. He seemed like that kind of guy.

ISTANBUL
By Jay Starre

A city of nearly thirteen million, Istanbul straddles Europe and Asia. It has been a crossroads of culture and trade for millennia. At only nineteen miles long and less than two miles wide, the Bosporus Strait that bisects the metropolis is a tight conduit between the oil-rich countries bordering the Black Sea and the Mediterranean. It is a prime target for terrorists looking to disrupt world trade for their own nefarious ends.

Johnny Bond was in the Turkish city because of just such a rumored threat.

Istiklal Avenue was bustling with crowds. A favorite strip for the city's night life, this warm spring evening was no exception. Johnny had some trouble finding Il Greco the first time, but this was his third excursion to the night spot in a week, so he knew exactly where to go. He strolled through the unmarked doorway on the street level and quickly ascended the winding stairs up to the fourth floor where the restaurant enjoyed a favored rooftop location and a devoted clientele.

Abu Laden supposedly frequented the place. Johnny discovered this information by word of mouth, and with all these millions of Istanbul residents crowded together cheek by jowl, word of mouth was a ready and surprisingly reliable source of information.

"Third time's the charm," Johnny muttered to himself as he spotted his prey leaning against the parapet across the crowded floor.

He knew it was Abu immediately, even though he could see only his back and a glimpse of his profile. His briefings at CIA headquarters had been thorough. He'd poured over numerous photographs and more than a score of videos of the Iranian and had mentally catalogued all the nuances of his physical attributes.

More athletic than burly, he was neither tall nor broad. Tailored designer jeans belted closely at the waist emphasized a taut ass. Neatly trimmed black hair was swept back to reveal a classically handsome profile, sharp nose, round eyes and mouth, prominent chin. It was Abu, without question.

A little rush of satisfaction coursed through his nads and cock, which was appropriate considering his next move. He casually strolled through the crowded tables and approached the parapet. A fortunate opening allowed him to slip in right beside Abu.

"Nice night. Uh, I couldn't help noticing your jeans. They're cool. I hope you don't mind me asking where you got them?"

As the Iranian turned to look at him, Johnny offered a winning smile. It was one of his best assets, and he employed it shamelessly. With his round face and dimpled cheeks he looked practically cherubic, though he had grown a closely-cropped beard in an attempt to counter his college-boy looks. His blond hair and beard were accented by pale blue eyes and a round mouth with plump pink lips. He was a big man, a few inches over six foot and husky from his college years playing football. But for all his size, he looked somewhat gentle. His slow walk and languid movements gave the very false impression he was easy-going and unassuming. At only twenty-nine, he looked even younger.

He looked Abu directly in the eyes and pressed his thigh and knee ever-so-slightly against the suspected terrorist's as he awaited a response. Although a lot was riding on this moment, he was not the least bit nervous. Nervousness was not his style.

"Thank you for the compliment. I purchased them in the Grand Bazaar. A jean shop named Gio Jeans. Tell the proprietor Mahmoud Ali sent you. He will provide you with a deal. Isn't that what you Americans are always after?"

The voice was light and clipped with an impeccable English accent. Johnny had known to expect this, but not the hint of mischievous teasing. The thigh did not move away, and he pressed ahead.

"Awesome! I'll beat a path there tomorrow afternoon. Shall I expect to see you there? Maybe you could get me an even better deal in person?"

"Perhaps. Good evening to you."

He moved very quickly, turning to rapidly wind his way between the crowded tables like a runner leaping hurdles without actually leaving the ground. Johnny knew it was possible he had scared him away, but thought it more likely it was the man's nature. He didn't seem one to stay in any place too long.

It was no surprise that Abu had provided a fake name. Nor was it a surprise he'd guessed Johnny was American. The blond spy made no effort to hide his nationality. It was an easy cover to maintain. He looked and acted like a young and cool American businessman. Abu himself probably had a number of aliases he employed, much as Johnny did.

The Grand Bazaar was an American shopper's dream come true on an exotic scale. With more than three thousand shops and sixty covered streets, it was definitely not easy to find the single shop Johnny sought. But once again, word of mouth served him well, and the following day he swam his way through a treasure trove of gold, silver, silk, spices, porcelain – and yes a whole street of jeans.

Whether the shop owner really knew someone named Mahmoud Ali or not, he was quick to offer up his wares. At a great deal naturally. Jeans hung in racks from the floor to the fifteen foot ceiling in the narrow, cramped shop. Johnny was hardly on a budget, and he chose an outrageously overpriced pair that actually fit his husky lower body.

"You should choose these. They fit you well. Very well. Give my American friend a deal, please."

The shopkeeper bowed toward the voice behind Johnny as a pair of hands settled on his waist just above his jutting ass. The voice belonged to Abu, so the hands had to be his as well. They didn't grope, but they squeezed just slightly, almost exactly mirroring the pressure of Johnny's knee at the restaurant the previous night.

He turned to offer his brilliant smile only to see the slender Iranian turning and departing in the swift glide he favored. Johnny was quick, too, when he wanted to be. He tossed a generous wad of cash at the grinning shopkeeper and raced off after his disappearing prey.

The game was afoot, and it was quickly apparent the Iranian was teasing, or testing Johnny's resolve. For his part, the American spy didn't want Abu to know he was following him, but didn't want to lose him either. The hordes of locals and tourists wandering the Bazaar's lanes were both an impediment and an aid as Johnny waded through them in his pursuit. Abu played along by staying just far enough ahead to force the young spy to move quickly and keep his wits about him.

Nearly half an hour of seemingly aimless meandering finally led them to the entrance. Johnny had parked his motorcycle nearby and was forced to make a split-second decision. He chose to mount up to continue the pursuit. Only a block later, Abu did the same and Johnny was smugly pleased at his intuitive choice.

CIA had known the Iranian's preferred mode of transportation was a motorcycle. So Johnny had been provided a tricked-out CIA bike with all the spy bells and whistles necessary. He'd been in the city for a week already and made it his priority to explore. Good thing.

They wound their way through streets crammed with honking vehicles, down narrow alleys jammed with pedestrians, and past amazing monuments like the surreal Blue Mosque and Hagia Sofia with their towering minarets and impressive domes. But sight-seeing was not an option as the Iranian cut in and out of traffic, blasted through irate walls of citizenry, and did his best to confuse and confound his pursuer.

Johnny's bike had the best GPS the CIA could provide, which was without question the best in the world. He knew where he was at all times, and was as good or better at driving his motorcycle than Abu.

The American was a champion mountain bike racer. Growing up in Colorado, he had dared Rocky Mountain trails that would frighten the bravest. Still, this wild ride through Istanbul's streets rivaled some of his most dangerous races.

They ended up somewhere in the upper city where commercial and residential co-mingled in an indistinguishable and tightly-packed chaos. Abu parked in front of one of these brightly-colored buildings and disappeared into the shadows of a deeply inset doorway.

Johnny parked a short distance away and boldly approached the building. It was abundantly clear to him that Abu hadn't really intended to lose him. If he had really wanted to, he probably could have.

So, taking a deep breath and putting on his best smile, he entered the shadowy alcove to confront what lurked there. A doorway blocked his way, the upper half made up of iron bars. A large Turk stared at him from behind the ornate iron work.

"Uh, I'm a friend of Mahmoud Ali's. May I come in?"

The dour expression on the plump face gave no indication Johnny's bold lie meant anything to him, or whether or not he understood English. Regardless, the man backed away, and the door opened. The moment Johnny entered, he realized what the place was. The smell of steam lingered in the air, and the doorman's open hand and demand for five American dollars told him it was a hamam, a public steam bath.

It couldn't have been more perfect for his plans! He slipped into one of the curtained alcoves and removed his clothes quickly. He only wore his helmet, his new designer jeans and a T-shirt, the rest of his stuff left behind and locked inside a compartment on his motorcycle. He hadn't even brought his gun, but he did have the most important tool in his arsenal with him. Even being totally naked would not reveal it, so he smugly wrapped the towel placed on the little counter around his substantial hips and paraded out into the narrow hallways.

It was early afternoon, but you wouldn't know it from the dim lighting – and the surprising number of unclad patrons. At least a score lounged in the first room, a steamy chamber with a splashing fountain against one wall and a dozen stone platforms scattered about where burly Turkish masseurs pounded energetically on prone, naked men.

As stimulating as the environment appeared, Johnny was goal-oriented and lingered only long enough to ascertain that Abu was not among the room's occupants. A doorway across the room beckoned. He padded barefoot across the slick stone floor into a hallway even more dimly lit than the previous ones. Fewer men seemed to have penetrated this section of the steam bath, and he only passed two or three before the winding passageway began to offer doorways on either side. Long strands of colored beads served as doors. He dared to part them and peer within as he passed each one. Beyond the glittering beads were small chambers with little fountains of their own and steamy jets rising from either the floor or the lower sections of the tiled walls. There were men in some of the rooms, and some of them were engaged in what could only be construed as light petting. They had their arms around each other as they sat on the wet tiles beside the fountain and steam vents, or they rubbed each other's naked limbs with slippery hands. Not exactly fucking and sucking, but definitely erotic.

Johnny's fat cock rose up stiff under his towel, and he smiled to himself. His keen intuition told him his prey was near. And he was right.

Beyond the next doorway he spotted Abu. This small room contained a fountain as well, and beside it a flat tiled pedestal at waist height. He was sprawled on his stomach, his towel unfolded and spread out beneath him, his naked back and rearing buttocks glistening with a sheen of steamy water droplets.

He faced the wall, so couldn't see Johnny lingering at his doorway. Nor could he see him as he entered quietly to pad his way across the small chamber and end up hovering beside him. His eyes were closed.

The naked back was all lean muscle. His skin was a golden amber, and it appeared he had a light tan. His paler ass was outlined by the tan and jutted up from the tiled slab in twin globes of firm perfection. He was smooth all over, and Johnny had to wonder if it was natural or he shaved his body.

He had been very quiet, a skill he had honed over the past several years of his training. Still, he couldn't be sure Abu wasn't aware someone was in the room with him. He discovered the answer to that question the moment after he dared to reach out and lightly run his fingers over the small of Abu's back.

Lightning-swift, the prone Iranian whirled around and reached up to seize Johnny by the upper arms. Regardless

163

of the huge difference in their body size and weight, Abu managed to drag and yank the big American forward onto the pedestal and then twist him onto his back. In a matter of seconds, Abu straddled the blond as he pinned him to the slippery tile beneath them.

Johnny had actually been prepared for the possibility of such a move. Without seeming to, he followed along with the tossing and rolling and allowed himself to be pinned beneath the slender terrorist. Still, he was surprised and impressed by the fierce strength of the man. He was even more dangerous than he seemed.

The dark eyes stared into his. The grip on his arms was implacable as Abu leaned down to whisper into his face."What do you want? Why are you following me?"

"Uh, sorry! I'm American, and we are a little more open about these kind of things. I was just after some fun. Sorry if I've offended you, pal."

"Some fun? All right, I'll give you some fun. My kind of fun," he hissed in his clipped British accent.

Again, he moved with unbelievable swiftness. One moment he was eye-balling Johnny and hissing in his face, the next he was facing the other way. His very-stiff cock banged against the American's chin and mouth while those fierce hands gripped his knees and yanked back on them. He buried his face between Johnny's hefty thighs and attacked his quivering asshole with a probing tongue.

All he could do was go along with the assault, and an assault it was. The tongue twisted and stabbed at his pink pucker while the hands on his knees slid down to seize his full ass-cheeks and squeeze them. His cock, a very lengthy rod with a blunt helmet, jabbed at his lips as the slender hips pumped up and down over his face. Johnny opened up.

There was no delicacy in the driving entry that followed. He slammed deep and choked Johnny with his stiff cock. The American spy gurgled histrionically to aid and abet Abu in his apparent need to dominate. He had little gag reflex though, and opened wide to let the pipe-stiff meat slither in and out of his throat almost effortlessly. The fat nads banged against his chin while his full pink lips gaped like a fish out of water as the hot meat drove in and out.

Abu continued his attack on Johnny's butt-hole. His lips sucked it inside out. His fingers spread the pink rim wide open, and the tongue drilled into the yawning gap. He got even rougher. He lifted his hands and smacked them down over Johnny's round butt-cheeks with stinging exuberance. He even laughed between slurps as he dove his tongue into the American's yawning ass pit.

Running his own hands over the taut ass bouncing on his face, Johnny found himself in the perfect position to accomplish the objective in his pursuit of a sexual encounter with Abu. As his hands roamed over the heaving ass and he gurgled around the cock thrusting down into his throat, he placed his left fingertip strategically and pressed into Abu's slippery flesh.

The Iranian was not only dripping wet with steam, but was slick with some kind of oil he had obviously applied to his body. This was a good thing for Johnny. The invisible patch he pressed into Abu's flesh required body heat and moisture to seal. The spy pressed firmly and rubbed just slightly. The patch came away from his finger and adhered to Abu's ass.

With his knees on either side of Johnny's face, his ass was open enough for the spy to place the patch in a strategically perfect location – deep down in the crack on the left side of his crotch, above the dangling balls on the left of the ridged perineum. The patch was flesh-colored and mostly invisible, but a careful look might reveal the slight discoloration it created. It was unlikely Abu would spot it down there unless he lay on his back with his legs up and peered into a mirror. With any luck, it would remain in place and undiscovered for about ten days. Johnny had a similar patch under his left armpit, and it had remained intact and functioning for a week so far.

Elated at this important success, he lay back and allowed the brute attack to continue. Abu drilled his mouth with cock and his asshole with tongue. Johnny's lips gaped wide, and his loud gurgles continued. His size thirteen bare feet bobbed in the air near his head as he squirmed upward off the platform into that thrusting tongue. Abu smacked his pale butt enthusiastically.

The sprawled American hardly minded the savage treatment. In fact his own stiff cock thrust against Abu's smooth belly in a oily glide that had him nearing a precipitous orgasm. But the Iranian forestalled that release with a sudden re-positioning that left Johnny open-mouthed and gasping.

He was up and off the table to stand at the foot of it. Dragging Johnny toward him, he then gripped his legs again and shoved back on one knee so hard it pressed against the sprawled blond's furry chest. With his ass wide open, the jerking pole between the Iranian's lean thighs had easy access to the spit-gobbed hole quivering in the center. Drool coated the reddened lips, but it was not enough for the dark-eyed terrorist. He grinned as he smacked Johnny's lush butt-cheek with one hand and reached over to the lip of the splashing fountain beside them with the other. He snatched up a small silver urn then upended it over the spy's splayed crack.

It was some kind of scented oil, rose and lilac and some earthy odor mingling as the slippery stuff cascaded down over his ass and the rearing cock lying against it.

There was a moment of suspended confrontation as the pair eyed each other in the dim light. Abu's bulbous-headed cock lay in the center of Johnny's spread crack, poised to drive home. Johnny was keenly aware much more than sex was at stake. He had to wonder if Abu had any inkling of the same. For some reason, Johnny felt an odd kinship with the supposed terrorist. Their hidden agendas, their secrets, even this savage sex, all seemed to bring out similarities rather than differences in them.

Yet the two couldn't have been more different physically. The blond's powerful body was huge. Packed with muscle, he was also fleshy and hardly lean like his assailant. Abu's belly rippled with smooth muscle, his stiff cock a jutting spear rising up between thighs that also rippled with slender muscle. He was almost entirely hairless while Johnny's big body was coated in a light down of soft blond fur. Johnny seemed almost lazily languid, while the Iranian appeared wired and taut, from head to toe.

Appearances certainly can be deceptive, as any spy can tell you. Johnny did his best to cultivate his lumbering, nonaggressive look as a disguise. He was absolutely certain there was more to Abu as well.

The Iranian smiled, a devilish smirk that lit up his dark eyes. Then he slammed forward with his hips and impaled the blond.

"Ohhhhh!!! God almighty, pal! Are you trying to kill me?" Johnny hissed. He was trying not to make too much noise, as he was aware only the beaded doorway gave them any semblance of privacy.

Abu was deadly-quiet as he continued to smirk and stare down into Johnny's wide blue eyes. He rammed his cock balls-deep, yanked it out, then shoved it right back in. He offered no finesse, nor any mercy, as the stiff spear gutted the blond in a series of rapid-fire strokes.

Johnny had no intention of lying there passively and just taking it. His long arms reached out to grasp the firm cheeks of Abu's thrusting ass and pull on them, thus increasing the force of that pummel-fuck. His own fat cock throbbed and leaked on his belly while his pink asshole sucked and squeezed the rod jabbing it.

It was Abu who brought them to a crashing orgasm. He seized Johnny's plump meat and yanked on it with an oily hand. Savage pumps had him squirming up off the tiled platform and huffing for breath. With that constantly ramming cock up his gut and that fierce fist pumping his cock, he was done for.

As soon as he began to shoot, Abu pulled out and sprayed him. Cum erupted in a violent spew that coated Johnny from crotch to chin. Breathless and shaking all over, Johnny couldn't help giggling hysterically as that wild spray continued for much longer than he thought possible. Cum was everywhere.

"I go to clean up. Good afternoon, American. I hope you had your fill of fun."

With a final slap to Johnny's beefy butt and before Johnny had time to respond, he turned and fled. The blond rose immediately, and with trembling knees quickly washed away the cum, oil and sweat from his naked body in the room's fountain. The first part of his mission had been accomplished, and part two was about to begin.

Abu's frequent though discreet encounters with other men had been documented by the CIA, as well as his propensity to go for the bigger men, and blonds in particular. Johnny had been chosen for the mission in part because of his physical appearance – and of course his willingness to attempt a seduction of the man.

Although the Americans were aware of Abu's many affairs, they had been unable to trace him back to his headquarters in Istanbul. He had managed to ditch any and all tails they put on him. Thus, Johnny was dispatched.

Now he rushed to dress and get back to his motorcycle. He intended on following Abu from the hamam to his lair. With the aid of the patch Johnny had planted, that goal might also be accomplished.

The patch was an ingenious new type of tracking device. Outside, the blond spy mounted his bike and took off to circle the neighborhood while he waited for Abu to emerge. The GPS on his bike also now tracked his prey. This time he need not follow closely, and definitely did not want Abu to know he was tailing him.

The afternoon was turning into evening by the time Johnny closed in on Abu at one of the ferry docks that offered transport across the Bosporus from the European side of the city to the Asian side. He had followed Abu in a circuitous route for nearly three hours around the bustling city until the Iranian had finally setteld in at one location.

Johnny parked a few blocks away and discretely moved in to scope out the situation. He carried a pocket version of the GPS tracker from his bike and was thus able to keep an eye on Abu's movements as he lingered in the shade of a bank of blooming azaleas and peered at the row of crowded buildings opposite the ferry terminal. Abu was inside the third from the corner and had been there for half an hour. Was he eating? Meeting with someone? Or was this his secret lair?

The red blip on his tracker alerted him that Abu was on the move again. He looked up from the device to the doorway of the building fifty yards away. A trio of figures emerged simultaneously.

Two men appeared, both of which looked remarkably like Abu! The third was a woman. After a few steps, all three separated to head off in different directions. Johnny's mouth dropped open. The tracker blipped brightly as the woman made her way straight across the street toward the ferry terminal.

Johnny touched the left side of his sunglasses beside his ear and the special lenses immediately zoomed in on the strolling woman. Long auburn tresses fell to her shoulders. A pale-green silk dress fell to just above her knees and was cinched at her narrow waist with a large brown leather belt. It was long-sleeved and hid her arms. She wore green silk stockings and brown leather high heels. She walked with a gliding roll all too familiar to the watching American.

It was Abu! No wonder he had managed to elude his previous tails – he really did look like a woman! Johnny laughed out loud. Not this time, he thought. Not this time.

He boarded the ferry after Abu at the last possible minute. With the aid of his tracker, he managed to keep well away from the silk-clad damsel while they crossed the strait. Once they landed on the Asian shore, he followed closely but discretely as Abu walked up a few blocks to finally enter one of the sea-side homes that faced Europe. He recognized it for what it was, a Yali, one of the numerous homes built in the 1800s by the current Sultan and other aristocrats as summer residences. Over the years many of them had fallen into disrepair, but in the last few decades most had been renovated and turned into expensive waterfront properties.

This one was plastered in a lovely pale yellow and surrounded on the land side by gardens and shrubbery. The moment Abu entered the small door at the side of the building, Johnny leapt into action. He intended on surprising the Iranian, and wasn't going to wait for him to settle in.

Racing to the door in surprisingly swift bounds, he arrived to bend over and pick the lock in less than thirty seconds and slide inside quietly. He raced up the stairway he found with surprising lightness for all his bulk. Another doorway blocked his path on the second floor. A quick glance at his tracker told him Abu was just inside. He was still running when he smashed open the door with all the weight of his big frame behind him.

Abu whirled to confront him, and was on the verge of pulling out a weapon when Johnny shot him. He toppled backwards onto the bed, instantly unconscious. The drug in the dart Johnny had shot him with would render him helpless for a good hour.

That hour passed swiftly, but gave the tall spy the time he needed to discover some interesting and shocking details of Abu's surprising secret identity. He stood at the sliding glass door that opened up to a small balcony and gazed out at the busy Bosporus below. Such an important waterway, and from what he'd discovered, definitely at threat from the radical Muslim terrorist group called the Righteous Angels.

It had taken nearly a half hour to discover the secret panel that opened up to a compartment containing a laptop that was password protected and not easily compromised. That hardly mattered. He could either force Abu to reveal the password when he awoke, or take it back to his bosses and hand it over to the experts. It took another ten minutes to discover the secret compartment behind the secret compartment that held the treasure trove of documents and other goodies that revealed Abu's true identity and goals.

The most telling among the rather contradictory pile of fake passports, foreign currencies, enigmatic dossiers and misleading letters was one precious item that convinced Johnny he had discovered Abu's greatest secret. It was a small gold necklace. Attached to it was a tiny Star of David.

Abu was Jewish. He was an Israeli spy, not a Muslim terrorist. This was the most plausible conclusion at which Johnny could arrive. Abu had been among a group of infant orphan refugees from Iran who had been adopted out. An Iranian-American couple had adopted him, and they had moved to Britain where he had been raised.

There were a number of Jews who lived in Iran before the revolution, and it seemed that Abu's original family was among them. Somehow Abu must have discovered this, and the fact he was Jewish himself. What an interesting story!

Behind him he heard Abu call out to him. "What do you want? Release me and we can talk."

He was awake. Johnny turned to him and crossed the tiny room to the bed. He sat down beside the sprawled spy. Johnny had removed the wig, but Abu was still wearing the dress. He'd found a number of silk scarves in Abu's drawers and used them to tie the Iranian face down to the bed before he went about ransacking his room. He wasn't taking any chances.

His ankles and wrists were bound wide apart and held him securely. The silk dress he still wore did little to hide the round firmness of his spread butt-cheeks. The lean muscularity of his arms were revealed now with the long sleeves slipped down to his shoulders. The green silk stockings on his legs softened but didn't really alter their muscular shape.

He smiled as he gazed at that helpless body, just now beginning to struggle slightly. The possibilities were enticing.

He had a decision to make. The Israelis and Americans were allies, but their spy folks were often not prepared to share secrets. Johnny's people would treat Abu like an enemy more readily than a friend.

He could call in his backup and abandon Abu to their not-so-tender mercies. That was not going to turn out well, he felt. This dude reeked of tough and smart. He wasn't going to be giving away anything more than what Johnny had already discovered. And so far he had managed to completely fool the CIA into believing he was an Iranian terrorist, not an Israeli spy. Yes, smart and tough.

Abu could guess what he was thinking.

"I am not stupid. I realized you were an American spy the moment we met. We can work together. You know there's nothing here you've found that compares to what's in my head. I'm to meet with the Righteous Angels tomorrow at eight in the morning. You can come with me, or follow me and observe. And you can share what you know with me. Together we've got to be better off than as it stands now, at each other's throats."

Johnny smiled. "Something to think about. Yes, something to think about. But for now, it's payback time."

He reached out with both hands and grasped the hem of the dress just above the backs of the knees. He yanked upward on it. The material was true silk and didn't rip, but it easily slipped upwards to reveal the flesh beneath from the belted waist downward.

Instead of underwear, he wore a snug-fitting jock-strap which served to hide his goodies under the silk dress. The garters that held up his nylons rose up to fasten just beneath his ass. Along with the jockstrap, they outlined the firm globes of his smooth ass. Johnny grinned wickedly as he reached over to the open drawer of the night stand and pulled out the bottle of expensive lotion he had noticed there when ransacking them earlier. He flipped open the lid and upended it over Abu's naked butt, right along the divide between those parted globes.

He unzipped at the same time and pulled out his stiff cock. Dropping the lotion on the bed, he shoved down on his brand-new designer jeans and underwear and squirmed out of them. In seconds he was on the bed again, naked from the waist down and kneeling between Abu's spread legs.

Abu hadn't been gentle at the hamam. It probably wasn't his nature. Johnny sensed what he needed – a good hard fuck. He obliged. Spreading the marble-hard cheeks even wider apart, he had a good look at the twitching amber slot. It was coated in a slippery sheen of the creamy lotion. He drove forward with his hips and slammed into the gooey mess.

The hole offered no resistance. Abu might have seemed helpless tied hand and foot, but he managed to rear upwards with his taut hips and add impetus to the rough violation. There was no question he willed his sphincter to open for that thrusting cock-head. It burrowed half-way home in one violent drive.

"Yeah! Take it," Johnny cried out.

"Is that all you have? Can you not fuck harder, American? Unnggggh!!! Harder! This is nothing-unnnggggh!"

The hole pulsed around his buried cock. It opened up for his thrust, but then clamped down over his buried meat to squeeze and grip it with relentless force. It was absolutely amazing.

They fought it out. Sweat flew from Johnny's forehead, dribbled down his pits and pooled in the crack of Abu's delectable ass. Sweat blotched the silk dress from Abu's neck down to where it bunched along his waist. The garter belt actually snapped apart as the pinned spy reared and bucked and Johnny slammed down into him. The American tore at the stockings, yanking them down to Abu's ankles as he continued to pummel-fuck his heaving butt-crack.

His cock and balls, trapped in the jockstrap, bounced on the bed between his spread thighs, receiving a good pounding as the two rose and fell atop the bed, springs creaking and headboard banging against the wall.

The squishy hole Johnny assaulted grew looser and looser until he was easily ramming home with every thrust – and then yanking all the back way out. For all Abu's grunting and gasping, he managed to spur on his partner/adversary with continual abuse. Even though his hole seemed to have capitulated, he wasn't admitting any such surrender aloud.

In the end it was a draw, to neither men's surprise. The slippery friction of that seething hole drove Johnny to the edge and beyond. He couldn't hold back from spewing as he pulled out of Abu's seething hole and let loose all over his sweaty, solid butt cheeks.

But Abu wasn't left in the lurch. Gasping for breath and still spraying, the blond spy crammed a trio of fingers deep into the leaking hole he'd just been fucking and cork-screwed them deep. At the same time, he shoved his other hand under Abu's belly and under the jockstrap to find his cock. It was stiff as hell and dripping pre-cum. A good pump on it as his fingers twisted and jabbed, and it was all over for the bound Iranian. He emptied his load all over his own bed, thrashing and cursing.

Johnny kept his fingers buried in the creamy hole and lazily probed as he allowed his captive to finish off. The steamy heat of that quivering slot begged for another round and his cock remained stiff, regardless of his all-to-recent orgasm.

"Not satisfied, American? There's more where that came from. We will make an excellent team, and you will get much of that fun you are looking for."

Evening had settled in and cool sea air wafted in over them from the balcony. It was growing dark as he gazed down at his prisoner. That ass! He fingered it deeper and laughed out loud. It was probably foolish, and definitely risky to make a deal with this tricky character. But wasn't his business all about risk?

"And you'll get some fun of your own out of the bargain, I believe. Well, perhaps. Perhaps. And speaking of fun, we may as well have some more right now."

He was still laughing as he slipped his fingers from the juicy slot and replaced them with his fat cock. The big blond started fucking all over again.

Time enough later to make any final decision, he thought.

"Fuck me, American! Have you no balls? Show me you are a man!"

He slammed deep in response. Then he laughed again. Who was playing who? Only time would tell, he guessed.

The Istanbul evening descended as they continued fucking in the darkness. It looked like a long night ahead of them.

MASSAGING THE TRUTH
By Landon Dixon

Dixon's stories have been published in several magazines and anthologies and compiled in the short story collections *Hot Tales of Gay Lust 1, 2,* and *3.*

I cast a furtive glance up and down the dark alley then knocked on the grey metal door.

A slot slid open in the door, and two brown eyes stared out. "Yeah?"

"Washington had wooden teeth."

"How wooden?"

"Wooden you like to know."

The slot slid closed. The metal door clicked open. I slipped inside the squat brick building.

The corridor was dimly-lit, the air warm, almost sticky.

"Who sent you?" brown-eyes asked, a big, burly guy in a tight white T-shirt and tight white pants, white sneakers. Black hair bristled in a brushcut off his block head, and muscles bulged on his arms and chest and neck. He looked like an attendant in a mental hospital. And, again, I doubted the sanity of the plan.

"I, uh, heard things ... on the street," I responded nervously. "Thought I'd check it out." A grin fluttered across my trembling lips.

Brown-eyes grunted and turned and led me down the corridor. His huge buttocks strained the stitching on the back of his pants, the thick mounds clenching and jostling and bunching, powerfully.

The parade stopped at the end of the corridor under a bright white hanging light. Brown-eyes gave me the once-over, twice, looking up and down my slender, suit-clad frame, examining my thin, bespectacled face; checking form and function. I thought I saw a twinkle of recognition in those hard brown marbles set in that stern stone face.

He pointed a blunt finger down the hallway to the right. "Third door on the left. You want basic or full-service?"

I peered down the hallway, flicked my grey eyes back up at him. "Uh ... full-service? Does that include ..."

"Everything."

He trundled off down the corridor, his giant white body dissolving into the dimness.

The place didn't have a name or a number. But word on queer street was that a man could get a good, deep-body massage that catered to his particular bent. Rub and tugs, and suck and pumps, were illegal, but in the nation's capitol, services could be found for every need, for a price.

I walked down the hallway to the third white-painted door on the left. I turned the brass knob and slipped inside.

A tall, lean, tanned blond was waiting for me, smiling and rubbing his hands together. "I'm Kurt," he said, his clear blue eyes taking in every inch of me.

He was dressed exactly like brown-eyes. Except there was a bulge in his front, as well as the pair at the back. My dry mouth suddenly slavered saliva, my eyes going misty behind my horn-rims. "H-Hi, Kurt. I'm, uh, Colin."

His smile spread wider, the plush red curtain of his lips parting to reveal shiny white teeth. "Take off your clothes, Colin."

I closed the door behind me. It sucked tight and locked. The room was small, narrow, stuffy, dominated by a brown padded massage table right in the middle. White towels were piled up on a three-legged stool in one corner, three large bottles of baby oil standing on the white tile floor next to the stool. Two banks of florescent beams flooded the white-walled room with light. There was a sprinkler head set up in the ceiling, directly above the massage table.

I took off my suit jacket, stripped off my tie, unbuttoned my shirt, my shaking hands making it fumblesome progress. Kurt stepped closer and took the garments away from me, hung them on a hook on the door. I unbelted and unzipped my suit pants, pushed them and my shorts down, stepped out of the pile of fallen silk. My cock hung down over my shaven balls semi-erect and tingling. Kurt scooped up my lower garments and hooked them, as well.

"Lie down on the table," he instructed, his voice soft and rich, like honey. "I'll take care of the rest."

He didn't specify how I should lie down – on my stomach or back. It was my option. I climbed up onto the table and sprawled out on my stomach, sticking my face into the padded opening at one end.

The table didn't move. It was bolted to the floor, heavy-duty construction. My nude body shimmered in the warm air, under the bright lights, my surging cock pressing into the padded vinyl.

Kurt grabbed up a bottle of baby oil and squirted a stream onto my back, making me jump and grab onto the edges of the table.

His hands were firm and knowing. He massaged my neck, working the tension out, kneaded the knots out of my shoulders. My face reddened in the hole, my cock pulsating against the padding.

Kurt rubbed his way down my back, straightening my spine, stiffening my cock. He skipped over my trembling butt cheeks, applying oil to both my legs, working and loosening the hamstrings and calves, lacing and rubbing my ankles, knuckling the soles of my feet, pulling on my toes. He was skilled in the art of massage and not-so-subliminal seduction, built for both jobs.

179

Oil splashed down onto my ass, and I moaned.

"Here we go," Kurt said. "Full-service."

He gripped a buttock apiece and plied with both hands. The force, the feel, the fondle of his hands on my ass drove my erection hard into the table. He rode his squeezing hands up from the start of the swells at the back of my legs, over the humped flesh, down to the small of my back; again and again. My knuckles burned white on the edges of the table, cock pumping.

Kurt dug his fingers into my butt cheeks, crossways, and spread them apart, open. My pucker flowered in the hothouse. Then something wet and warm hit it bang-on – Kurt's tongue.

"Jesus!" I squealed through the face-hole.

Ripples of delight raced up and down my sensualized body, my buttocks quivering and buzzing in the blond's clutching hands, my manhole burning on the end of his licker. He teased my ring with his swirling tongue, rimming. Then he formed the mouth-organ into a spear and fired it into my anus, deep. I jerked, the guy's tongue plugged into my rectum.

He pulled his tongue out, plowed it back in, fucking my joyous chute with at least three inches of sticker. I thrust my ass up to take all I could, my cock and body throbbing with heated emotion. Until Kurt pulled his tongue out of my anus for good, applied it in long, moist, dragging strokes to my sensitized crack.

I shuddered, the buff blond absolutely painting my shaven butt cleavage, lapping between my cheeks and over my manhole. I shivered with each budded lick, my entire body and being shaking out of control.

Kurt said, "Roll over."

I jerked my head out of the face-hole with a wet pop and jumped up and spun around in mid-air, landed with a splat on my back, exposing my front. My nipples and cock burst outward with engorgement, brimming with awesome excitement under the bright lights.

Kurt smiled down at me. He licked his lush lips. Then he went back to work and play with his skilful, sensuous hands.

He gripped my ankles and slid his hands up my shinbones, planted them in the sinuous masses of my thighs, and plied. My cock sprang up like a missile from a ground launch, as the blond played my taut string muscles with his fingers.

But his hands swooped up and glided over my red-alert erection, slid onto my stomach. Where they swirled, then spun up onto my pecs.

Kurt's handsome face hung over my flushed face, as he scooped up my pecs and squeezed them, massaged them, piled them together and kneaded the pair. My nipples flared up wildly, sticking out hard and pink like my cock. Kurt bent his head down and lashed one propped-up bud with his thick red tongue, my other nipple. I gripped the table on either side like before, arching my chest and body upward, offering myself to the man's talented tongue; glaring up at that sprinkler head mounted right over the table.

Kurt sealed his lips around one stiff spit-shined nipple and sucked on it. My cock and brain vibrated. The beautiful blond sucked up my other nipple and tugged on it, his hands clasping my pecs. I closed my eyes, shimmering with that strange, ball-streaking, cock-humming buzz I get whenever my nipples are fingered and fellated.

Kurt released my pecs. The reddened flesh sagged back to normal position, smoldering with the memory of Kurt's grip and tongue. He wound his long fingers around my cock, pulled it up, poured his plush lips down and over.

"Sweet Jesus!" I bleated with even more of a Texas twang.

Kurt's silky blond head sunk down onto my groin like the blazing sun, his cauldron of a mouth consuming my cock whole. I craned my neck and stared at the melting point of man-on-man. My cock pulsed molten in his mouth, hot air from his nostrils flooding my balls.

He kept me locked down, quivering, in his superheated velvet vise for a good/great half-minute or so. Before he finally pulled his head up, slowly, his wet lips and tongue dragging along my throbbing shaft.

He slid his left hand up onto my chest, squeezing my pecs, pinching my nipples, his right hand cradling and massaging my balls. As he bobbed up and down on my cock, sucking with a fearsome intensity. It felt as if he'd pull my foreskin right off, blew my mind and my grip on reality.

But he only kept it up for a minute or so, leaving me gasping. He'd sensed the boil in my balls and the come-hardness of my cock, expert sexnician that he was. "You want me to fuck you, Colin?" he asked, noosing my shaft at the hood with his fingers, to cap my impending explosion.

I gulped, "Yes, please!"

He dropped my dick. He peeled off his T-shirt and pants like they were tearaway. His entire body was tanned bronze, a lithe caramel-coated length of lovely man that boasted mounded pecs and pointing nipples, a washboard stomach, a trim waist, long supple legs, blond-dusted balls, and a smooth, clean-cut cock that seemed to rise up and jut out forever – straight at me.

I stocked up on the delicious eye-candy then he barrel-rolled me back onto my belly, sprang me up onto my hands and knees like an eager little doggy. Kurt mounted the table in behind me. The padded platform took both our manly bodies with ease.

Kurt sluiced oil off my bowed back with two fingers and swept it in between my arched buttocks. He lubed my hole outside and in, his digits squishing inside and squirming deep. I gleefully sucked on his probing fingers with my panting ass muscles. Until he unplugged, greased his cock, pressed the head of that sculpted tool up against my manhole.

I exhaled and tried to relax. He punched his mushroomed cap through my ring and surged swollen shaft into my anus. I inhaled and went rigid. Inch after bloated, pulsating inch plunged into my chute, stuffing me full of wild sensation, ballooning my bum and body. His balls kissed my clenched buttocks, and his hands gripped my frozen hips. And I almost swallowed my tongue. The guy's bone was buried in my ass.

He pumped, once. Again, his corded thighs banging off my butt cheeks, rocking me forward on the table, his cock stroking full-length and fiery in my ass. He thrust repeatedly, rhythmically, sawing back and forth in my electrified chute, fucking me. I tilted my head up and yowled.

Kurt slammed me faster and harder, sending his pipe shooting right into my very soul. I hung onto the table, hammered at the sexhole. The sharp smack of his thighs against my buttocks echoed in the crackling air, just above my high-pitched moaning, his throaty groaning. He pounded into me, reaming me into sexual oblivion.

My flapping cock shot up between my legs and spouted semen, pressurized and propelled by the pistoning stroke of meat in my ass. I shuddered and cried out. Kurt grunted and gushed, his thundering dong exploding inside my seared anus and blasting liquid lightning against my bowels.

When I finally staggered out of the steamy sex-cell into the dim hallway, brown-eyes was waiting for me under the hanging light at the juncture of corridors. He held a small white packet in a beefy paw. "A DVD of your session with

Kurt, Mr. CIA Assistant Director," he smirked, handing me the packet. "We have copies, of course. If we need them." His smile turned grim. "You will be contacted how to proceed."

My fallen face reflected astonishment. I stumbled out the back of the building and into the Washington night.

# # # # #

"Good work, Thompson," CIA Assistant Director Mort Callahan congratulated me, when I made it back to the office. "Now we know for sure that massage parlor is a base for Russian spying – luring federal officials and politicians into compromising positions and then blackmailing them for state secrets." He smiled sympathetically at me. "You'll get a promotion for this. For going, uh, below and beyond the call of duty for your country."

I looked just like the guy – same build, same age, same facial features. A little hair-dye and make-up, a few acting and voice lesions, made the ruse complete. And the Russians had bought it hook, line, and sucker (and fucker). Only, the real Mort Callahan had a large purple birthmark on his lower right abdomen, which I didn't; a birthmark that could be revealed for the press to prove that he wasn't the one given the full-service treatment at the illicit massage parlor. If the Russians went ahead and released the evidence of their scheme.

"We'll shut their operation down and expel the lot of them."

He stuck out his hand and I shook it, proud to go gay in defense of the American way. Excited to be on my way up from a clerk in the corporation. Enthralled by what Kurt had done to me, for me, how he had done it to and for me; knowing I just couldn't walk away from a man like that, spy or no spy.

# # # # #

It was super-surreptitious even by counter-espionage standards. I sheltered Kurt from the fall-out, kept on meeting him in the back of a Russian deli. He fondled me, sucked me, fucked me. And I fed him low-level intelligence from my new desk job as a thank you, a lewd lust-struck traitor.

It was bogus information, of course, meant to confuse and subterfuge the stud and his handlers. That's how I got Callahan to play along, so I could still play along with Kurt.

Honestly, though, I don't think the blond bombshell even passed on the phony intel to his bosses back in the Kremlin. We were in love, after all.

Not that I told my bosses any of that. Sometimes the truth has to be massaged a little, so that work can become play in the treacherous world of espionage.

DOUBLE-DOUBLE
By Landon Dixon

Schottz cracked the young man over the head with his cock.

Hanniger almost plunged face-first into the open filing cabinet, a micro-camera spilling out of his hand and onto the floor. He jerked his blond head around, stared up at Schottz's lethal looking hard-on with frightened blue eyes.

"You don't have authorization to access this office," Schottz growled, wagging his engorged dong in a threatening manner over the cowering file clerk. "This is the Soviet attaché's office."

With the post-war situation in Berlin so unstable, an unprecedented Allied airlift underway to relieve the starving citizens of West Berlin, all untoward unsanctioned activity had to be monitored and stopped by all means necessary, if necessary. The Allies would love to get their hands on East German and Soviet troop and military hardware data, the resolve of both parties to maintaining the blockade. As the Stasi second-in-command in the Berlin sector, it was Schottz's job to plug any leaks, before they trickled over to the enemy.

Hanniger gulped, blinked his eyes, looking into Schottz's hard, uncompromising cock. He still clung to the sheet of paper he'd pulled out of a file, was about to take a picture of. It shook in his left hand. He suddenly stuffed it into his mouth and started rapidly chewing.

Schottz grunted. Then the big man bent down, pressed his thumbs into the sides of Hanniger's throat. The younger man gagged, coughed up the crumpled wet ball of paper. Schottz drove his cock into Hanniger's mouth, a more than fair replacement.

Hanniger clutched Schottz's wide hips and eagerly sealed his lips around the big man's vein-popped pink shaft, sucked with his mouth. And Schottz grunted again, with satisfaction this time. He dug his meaty hands into the young man's fine, blond hair and helped him suck cock, pumping his hips, Hanniger's mouth and throat.

Hanniger beamed up at Schottz in the dim light, his pale throat bulging with the thrust, his reddened cheeks billowing with suck. He'd always admired Schottz, the big man's tall, muscular body, his chiseled, impassive face, the sheen of his close-cropped black hair and the authoritative strut of his walk. Schottz was fifty years old, wore black horn-rimmed glasses and a small hearing aid behind his right ear, but he carried himself with the power and grace of the career military man.

The wet, hot tug of Hanniger's mouth on Schottz's cock made the older man's nipples stiffen and tingle under his white shirt, his hanging balls tighten and buzz. He glanced at the sodden ball of paper on the floor next to Hanniger. He could guess what that was all about – a communiqué from the Soviet attaché to his bosses back in the Kremlin. The Soviets told their East German comrades little, treated them with the contempt of the conqueror, giving orders rather than advice. What Schottz wanted to know was who Hanniger was working for, where the illegally obtained information was destined, and why.

Hanniger's slim fingers bit into Schottz's hips, his head bobbing faster and faster, mouth and throat vaccing harder. He couldn't believe he was sucking the big man's cock. The sledge of beef tasted so good, so filling, throbbed so powerfully inside his mouth. He desired with all his heart to be doused with Schottz's hot, spurting cum, to eat, to swallow the man's erotic discharge. To have the living legend of the former Third Reich let loose in his face and soul.

Schottz sensed the need, felt the passion. Hanniger sucked with a commendable verve and precision, anxiously but effectively. Schottz's big body shimmered, his big cock forging molten in the younger man's tugging mouth and squeezing throat. He jerked his hips back, yanking his boiling dong out of Hanniger's gasping mouth.

"Who sent you in here to snoop on the Soviets?"

Hanniger gulped, his mouth gaping empty. A teaser of salty pre-cum slid down his throat. "N-No one. I was I-looking all on my own. I was just curious about ..."

Schottz slapped the man's pretty face with his dripping slab.

Hanniger squealed, with pleasure. Took the backhanded stroke of beef off his other cheek with equal delight.

"Tell me," Schottz growled. "Or you won't taste my fulfillment."

Hanniger licked his lush, red lips, his blue eyes gone frightened again. "It was ... just like I said. I ..."

Schottz crammed cap into the man's mouth, pulled it back. Leaving a string of pre-cum linking the two men. Which Hanniger excitedly sucked up.

"It was Munchen! He instructed me to break in here and go through the files, take pictures of any useful communiqués!"

Schottz's thick lips formed a grim smile. "For what purpose?"

"I-I don't know that! I'm just a low-level file clerk. Munchen wouldn't confide in ..."

Schottz jammed his gleaming dong back into Hanniger's mouth, cutting off the pleaful speech. Munchen was Schottz's boss, the head of the Stasi, Berlin Sector. He didn't even confide in Schottz. No one could be trusted these turbulent days, with the new world order hanging in the balance.

Schottz grabbed onto Hanniger's head and pistoned his hips, driving his cock deep and true into the younger man's urgently sucking mouth and throat. Then he grunted, softly, sprayed semen inside Hanniger, in torrential waves. Hanniger swallowed exuberantly, expertly, his shining face stuffed full of cock and cum, eyes watering tears with the wonderfulness of it all.

Schottz shook his dong off and holstered the tool back in his grey pants. He pointed at the ball of paper on the floor. And when Hanniger turned on his knees to pick it up, he slammed the man's head against the metal filing cabinet, knocking him cold.

"Pleasant dreams," Schottz commented, striding out of the office with satisfaction.

# # # # #

Schottz jabbed his iron erection into the small of Teldov's back, banging the man up against the urinal. "You frequent gay bars, eh, Teldov?" the big man snarled.

The MGB-Stasi liaison officer jerked his head around, his body pinned against the white, wet porcelain by the force of Schottz's cock. He shrugged his bony shoulders, his thin face coloring. "It's-it's just a bar. Like any other. I ..."

"It's a pick-up spot for men." Schottz glanced down at his steel dong, back up into Teldov's twitching face. "I'm looking for a man, myself."

Teldov eagerly smiled, his ginger eyebrows jumping. "Oh, yes?"

"Yeah," Schottz rasped. "You, Teldov." His hard, black eyes behind his glasses slid down to Teldov's bare, mounded ass. "I think you've got just what I'm looking for."

Schottz jerked his rod back and banged down to his knees on the black and white tiles, yanked Teldov's unbuttoned pants all the way down. The Russian's buttocks trembled, round, soft, succulent. Schottz slapped his big hands onto the plush pair and pulled them open, planted his stiffened tongue in between.

"God!" Teldov yelped, violating Soviet state atheism like Schottz was violating his butthole.

Schottz pumped his head, spearing the rounded tip of his wet, pink sticker into Teldov's puckered pink hole. His hands mauled the smooth, satin flesh of the Soviet's buttocks, his breath steaming hot and humid against the man's wettened starfish. Then he bent his head down lower, flattened his tongue out wide, licked up along Teldov's shaven crack from deep in between the man's legs to the tip of the tailbone.

Teldov shuddered with delight, his clutched cock leaping in his hand, up against the slick porcelain. He took stroke after stroke of the East German's bold, budded tongue, his body blazing with pleasure, mind gone to jelly under the oral onslaught. So, when Schottz split Teldov's quivering cheeks even wider, speared his tongue back in, even deeper, it seemed only natural, wonderfully so.

Schottz drove his bladed licker as far as it would go into the man's opened-up ass. And that was three inches or more. He felt Teldov's resolve totally dissolve on the end of his tongue, the man's sphincter loosen with surrender. And that's when the capsule popped out of Teldov's rectum and onto the end of Schottz's searching, sensual tongue. The East German sucked the small metal container into his mouth, transferred it to the three hollowed-out teeth on his lower right jaw without the Russian even noticing.

Schottz writhed his tongue around in Teldov's anus some more, setting the man to trembling out of control. Then he pulled his pink snake right out of Teldov's tunnel, lapped the man's crack briskly some more, before bounding up to his feet.

191

He played the mushroomed purple hood of his dong along Teldov's slickened butt cleavage, up against the Russian's panting manhole. "You and I – we should liaise more often," he gritted in Teldov's reddened ear. "This way and other ways."

Teldov groaned, jacking his cock, gripping the side of the urinal with his other hand. "Yes! Please! Fuck me!"

Schottz greased his rod, swirled a blunt, slick finger around Teldov's already saliva-moistened ass ring. Then the big man drove his heated point home, jabbing the crown of his cock through Teldov's pucker, burying the massive German bratwurst in the Russian's burning bung.

Teldov was flung up against the urinal by the butt-busting strength of Schottz's cock. He kissed the tiled wall, thrust his own cock against the slick porcelain. As Schottz rutted his mammoth dong around inside Teldov's electrified anus.

But Schottz had places to go and people to seduce, plots to foil, before his night was through. So he didn't waste a lot of time ass-climatizing Teldov's chute to his Communist member. Instead, he planted his big hands on Teldov's narrow shoulders and powered his hips back and forth, pounding his cock into Teldov's butt.

The redheaded Red groaned, shuddered, getting banged, his own surging erection getting shunted up and down the porcelain in rhythm to Schottz's cock in his rump. The two men, suspicious colleagues at best, had struck a fucking chord.

Schottz hammered Teldov's ass, his cock plowing the man a new one. His balls slapped buttocks, his own body burning with the urgency of the bathroom reaming. Zither music shrilled out in the bar, but the two men were hearing none of it, engaged up to their cocks in loving one another. Teldov through back his jerking head and howled, semen jetting out of his urinal-skimming cock and up into the air.

Schottz rammed the desperately shaking man as hard as he could a few dozen more times, driving the sperm out of Teldov's shooting prick. Then he grunted, was jolted by his own orgasm, his ass-enveloped cock exploding, firing searing jizz up against Teldov's bowels.

Schottz gripped Teldov. The Russian clung to the urinal, contracting his butt muscles to milk every last drop out of Schottz's lodged cock. "Where were you going tonight?" Schottz breathed in the man's ear.

Teldov glanced back. The German thumped up against Teldov's ass, wallowing his cock in the stew simmering in the Russian's chute, making Teldov sigh, spill. "I was going to see your boss – Munchen," he confessed. "We had some ... business to discuss."

Schottz pulled his cock out of Teldov's ass with a wet pop, chopped the man on the back of the neck with his bladed right hand. The Russian slid down the urinal to the bathroom floor, out cold.

# # # # #

The capsule contained microfilm. The microfilm dealt with the details of Soviet atomic research. Explosive stuff, literally and figuratively.

Schottz smiled to himself, as he wheeled his car up the long drive to Munchen's house, parked and got out. Munchen's personal secretary answered the door, wearing a bathrobe. Schottz clipped the effeminate man on the side of the jaw, caught him and let him sag to the floor. He wanted to catch his boss by surprise. He knew just where Munchen would be – in his bedroom on the second floor, waiting for his able and willing assistant to return to his bed.

The room was dark, like the night. Schottz slipped inside, into Munchen's spacious bed, wrapped his arms around Munchen's thin, supple body from behind and kissed the man's lush earlobe.

"Ah, Heinrich, you've returned," Munchen murmured, pressing his nude, fetus-positioned body up against Schottz's spooning bare body. "Good. Who was at the ..."

His words trailed off, as he felt Schottz's massive erection slide up and fill the silken gap between his buttocks. "Schottz!" he whispered.

"Right, sir," Schottz confirmed, pumping his pulsating pole in between his boss's buoyant cheeks. "I've brought you some information from Hanniger, and Teldov."

Munchen stiffened in Schottz's strong arms, front and back.

Schottz released the man, turned on the bedside lamp. Munchen scrambled around on the sheet to stare at his underling. Schottz regarded his boss impassively, his dark eyes unblinking.

"What do you mean!? What information!?" Munchen protested, dragging the bedspread up to his chest. "I don't know what you're talking about! Get out of my bed!"

Schottz's grin was that of a death-head's. "You've been passing secrets to the Allies, Munchen. You're a double-agent. I've got the evidence, and I'm going to use it. Unless ..."

Munchen's grey eyes went wide with panic, his handsome Prussian face flushing. "Unless-unless what!?"

Schottz slid a big hand under the bedspread and grasped Munchen's cock, squeezed the smooth-shafted appendage. Then he moved closer, opened his hand, slid his own erection up against Munchen's, closed his hand over the pair of hard, beating cocks. "So you admit it. You instructed Hanniger to break into the Soviet attaché's files, take pictures, used Teldov to secure Soviet atomic research secrets – so you could pass the information on to the West, for a price." He squeezed their cocks together,

194

pumped the engorged pair. "Admit it. I've been onto you – after you – for awhile, Munchen."

Munchen grimaced, groaned, Schottz jacking harder, hotter. The aristocratic German at last nodded. "I admit it, yes." He dove a hand down beneath the covers and closed it over Schottz's hand on their cocks. "And now you're in on it, too, Schottz. Join with me!"

Schottz stared at the man, his hand no longer pumping.

Munchen threw back the bedcovers and scrambled around again, this time diving his head down to Schottz's groin. He brushed the man's hand away and grabbed onto the hard-on, himself, stuffed the beefy cap into his mouth, desperate to seal the sordid deal. Schottz grunted, thrust two-thirds of the rest of his enormous member into Munchen's moist, velvet-lined mouth.

Munchen smiled around the vein-ribboned shaft. Then he sucked, calmly, confidently. He smiled again when he felt Schottz's hand close over his cock at the base, felt Schottz's mouth consume most of his shaft.

The two men orally consummated their tacit agreement, sucking earnestly on each other's cocks. Munchen couldn't wrap his mouth around all of Schottz's meat, but he did his best, and did it well. He played with Schottz's hairy balls, squeezing, twisting the laden pair, as he vacced up and down the man's pipe. He filled himself with cock, feeling the heavy, wet, foreskin-dragging tug of Schottz's lips and tongue and mouth on his own wickedly pulsing cock.

Schottz pumped his hips, helping his boss cock-suck. As he expertly sucked Munchen's surging erection. He slid a hand over the man's rounded butt cheek and a finger into the man's butthole, plunging it in to the third knuckle. He felt Munchen jerk, the man's cock jumping in his mouth, butt muscles seizing Schottz's deliciously invading finger.

195

Schottz pumped Munchen's ass in rhythm to his cock in the man's mouth, sucking quick and hard on Munchen's dick.

It was too much for the Prussian. He groaned around Schottz's dong, spasmed around Schottz's finger. Semen flooded Schottz's throat in hot, salty bursts. The big man hungrily swallowed, plugging Munchen's ass and mouth.

Then Schottz's handled balls boiled over and his mouthed cock erupted. He tremored with the heated gushes of orgasm, almost blowing Munchen's head off with his shooting ecstasy.

Schottz caught Munchen's gourd between his powerful thighs and violently twisted the man's neck. Munchen snapped into unconsciousness.

Schottz had the evidence he needed to make Munchen disappear now. His hearing aid with the microphone and his glasses with the embedded camera had captured the man's treasonous confession. He would turn it all over to his superiors in the East German secret police, along with the other evidence, and they would "retire" Munchen.

But first, Schottz opened up the secret panel in Munchen's bedroom wall and sat down at the transmitter. His message to the Western allies was simple: "double-double." Now that he was in charge, he would be able to pass higher quality intelligence on to the British and Americans, not the low-level stuff Munchen had been jerking them around with.

CODE NAME: GOLDEN ROD
By Landon Dixon

I was supposed to be briefing the President on the clandestine raid we at the Corporation had conjured up. But when he'd excused himself to use the presidential toilet just off the Oval Office, and then invited me inside, how could I refuse?

Now, I was sitting on the porcelain throne of power, Mr. President down on his knees on the linoleum sucking my dick. He had my tool stretched out long and hard thanks to his firm handshake, dripping pre-cum out the slit thanks to his tireless speechifying mouth. I grabbed onto the guy's baby-elephant ears and pumped off my seat, shunting my golden cock back and forth in his wet, hot, sucking maw.

The agency tagged me "Golden Rod" because of my yellow-gold dick. My skin is light-brown, tan, except for my cock, which for some reason (maybe childhood radioactive play around Los Alamos, maybe just an aberration in coloring thanks to my Italian/Irish heritage) is a bright, shiny golden hue when fully aroused. And it was aroused now, the President's urgent sucking and slurping making it gleam.

I twisted his ears, forcing his mouth deeper, holstering a part of my rod in his velvet-lined throat. His oratory was just as good as it'd been during the campaign, and he readily bent to my carnal cock wishes like he bent to almost anything Congress handed him. I pumped his face, making his big brown eyes water, his plush purple lips leak drool at the sides. My mission could wait; the President was being taught the "golden rule."

He jerked his head back, shook his ears out of my hands. Saliva streamed in a string from his lips to my dick. "Would you mind doing some in-depth polling for me?" he

197

quipped, giving me that endearing grin that had won the hearts, if the not the minds, of the American public.

"Sure thing, Mr. President!" I responded. Always up for a call to duty.

He rose to his feet and helped me to mine. We traded positions. He gripped the tank of the toilet and straddled the bowl, sticking his butt out at me. His presidential pants were down around his ankles, his executive dong jutting out from his pube-pebbled loins like the west lawn flag at full breeze. His bum was just as cute as his face, taut and cheeky.

I got in behind the leader of the free world, spanked his back mounds with my slickened staff. He grunted and gasped, "Stick it in! Fuck my ass!"

Like every good green beret boy scout, I came prepared. I plucked the CIA-issue tube of lube out of my lowered pants pocket and sheathed my golden dong in glistening oil. Then I poked a slippery digit at the President's manhole, probed inside, and around. He moaned and rotated his dark moon on my sunken finger. We were good to go.

I unplugged my digit and grabbed onto my cock, steered bloated head up against the President's ass ring. He shuddered. Shaking the toilet. I gripped his narrow hips and thrust out mine, squishing my cap against his pucker, trying to bust through.

"Yes! Yes we can!" he exulted.

Just the inspiration I needed. I pushed my pelvis hard and my hood stretched his ass ring and popped through, plunged inside. I poured throbbing, swollen shaft in after my hood, stuffing the President's anus with cock like ACORN maybe stuffed ballot boxes. He took it and loved it, pushing back with his butt, ass-eating up every inch of my golden rod.

I fairly glowed in his anus, sealed tight to the balls.

"Fuck me! Fuck me!" he rasped.

And I stroked his ego with my cock and kissed his ass with my balls, like the best of sycophants. He was surprisingly tight for all of his liberalism, blisteringly hot. My dong went molten in his gripping butt-sleeve, as I churned back and forth, ass-fucking the President in the White House toilet.

"Faster! Harder!" He wasn't above pleading.

My knuckles burned white on his dark flesh. I cranked my powerful hips more powerfully, boring the man the best way possible. It wasn't the audacity of hope; it was the awesomeness of reality. I hammered his butt, reaming his chute.

He gripped his own flapping nightstick and shot up onto his toes like in the presence of the First Lady. "Yes! I'm coming!" he bleated above the blatant, brazen smack of my corded thighs against his tightened cheeks.

He jerked on the end of my jamming dong, jetted semen out of his handled cock. I couldn't hold back. I slammed the sworn-in swearing man in a frenzy, then bellowed my own joy, blasted my own ecstasy. I spurted the shuddering President's convulsing ass full of my heated appreciation.

He could have four of more of my years whenever he wanted.

# # # # #

I caught a nuclear sub bound for the Mediterranean. No one knew what my mission was. I was just one of the crew, with extremely light duties. And to really fit in, and arouse as little suspicion and as many cocks as possible, I huddled in a threesome in the torpedo room.

Their names were Sully and Hernandez. Sully was a redheaded lad with a freckled, eager face and wide, open and accommodating blue eyes, smooth pale skin.

He was built small and slim as befitted his tin can consignment, just like his submate Hernandez. Only Hernandez had short, bristly, black hair and liquid brown eyes, brown skin. They put into practice the new naval policy "please ask, don't tell."

They were inspecting my depth charge with their hands and lips and tongues, on their knees at my feet, even before they'd finished giving me a tour of the tub. Sully sucked up my golden prong with a vengeance after the usual oohing and aahing. His full, red lips torqued up and down my pipe. While Hernandez occupied himself with my balls, popping the pair around with his neon-pink tongue, juggling, licking, then swallowing whole and sucking.

It was cramped in there, hot and stuffy. I hung onto a hanging torpedo and gently pumped my hips, stretching Sully's mouth and throat and imagination, smacking Hernandez's lips with my nuts. Then the crew members exchanged my member, Hernandez deep-throating my dong, Sully lip-loving my balls. I groaned Anchors Away, ready to blow off steam.

But the boys weighed my genitals before I could fire any protein torpedoes, and we were off on a hitch together. We all greased up for action and Hernandez hit my ass at ramming speed while I sunk sub into Sully upfront.

My cock penetrated the redhead's pale cheeks and plunged into his pink anus in a golden splash nine inches long. We groaned, and then I gulped, as Hernandez uncorked my ring with his mushroomed dickhead and drove the length of his smooth-shafted cock into my anus.

We were bound together front and back, coupled into a threesome. I wrapped my muscular arms around Sully's ginger-fuzzed chest and humped my hips, pumping his ass. Hernandez gripped my hips and swung his, churning my burning butt-tunnel with his dick in rhythm to the ass-stretching I was giving his crewmate.

The air grew thicker, heavy with our grunts and groans, the crack of sweaty taut flesh against flesh, the sluice and slide of dongs sheathed in chutes. I pinched Sully's nipples and spun them, slamming his ass. Hernandez crowded closer and bit into my neck, licked at the back of my ears, stoking my anus to thermo-nuclear temperatures and temperament.

"Ohmigod!" Sully yelped, slapping his hands onto my hands on his boyish chest, free-firing semen out of his manly cock.

His jetting glee sent me prowing prick-long into sexual oblivion. I blew my top, blew out my balls. Blistering orgasm jumped my blazing cock still deeper into sweet Sully's rectum. I doused his bowels with my lust. Just as Hernandez tore me a new one with his exploding dong, almost tore my ears off with his howl of delight. He splattered my shattered insides, as I shot Sully full of liquid orgasm.

# # # # #

I hit the sandy shore two miles south of Haifa just past midnight. Then I slit the small inflatable craft I'd arrived in, sunk it. And when I turned around, a woman had materialized in the Hebrew moonlight.

She was wearing a tight khaki uniform and cap with no identifying insignia, just the swells of her breasts and the flare of her hips identifying her as a woman. "You are Golden Rod?" she asked.

The fact she even knew of the existence of Golden Rod spoke volumes. But I spoke far less. "Perhaps."

"Prove it."

"And you are?"

"Golda. You're liaison with the IDF."

I hesitated, always cautious, especially on foreign, though friendly, soil.

Golda pulled an Uzi out from behind her back, and I unbelted my waterproof pants in a hurry.

My dong hung down, low, winking slightly in the dim light, but certainly not turned-on to its full glow by the presence of such a shapely woman. Golda dropped the Uzi, and then her khakis. She had large breasts and rounded hips, all right, and a semi-erection dangling between her slender legs.

"We liaise?" she asked.

Surprises are par for the off-beaten course in my line of work. At the moonlit sight of that smooth, hooded cock, my own hanger swelled to dong, pulsating gold under the stars.

Golda gasped. "You are Golden Rod!"

"In more ways than one." I went down to my knees in the sand, sucked Golda's dick into my mouth.

She moaned and bit her fingernails into my shoulders. I bobbed my head back and forth, power-sucking her power pole. It stiffened to full rigidity under my oral onslaught. I shot up a hand and grasped one of the lovely tranny's tits, squeezed the bloated chest hump, tweaked the rubbery nipple.

She bucked in my mouth, plugging my throat. I swallowed all she could give me – swallowed and sucked, playing with her jugs. The contrast of man-meat and woman-lumps was stunning, mucho stimulating.

Golda spilled over onto the sand on her back. I never stopped sucking. She grabbed onto my dong, stuffed it into the red, wet furnace of her mouth. We were joined in the international number of lust: sixty-nine.

I gripped Golda's lean-muscled thighs and sucked hard on her pulsating prick, pumping my head up and down like a Saudi oil cricket. Golda dug her nails into my bold, round buttocks and burrowed her head up out of the sand, vaccing my cock with the same wicked intensity.

I pulled her out of my mouth with a wet pop and licked at her sweet shaven balls. She spat out my hanging and humming meat and slurped my nuts, stroked up my smooth-shaven crack with her tongue. I groaned into her sack, squirming my own licker down her perineum.

We went back to sucking, hard, our heads rising and falling like Middle Eastern dictators. The moon and the stars shone down, the warm waters of the Mediterranean lapping at the shore. Then my cock pulsed pure gold into Golda's squeezing mouth, and I spray-painted her throat with hot semen.

She arched up into my mouth, coating my own throat walls with sticky sperm.

Dude looked like a lady, came like a man.

# # # # #

Eron piloted the other F-35. We swung in low over the target, then let fly with our Sidewinder missiles. The Iranian mountainside nuclear facility at Qom went up like the fourth of July. Giant orange fireballs chased us back up into the wild blue yonder.

But we swooped down for seconds, just to be sure, to put the final nails in the coffin of terrorist atomic testing. Like had been done in the deserts of Syria and Iraq previously.

Iran needed a nuclear reactor for "energy" purposes like the Saudi princes needed sand for beach-building. I had the crucial coordinates thanks to the good ole U.S. high-sky surveillance spying, so I rode along with our one true Middle East ally.

Eron and I reduced the enriching facility and Iran's dastardly atomic aspirations to rubble. Then we soared back up into the sky. Black clouds of feeble anti-aircraft fire dotted the heavens ten thousand feet below us, as useless as puffs of smoke in a whirlwind. Two IDF jets had taken out the SAM sites around the facility two minutes before we'd stormed onto the scene with our payloads.

I jutted my thumb up at Eron, and he victory-signed me back. Then I blew the remains of a flock of albatrosses I'd thought I'd missed out of my left engine and my plane spiralled out of control.

I just managed to crash-land across the Iraq border, hitting the eject button in the nick of time. I floated down to rocky earth, right into the angry arms of a waiting mob of mountain tribesmen.

There were thirty of them, rough, bearded men dressed in tan robes and golden turbans. They hustled me off to their village, set me up before a tribal council of six ancient men who seemed to be hewn from the very stone all around them. They spoke one of the five-hundred-forty-six dialects of the Middle East I wasn't familiar with.

An old guy as weathered as the dust he squatted in, drew a gnarly hand across his waddled throat, passing sentence. The two men gripping my arms ripped my flight suit right down the middle, baring my body, the golden appendage between my legs.

The old guy almost swallowed his tongue. The other ancients used theirs, setting up a high-strumming wail that echoed from the mountaintops all around. And then they, and the rest of the men of the rugged village, prostrated themselves on the ground, all about me.

The old guy finally explained the bizarre situation by drawing back a curtain covering a section of cave wall, revealing "Turzak Gold'un," the founder of their obscure sect. He was a tall, dark-haired, good-looking man, as buffly naked as I was, with a staff between his legs – a golden staff, which he had used to seed his followers.

I was the second coming, sent from heaven. Twelve of the most beautiful men and women of the village were offered up to me to be sanctified. I dismissed the women and examined the men. They were lovely specimens of malehood, young and smooth and ripe and brown-skinned, supine on their hands and knees facing away from me, their rumps raised to me. I used the holy oil to bless my hardened cock, then speared it into the first man in line.

He grunted and shuddered but didn't raise his head from his folded arms, just his gorgeous ass a little more, to meet my thrust. I slid in deep and long and sure, a fiery gold to the hilt. Then I gripped the man's narrow waist and pumped my hips, consecrating his ass with my cock.

I pulled out, slotted my rod into the next beautiful butt in line. This man was even younger, tighter. It was a hot, hold-your-breath squeeze, but I burst in, barged deep; then banged his butt with a righteous fervor.

My head was spinning, face watering, balls seething and cock surging, when I stuck and fucked the next three men, plugging their hot, gripping anuses and stoking. The only slight turn-off was the old guy watching me from a corner of the cave, his milky blue eyes focused on me, ancient mouth drooling and wooden tongue hanging out, creased head bobbing.

I barely had a hold of my senses, my body burning with male fever and my cock steeled come-hard, when I shoved gleaming cap into the last man in line, sunk golden treasure into his ass. His body shone almost as much as mine, smooth tawny skin glistening with perspiration, pert rounded buttocks rippling delightfully as I banged against them. My pistoning cock seized up like my mind, my butt-slapping balls blowing apart.

I threw back my head and roared, blasting raw, rugged joy into rump. The old guy threw up his withered limbs and shrieked to the heavens, welcoming the gush of golden seed I poured into his compatriot, burst after glorious burst.

# # # # #

I snuck out of the mountain village the next morning, hitched a camel train into Turkey. I had no desire to become a golden tribal idol, not when the Corporation still needed me.

A few sessions of full-body Turkish massage and I'd be back in shape and ready for more action. Serving my country anyway I can. That's my golden rule. Code name: Golden Rod.

ENTER THE DRAG QUEEN
ByLogan Zachary

Logan Zachary (LoganZachary2002@yahoo.com) lives in Minneapolis, MN. His new book *Calendar Boys* is out, and his stories can be found in dozens of anthologies.

When I received the message, "Help me, Layah Mann, you're my only hope," I figured it was an over-dramatic drag queen's prank, but when "The Queen" herself signed her name to the note. I knew this was serious.

It turned deadly serious when my younger brother, Bedda Mann, died in the filming of season seven of *Top Bitch*, the cheap rip-off version of the "real" first drag queen contest developed by "The Queen" herself. During my brother's elimination, his leash tragically caught on the trapdoor when he fell into the flea dip. It got caught and broke his neck.

I always felt his accident happened on purpose. When the incident was investigated, they found nothing suspicious, but my brother's last text message told me something else. "They know I know, and they're after me. HELP!"

But I was too late.

So after my meeting with "The Queen," she convinced me to sign up for season eight of *Top Bitch*. She would help me behind the scenes and send her best drag queen to help me in the competition. So that's how I came to be here, one of the top three drag queens vying for the diamond studded collar and tiara of *Top Bitch*.

"Bitches, you've come up from puppies, to dogs, to pedigree show dogs, and this is the final challenge for the Breeder's Cup," Brittany Spaniels said. Brittany was a wanna-be celebrity, runner up from *The Queen's Race* show, but she was kicked off for cheating, poor sportsmanship, and leaking nude photos of the other contestants. Brittany was worse than that slimy reporter who outted gay celebrities and reported the most disgusting news reports.

The dog pound doors opened up. The three PitBulls, Michael, Scottie, and Steele, strutted out on stage wearing only a leather studded jock strap. Each carried a bottle of lube and bag of dog toys.

Brittany wore a pink collar, and her hair was pulled up into two pigtails that rode high on her head, like the ears of a dog. "Bitches, your task for today is to be the first queen to obtain a winner's cup full of PitBull breeding fluid. You may use your hands, your mouth, or anything in the bag of dog toys. The first bitch to fill her bowl will be the Top Dog and have a 50/50 chance of being Top Bitch. The Loser will be picked up with the pooper scooper and dumped into the flea dip."

PitBull Michael stepped in front of me and thrust his jock into my face. I looked at the two other competitors and readied myself as did Shaggy Divina and Fleas Navida with their PitBulls.

"Bitches, go give your dog a big milky bone-er," Brittany barked.

The whistle blew, and we were off. I threw PitBull Michael back on his tight ass and ripped off his jock strap with my other hand. No fucking romance here. I poured lube over his cock and started to stroke his dick. I kicked the dog toy bag over and saw a huge red rubber fire hydrant. My free hand rolled the toy in lube and teased his hairy ass with the hydrant. I licked his heavy balls as my hands worked over his sensitive areas.

I felt his cock swell and grow in my hand, six inches, became seven, eight, and a whopping wet nine. My fingers could barely get all the way around it. I sucked on one low hanger and drew it down my throat. It was fuzzy like a tennis ball and almost as big. He tasted like all man. I nuzzled down to his hairy hole and licked the pink pucker.

His whole frame flopped on the floor as his leg involuntarily shook his body.

I knew I hit his sweet spot. I lapped my tongue on his opening and sought entry.

His circle opened a little, and my tip went in. I felt for the hydrant and guided it to the hole. I twisted and turned it, and it slowly entered him. His legs straightened and hovered above the floor.

I ignored Shaggy Divina to my right and thumbed PitBull Michael's balls as I jacked his bone. I knew that I had flirted with this PitBull throughout the season, and he liked my attention. He did disclose his kinks, on ass and nipple play, and one sure fire thing that would get him to shoot and drain his balls faster than fast.

Fleas was struggling with her PitBull's jock strap and hadn't even gotten her PitBull hard. His snausage was dangling like an old rope chew toy.

Pre-cum started to flow out of PitBull Michael, and I knew his bone would be milky soon. I pulled the hydrant out of his hairy butt and tossed it away. The camera crew zoomed in on his gaping hole. I slipped my cock out of my shorts and stroked over it with lube. I lifted my leg and dove for his opening. My cock slipped in just as his ass started to tighten back up. I plunged in a few times to tap his prostate, and then I let my urine flow. I filled his ass, marking my spot with a hot enema. I grabbed the doggie bowl and positioned it on his sculpted six pac.

His body tensed, cum shot out of his dick, and landed in the dog dish. Wave after wave of thick hot doggie juices poured over the lip of the bowl and filled it up. PitBull Michael growled with pleasure.

I emptied my bladder into him and felt the warm back-wash cascade over my inner thighs. I didn't care, all I was focused on was winning. I needed to get to the final two to find out who killed my brother and why. Bit by bit I found out a little more of what was going on behind the scenes.

"We have a winner, and we also need a piddle pad for one of our dogs. He doesn't seem to be housebroken yet." Brittany whistled for her canine clean-up crew.

PitBull Michael came again as I continued to stroke his cock. His ass released, and the stage was awash with my fluids.

"We'll need a mop and a few more piddle pads," Brittany shrieked.

Fleas was still trying to get her dog's bone hard, as Divina spat out the load that she sucked out of her PitBull Scottie's balls. She high fived me and lube splattered over us.

A cat screeched, and the event was over. "We have our final two bitches, and Fleas Navida will be dumped into the flea dip with the pooper scooper." Theme music blared to life and director yelled "Cut."

# # # # #

After the day's events, I waited for everyone to leave the studio. I searched the workroom, looking for anything that my brother would have left for evidence. I looked at myself in the mirror next to the life size picture of Brittany Spaniels. What was I missing? I moved over and looked into her eyes. "What are you hiding, bitch?" I noticed a bump on her wrist and the spot looked worn. I pressed the bump and a metallic click sounded as the mirror swung into the wall. I had found a secret entrance into a hidden room.

At first, I thought it was a storage area for extra make-up, which was used for the show and the commercials, but on second look, the packages looked different. I opened a golden compact, and the mirror inside fell out. It shattered on the floor. I kicked the glass pieces under the shelf and looked at the white powder inside. It didn't look like Midnight Dreams as the label read. The powder was pure white, not a smoky gray. I stuck a finger into the powder and tasted it. It was bitter and made my tongue go numb. So I knew it wasn't a cosmetic powder, this was a grade A drug. Heroin, cocaine, I wasn't sure, but the chemical tingle told me it was strong.

I kicked the rest of the mirror under the shelf and noticed something red and shiny. I bent over, picked it up, and saw it was a red bracelet. I pulled it out and saw my brother's name, Bedda, on the name plate. Fuck, he had found the drugs, too, is that why they killed him?

I slipped the compact into my pocket and slipped out of the room. I looked around the room, the cameras were off and hopefully, no one had seen me. Could I be so lucky?

Sneaking across the parking lot, I entered the back door of the hotel the show had put us up in. I headed to my room and stripped off my clothes. Standing in the shower, the hot water scalded my skin as I washed sweat, lube, and cum off my body. I shampooed my hair and closed my eyes as the water rinsed me.

A cool breeze blew around me as the shower curtain rustled.

I opened my eyes and spun around to see PitBull Michael step into the shower. He was buck ass naked. Immediately, I looked to his hand to see if he carried a weapon. Only a raging hard on threatened me.

"I've come to finish what you started this afternoon." He grabbed my cock and started to rub up and down. Body wash made my dick more slippery, and the sensation grew and grew.

I kissed him and nibbled on his lower lip.

His tongue entered my mouth, and he kissed me deeply.

The shower water started to cool off, and I shivered. I tried to turn the water hotter, but it didn't help. I pushed him away and turned off the shower. "We're out of hot water."

PitBull Michael pulled the shower curtain back and pulled two towels off the shelf. He handed me one and started to dry off. His huge erection waved at me and his dark olive skin glowed.

How had I missed his good looks? My mind must have been too busy thinking about my brother than the man in front of me. As I dried off, I motioned for him to move over to the bed.

He walked over, and I watched his perfect ass as he headed to the bed. "You used some vital information I gave you against me today."

I hurried to wrap my arms around his narrow waist, and my hard on slipped between his cheeks. "I couldn't lose that event. I had to win at all cost."

Michael turned to face me. "There is something I need to ..."

I pushed him with all my might. He fell back onto the bed, and his balls and penis flipped up. I dove on top of him and straddled his waist.

"I really ..." he tried.

But my mouth came down on his and stopped all of his protests. Deep kisses and amazing tongue action caused my arousal to swell and throb against his torso. I felt his massive cock bounce up and down my crack as I sat on him. My hands massaged his muscular chest and circled his large copper nipples. They rose under my touch, and I pinched them. I could feel the holes in each, where his body jewelry usually stood proudly out against his dark skin, thick hair, and muscles.

I slid my butt back, pulling his hard cock back as I bent to suck on his nipples. My tongue entered the hole as my teeth rolled the hard nub. He tasted of man, salt, and caramel.

He rocked his hips, and his cock slipped between my cheeks and pressed against my hole. His hands spread my cheeks wide for more access to my tight backside. His cock missed my opening and pushed my balls up and against my belly as he surged deeper between my legs.

I felt a wetness brush along my sac as pre-cum oozed out of him. I slid lower on his body, enjoying the washboard that was his six pack. Despite the shower, the musky male ball aroma rose from him, and I licked my lips. His thick cock brushed my chin, and I licked the pearl of clear fluid at the tip, before swallowing his uncut head. My tongue traces in the fold of skin and circled his mushroom head. More pre-cum flowed out of him, and my lips pulled his foreskin back for better access. His thick bush tickled my nose. I reached underneath his ass and savored his hairy cheeks as I sought out his huge balls. I rolled them in my hand as my arms pulled his legs apart more, pushing his dick deeper down my throat.

Only half of his cock would fit in my mouth. He rocked his hips back and forth, threatening to gag me, but my breath came between thrusts.

Michael pulled the pillow from under his head and slipped it under his ass. "I had mine on stage; it's your turn to shoot your load. So give this dog a bone." He slapped his ass and spread his cheeks.

I bent over, kissed his pink pucker, and licked the tight opening. Reaching over to the bedside table, I pulled out a condom and a bottle of lube. I wrapped and lubed.

PitBull Michael rolled over, but played anything but dead. He offered up his butt.

I rose up onto my knees and knew doggie style was all I wanted. I pulled back on his hips and knew where his sweet spot was. I greased his crease and ran my hot dog between his buns.

He arched his back and pressed back against me.

I applied more lube and inserted a finger to grease inside and out.

"Do me," PitBull Michael growled.

I guided my dick to his opening and circled it. Round and round my cock slipped and teased him and finally started to enter him. I pulled back on his hips as I pushed my hips forward.

Michael couldn't wait. He backed up onto me and swallowed me inch by inch. He wagged his tail and encouraged me to speed up. "Deeper."

He was tight, but I slid in easily and almost shot my load as I entered him. I pressed in and held him pinned on my dick. Slowly, I pulled out and pushed back in. I could do this all night. Savoring the pleasure, I forced myself to move as slowly as I could, but Michael had other ideas.

He rocked back and forth, faster and faster. He pushed back, harder and harder.

My body wanted more. I needed to have him, all of him. I increased my speed and pulled on him harder. My balls swung between my legs and hit the bottom of his ass. Pound, pound, pound.

He rose up on his knees, his back to my chest.

I reached around him and found his beautiful cock. I stroked like I did earlier today, but this time with affection, with care, with love. I wanted it hard, fast and now, but I wanted it to last, too. "You are amazing," I nibbled on his ear.

The pressure was building, and I couldn't slow it down. "I'm ... I'm ..."

"Close? Me, too. Go for it."

I didn't need anything more. I doubled my speed and plowed into him. My hand worked his length and squeezed. Pre-cum poured out of him, making my hand slid faster and faster.

He jerked suddenly, and my hand was covered in thick hot cum. It dripped between my fingers and landed on my bed. His ass tightened and sent me over the edge.

I thrust into him and let the explosion happen. My balls emptied and filled the condom.

He felt the swell of heat in his ass and came again, rope after rope of cum flowed out of him. I thrust into him quick and sharp, send the nerve endings on fire. I pushed forward one more time and landed on top of him as he fell face down on my bed.

I stayed imbedded in him as we dripped, gasped and sweat. As I was able to move again, I rolled off him and screamed as I pulled out of his tight ass. The sensation was too great on my dick. I covered my cock, afraid of the slightest breeze in the room.

"You wanted to tell me something," I smiled at him. I traced circles in the sweat and semen on his body.

"You need to know this, so don't freak out. What we did, I wanted to do, and that has nothing to do with what I'm about to tell you."

"You're pregnant?" I joked.

"No. I'm an undercover cop. There have been many conflicting stories about missing people, your brother's death, and drugs. I'm trying to find out what's going on." He looked into my eyes.

"Why do you think I need to win? I want to know what happened to my brother, too. I feel that if I win, if I get to the end, I'll find out what is going on here." I pulled out the golden compact. "I found this in the dressing area in a hidden room."

Michael took the make-up case from my hand and opened it. "I knew it. It all seemed too simple, why didn't I think of that before?"

"It took me this long to find that," I pointed to the drugs.

"Better than I've done." He rolled onto his side and sat on the edge of the bed.

I moved behind him, sticky all over my legs, hands, arms. "Let's go hit the shower again, and then we can make plans for tomorrow."

He stood and stepped toward the bathroom. He stopped and looked over his shoulder at me. "Aren't you coming?"

I smiled. "I already did, but I love the sight of your ass. I wanted to savor it." I jumped off the bed and slapped his butt. "I want to wash every inch of you."

He spun around and his semi-wood brushed mine. "So do I."

I kissed him and felt my body relax for the first time since the contest started. I finally had someone on my side.

# # # # #

The next day, Shaggy Divina and I had our final contest. Last night after PitBull Michael left, I tried to warn my competition, but as I tried to wander around our rooms, the guards roamed the hallways all night. So I had no luck sneaking down to Divina's room. I wondered where the rest of the flea dipped contestants were. As soon as they went down the trap door, they were gone. No goodbye, nothing. Never to be seen again. Never back to pack their things.

Maybe there would be a time to tell Divina what I found, if the guards weren't around or if the PitBulls were busy. In my mind, the kicked off dogs had all met their horrible ends at the hands of the sadistic Brittany, just as my brother had. Hopefully, I was wrong, but who knew. At any cost, I needed to win the last event. The music blared, and the cameras started rolling.

"To be the top bitch, the alpha bitch, the dog has to fight and dominate the other dogs. So your last battle will be against each other. Dog eat dog." Brittany giggled and jiggled.

The PitBulls pulled a large sheet of plastic over the floor. Once the sheet was smooth, the three men poured four gallons of olive oil in the center of the square. They even poured some over their bodies, glistening under the lights.

"You may wear anything you want or don't want. You are top bitch. You decide your own fate." Brittany nodded to her boys, and they stepped back.

The pool of oil spread slowly across the sheet, and it waited for the final two.

I figured the less I had on, the fewer handholds Divina would have on me. I stripped down to my collar and jock. Divina took pride in her drag, never a smudge on her make-up or a hair out of place. She was a real lady. Her boots, whalebone skirt, leather corset, and wig made her look silly for a wrestling match. I knew this was going to be easy.

Divina took a step on the sheet and slipped, splashing olive oil all over herself. She tried to regain her legs, but only covered herself with more oil and fatigued her muscles.

I skated to her and looked down at the drown rat, not the victorious dog. I wanted this to happen fast and be done. I reached over, pulled off her wig, and threw it over to the corner and out of the oil.

Divina grabbed my leg, and his oily grasp slipped right down my leg. He flopped down on the sheet and sprayed me with oil. He spun around quickly and knocked my feet out from under me.

I landed hard on my ass and scrambled over him. I felt my erection grow as I crawled over him. My hand reached over his hip and realized he didn't tuck before the event.

Divina made an ugly woman, but he was such a handsome man. He would have been hairy if he didn't shave for drag. He had dimples in both cheeks and one in his chin, deep brown eyes and solid muscles and a sizable dick.

I wanted to lick him as I tried to hold him down. My hand hit his growing erection as we rolled around in the oil. I needed to pin him for a few seconds, so I could whisper in his ear what my plan was, but he started to work with the oil, instead of fight it. I untied his whalebone corset and flung it from his body.

He rolled onto his ass, and I pulled a wrestler move behind him. I placed my mouth to his ear. "The police are here, and they are investigating the show. I need to win to find my brother's killer. Do you understand?"

He nodded and rolled over onto his chest. His bare ass exposed for all to see. I rose above him, my hips cradled his magnificent ass and pinned him to the floor.

PitBull Michael knelt on the floor and slapped his hand in the oil. "One. Two. Three. Winner." He grabbed my arm and pulled it up over my head.

I stood and faced Brittany.

"Miss Layah Mann, you are the winner. You are the Top Bitch. So with your new position, what will your first Mann-Date be, get it? Mann-Date."

Olive oil dripped down my nose, and I wiped something away from my eye. "My first task as Top Bitch is to see," I looked around the room as the camera zoomed in, "who killed my brother." I pointed at Brittany. "You white slaver, drug dealing, killing bitch, who did it?" I jumped into a kung fu pose and waited.

"Miss Layah Mann, I have one thing to say to you." She raised her arm and pulled down on the lever for the trap door for the flea dip. "PitBulls," Brittany shouted, "Kill them, kill them all." She pointed her pink sculpted nail at them.

The floor behind me and Divina opened as the PitBulls approached.

Divina and I had our backs to the flea dip. I looked over my shoulder and saw one side had a slide down into the level below. The olive oil made my feet slid on the floor, and I knew I didn't have a chance to stand my ground. I pushed Divina to the side where the ramp was, so if we were knocked into the flea dip, we'd slid down the ramp, instead of falling down a story and kill ourselves.

The PitBulls charged us. Two hit me square on, my kung fu turned into kung pow, and they slammed me into Divina. She toppled over the side and slid down the ramp, shrieking all the way down.

I grabbed PitBull Scottie and Steele and pulled them down the ramp with me.

PitBull Michael stood at the top of the opening and watched as we rode to the bottom.

Divina had gotten to his feet and looked around the space for any weapons. A metal door was the only thing he saw. He ran to the metal bolt and threw it open. He waited and watched to see what he had just released.

I saw what Divina was doing out of the corner of my eye as I scanned the rest of the walls. Scottie and Steele pushed me back as I noticed a panel of buttons. I let go of them, but as they tried to hold me, the oil made me slip right through their fingers. I slid to the control panel and flipped every switch.

Lights flickered, music blared, ropes dropped from the ceiling into the pit and motorized cameras spun around in circles.

219

Divina yelled as she opened the door. She rushed inside, forgetting all about me and the two PitBulls. "Bitch," I swore, as a rope swung in front of my face. I grabbed it and wrapped it around my arm a few times. I backed up and ran to the wall, kicked off the bricks and swung directly at them.

PitBull Michael approached Brittany, who yelled orders at him, not understanding why he wasn't following them into the pit. He reached into his leather studded jock and pulled out his badge.

Brittany didn't need to see any more. She reached under her feather boa and pulled out a pistol. She aimed at him as he dove for the flea dip pit. The bullet hit his shoulder as he fell and a spray of blood distracted me for a second.

The other two PitBulls closed in on me as I backed into a corner.

Michael lay motionless in a pool of quickly spreading blood.

Divina pushed the metal door open and charged the PitBulls. She was followed by some pretty disheveled drag queens, the previously eliminated contestants.

The PitBulls turned as they saw the mob swarm toward them. As their attention was taken from me, I climbed up the rope and swung out of the pit.

Brittany spun and took aim toward me as I Tarzan swung at her with the rope. The gun went off in her hand as my olive oiled feet caught her square in the chest. The pistol flew out of her hand, and I let go of the rope. We skidded across the floor in a heap and landed at the base of her throne.

"You fucking bitch," she spat.

"Top fucking bitch to you," I said, and punched her in the face.

Brittany spun, but clung to the throne. She pushed a red button, and the floor disappeared underneath us. We landed on a pink pad. As I looked around, I realized it was Brittany's mirrored boudoir. A white tub sat in one corner, the mirrors formed a maze to her bed. The Top Bitch crown and studded dog collar were carefully placed on a white marble bust of Brittany. She crawled away from me, in search of something.

I figured she was looking for a weapon. I jumped to my feet and followed after her and bumped into my reflection in a mirror. She had me at a great disadvantage. She knew the maze. I didn't. Flashes of me in my leather jock and her pink furry outfit raced around me. Which one was the real one?

My foot slipped on the marble floor, and I landed hard. My foot kicked something. I reached down and found her scepter. A stiletto six inch heeled shoe embedded itself in a mirror above my head. I grabbed the metal staff and smashed a mirror. One image was gone.

I stumbled forward, trying to avoid the broken glass with my bare feet, but I need to stop her once and for all.

SMASH! Another mirror crumbled to the floor.

Brittany screamed in rage.

SMASH! I hit another one.

Where the hell was she?

Then it hit me, what meant the most to her?

That fucking crown and collar.

I smashed another mirror and searched for the prize.

Brittany's canopied bed loomed in the distance. I moved forward and noticed a screaming pink streak coming at me, claws and canine teeth flashing.

I swung the scepter with all my might.

BAMM!

221

HOME RUN!

Knocked her right out of the park.

The metal bar struck Brittany dead center in her chest. She stumbled backward on her heels, struck the pedestal with the crown and collar. She landed hard on her royal ass.

Her marble head wobbled back and forth.

She pushed back against the pedestal as she tried to stand up.

"Don't …" was all I got out before the marble crowned and collared bust fell forward.

Brittany's shriek was cut short as it landed on her.

SPLAT!

I turned away from the scene and went to find Michael. He needed me. The mirrored maze wound around and around, but I finally found the exit. As I found the flea dip pit, the police were arriving. I rushed to Michael and rolled him over onto his back. He moaned in pain, but I knew he was alive.

A drag queen ran by, and I snatched a ruffle from her prom dress. I ripped it off and applied pressure to Michael's shoulder.

"Ouch. Do you have to press so hard?"

"You didn't say that last night."

"I can see why you won."

I pressed harder again.

The police surround Scottie and Steele and saved them from the other drag queens that had been held captive in the cages underneath the stage. Sculpted nails and stilettos were used as weapons.

I looked up and noticed one drag queen with hairy legs, arms, and chest. She even had a full beard. She looked down at me and zombie walked to me. I touched his hairy leg. "It's alright, he'll be fine," I said, and then gasped. I knew those eyes. Those were just like mine. I let go of the bloody ruffle and hugged my brother, Bradford Mann.

He dropped to his knees and hugged me close. I knew Bedda Mann was still alive.

"You found me," he croaked, as he held me close. "They were going to sell me into white slavery for organ donations."

"You're safe now." I felt him recoil in my arms. I looked over my shoulder and saw PitBull Michael had joined us. He held the bandage to his bleeding shoulder.

I felt Bradford shrink away, but I soothed him. "He wasn't involved with the drugs and the slavery. He's an undercover cop working with me to find out what happened to you."

PitBull Michael moved closer and became the center of the group hug with Bradford.

Paramedics met us and took Michael and Bradford away on a gurney. They started an IV and covered both men with warm blankets.

Michael grabbed my hand and held it as they wheeled him and my brother up the ramp. "You did it, you were amazing."

"You helped every step of the way." I struggled to keep up with bare olive oiled feet.

"But you figured it out. So what's next Mata Hari?"

I slipped, let go of Michael's hand, and slid down the ramp.

I swore as I scrambled back up the ramp and climbed on top of the gurney with Michael. I smiled at Bradford and whispered into Michael's ear. "Once I get you boys out of the hospital, hot tub, champagne, you naked, and ..."

"You are such a bitch, top bitch." Then Michael's mouth covered mine. He got the picture.

THUNDERBALLS
By Logan Zachary

By the time I realized there was an intruder in my room, it was too late.

He dove for me as I tried to run. His arms wrapped around me, but as I was oiled up with sun screen, he slipped down my body and landed hard on the floor. His hands grabbed onto my shorts on the way down and pulled.

I felt my swim trunks slip down my ass and start to come off. I grabbed the waistband in front and tried to keep my dick covered. I didn't think to yell for help. My focus was just to keep my swimming trunks on and get the hell out of my room.

He pulled me down and scrambled on top of me trying to pin me down.

I turned, as I twisted in his arms and fought to free myself.

The setting Bahamas' sun shone through the blinds, revealing my intruder.

I stopped struggling. "I know you," I yelled at him. "You were on the plane and the bus tour to this resort. Why are you waiting in my room?"

Did he want to rape me? Kill me? What? I started to fight again.

"Mr. Rodgers, relax." He wrestled with me on the floor and tried to pin me.

I had wrestled a little in high school and college, but this was different. As I tried my escape moves, the thought hit me, he knew my name! I must have relaxed for a second too long, and he grabbed both of my wrists and pushed them down, finally pinning me to the floor.

I struggled underneath him and felt my swimming trunks slip down even lower on my legs. Despite the fear I felt, my boy was becoming aroused. My dick started to harden and threatened to poke out of my trunks.

He adjusted his position to sit on me, straddling my torso.

My cock tip slipped out of the waistband and pressed against the back of his pants. "What do you want?" I demanded, hoping he didn't feel my erection poking him in the ass.

"I'll release you if you promise to listen. I don't want to hurt you. I just need to get something back, and then I'll be on my way."

"My money is on the dresser. Please don't take my passport or credit cards."

He released my wrists and sat on me. His hand reached back and felt what was poking him in the butt. He felt my fat dick head and rolled it between his fingers. Pre-cum oozed out and wet the tip. He smiled. "So I excite you; that's good to know." He scanned my tan body and nodded. "You are very handsome yourself." He readjusted his position, and I swore I could feel his erection.

"You know I don't need or want your money, you know what I'm looking for."

I had never seen this man before the plane and bus ride. I didn't plan this trip. My twin brother booked this trip. The week before he was to leave, he crashed his motorcycle and broke both legs, but what would this guy want with a rare antiquities dealer?

"You're not Erik Rodgers?" the man demanded.

"No, I'm Derek Rodgers, his twin brother. Identical twins."

"What?"

"I'm Derek Rodgers."

"Shit." The man slipped off me and sat on the floor, staring at my cock.

I reached down and pulled my shorts up to cover my embarrassment. I brushed the tip of my cock and felt the burst of pleasure and warm wetness at the tip.

He pushed up to his feet and walked over to my suitcase. He rifled through the contents, throwing underwear, jock straps and Speedos around. "Where is it?"

"Hey, get out of my stuff." I crawled over to him and watched as he tossed my suitcase. My clothes fell into a pile on the floor as he searched for something. "So who are you? You know my name. I think I have the right ..." and a handcuff snapped around my left wrist. "What the hell?"

"I'm Matt Shelby, Secret Service."

I rolled my eyes. "No double 'O' something?" I didn't buy his crap.

"I'm working undercover and ..."

There was a knock at my door.

"Who's that?" he asked pointed to the door. "Were you expecting company?"

I glanced at the clock. "I was supposed to have a massage in my room right now. That's why I came in to shower."

The knocking came again, and a man's voice said, "Massage services."

"Just a minute," I called as I held up my handcuffed hand, pulling his along with mine.

"I left the key in my room."

"Great, some spy you are. He's here now, what are we going to do?" I shook my head.

"Open the door, tell him to set up on the bed, and we'll be right out." He motioned to the bathroom.

I turned the knob on the door. "Come on in and set up on the bed. We'll be right out."

Matt pulled me with all of his might and slammed the bathroom door. He turned on the shower and started to rip off his clothes. His shirt posed a problem for a second with the handcuffs and with one great pull, it tore, and it was off. His muscular body came into view as he took his clothes off. The thick brown hair on his chest became thicker as it went into his underwear.

I slipped my swim trunks off and stepped into the hot spray.

He kicked his shoes and socks off as he stepped out of his pants. Matt didn't wait to take off his briefs. He jumped into the tub and helped wash the suntan oil off me and then quickly scrubbed his body.

His white cotton briefs were see-through now, and he was amazing.

My erection swelled back to its full length.

His hand brushed against it, and I thought I was going to shoot my load.

He reached down and pulled his underwear off and let them drop into the tub. He rinsed his furry ass off and turned to face the shower. Once clean, he turned off the water and grabbed two towels. He handed me one, and quickly dried himself with the other one.

I followed his lead and once dry, I asked, "And this?" I offered up my handcuffed wrist.

He pulled a hand towel off the rack and wrapped it around our wrists and hands. "It's all I got. Ready?" He opened the door and dragged me to the bed.

Our masseur looked surprised to see two, but he just motioned for us to get on the bed and he said, "We can start face down if you'd like."

I stood at the foot of the king side bed and pulled the damp towel from around my waist. I let it drop and crawled onto the bed with Matt next to me, mirroring my actions. The hand towel still covered the handcuffs. I pulled my erection up and against my belly as I lay face down. My butt was exposed, but I didn't mind.

"Who should I start with?" he asked.

"He's the one paying for it, so do him," Matt said. His hand held my wrist and caressed it in the towel.

The massage therapist joined us on the bed, and he straddled my legs as he applied oil to his hands and warmed it up between his fingers. He started on my low back and worked up and over my shoulders.

Matt's hand sent warm waves into my body as the therapist worked.

The masseur wore shorts, and his bare knee spread my legs wider as his kneecap entered my crease. As he stroked up my back, it pressed against my opening and stimulated more tender nerve endings.

My erection grew underneath me, and I felt it start to ooze. I moaned in pleasure, as Matt's hand held me tight.

"Have you worked at the resort long ..." I waited for him to say his name.

"My name is Greg, and I've worked here for five years." He slipped over my leg and maneuvered his body between Matt and me, so he could use one hand on each back. He worked in long slow strokes, deep and powerful, relaxing the muscles below, and stimulating the nerves above.

I felt my body relax for the first time since Matt knocked me to the floor. What was his story? What did he think I had? What was Erik supposed to carry for him?

Greg's hand caressed low over one of my cheeks, his fingers road the crack and traced it as he went back to my neck.

The next time his fingers played between my crack, I pressed up and allowed him to go deeper into the groove.

He understood my permission and explored deeper with each pass. His oiled hand was warm and flowed easily over my skin; his finger brushed the tender bud deep inside and lingered for a second before moving up.

I didn't know if Matt was getting the same treatment, but at this moment, I didn't care. I moaned with joy as my body relaxed, legs spreading wider and all the previous tension leaving my body. A warm glow from the sun, the oil, and the massage allowed me to drift, but my erection never shrank.

Matt groaned next to me as he enjoyed his rub down.

I turned my face to see him. His body was chiseled from stone, rock hard, finely sculpted. This man was in tip top shape. His skin was golden brown all over; no tan lines marred his perfect flesh. Dark hair covered his arms and legs, with a small triangle in the small of his back. His ass was smooth and perfect; a dimple was low on his cheek. His hand still held my wrist and electricity flowed from his touch through every nerve in my body.

Greg moved lower and worked our legs. After a few strokes, he decided to work us over one at a time. He oiled my feet and rubbed into my arch, he pulled each toe and kneaded my calf, as he worked my thighs; his fingers dove back into my crease and teased my hole. He dug into my ass and released all of its tension. The process was repeated with my other leg, but once he finished the second leg, he returned to my butt. He kneaded the cheeks, spreading them wide and plowing deep, circling my opening as he ventured deeper and deeper inside me.

I arched my back and pushed back on him as he dug deeper into me.

He slipped off the bed, and I heard him remove his clothing. When he crawled back on the bed, a round object ran along my crease, it paused at my hole and slowly entered me.

At first I thought it was his cock, but he inserted a butt plug and filled my ass. He gently slapped my cheek. "I'll be right back." He turned his back to me to work over Matt's body. He rose up on his knees and gave me a beautiful view of his ass and dangling hairy balls. His dick was sticking straight up and bounced with each stroke.

His skilled hands preformed the magic he had just completed on mine. I watched and enjoyed the sensory play all over again, but this time I could smell the coconut oil and male musk that rose from his work.

I licked my lips as his ass rocked back and forth, his heavy balls swinging. I couldn't resist, I reached over with my free hand and cupped his sac. My grasp startled him for a moment and then he found his stride. My hand slid along his shaft and as it rounded the tip, a water fluid slipped out of his foreskin. My finger entered the uncut tip and circled the swollen head. I pulled back the skin and the pool of pre-cum lubed his dick and my hand. I pulled it back to his balls and guided my thumb to his hairy hole.

He widened his legs and rocked on my thumb.

Inch by inch, I went deeper into his bottom.

His hands were kneading Matt's cheeks open and exploring his tender bud.

I saw Matt's pink pucker kiss Greg's finger tips as the oiled digit circled and circled for entry. I rose up onto my knees and came behind Greg. My cock slipped along his crease as my handcuffed arm hugged his body.

The hand towel slipped off, and Greg saw the handcuffs. "You boys are kinky." He pulled on Matt's hips and drew his butt up into the air. He hung onto his pelvis and guided his dick to the well-oiled waiting pucker. He slipped a condom on and handed me one, too. He didn't have to say what he wanted.

I unrolled the rubber and waited as he entered Matt.

His low moan let me know he was in.

I crawled closer and pressed against his hairy opening. My thumb had relaxed him and inch by inch, I entered him. The three of us were connected and tingled with excitement. I started to pull out of his hot tight ass and felt him press forward.

Matt arched his back and moaned.

Greg bowed, and his ass moved toward me.

I thrust back into him and rabbit fucked his ass, short, fast bumps into him. My balls bounced and shook.

He pushed back against me, slowing my thrusts and surged back into Matt. He reached back and held me in place. He pistoned between us, gaining speed and depth as he went.

I started to synchronize my thrusts with his. Matt's body seemed to do the same thing. The smell of coconut covered the scent of man sex, which filled the room, and I felt drool escape out of my mouth. I wiped my lips with the back of my hand, tasting semen, sweat, and man.

Greg somehow reached between my legs and twisted the butt plug in my ass. He pumped it a few times and hit the sweet spot on my prostate.

I doubled my assault on his butt and felt the orgasm rise. I grabbed his hip and plowed as deeply as I could into him. My balls released, and the load exploded out of me.

It started a chain reaction, as Greg's orgasm ripped through his body and slammed into Matt's.

Matt had been jacking his own cock as Greg rode him. His back extended and stiffened as he growled a final moan and shot his spunk across the bed. Wave after wave of semen flowed out of him.

My cock spasmed one more time and emptied all I had into Greg. My legs gave out as I fell onto my back on the bed. My cock screamed from over-stim as I exited his hairy hole with a loud pop. Sweat bead over me as my breathing came in gasps.

Matt collapsed forward and landed into his pool of cum.

Greg's dick popped out of Matt's butt, and Greg lowered himself onto our handcuffed arms. His sweating body struggled to regain its breathing. "Wow, what a ride." His flat stomach heaved as he sucked in more oxygen.

Sweat and semen coated all of us, and Greg's coconut smelling body rose. "Do you mind if I rinse off?"

I waved him to the bathroom and turned to look at Matt. His ass was amazing. How I wanted to bury my face between those smooth cheeks, but I couldn't move. I watched as beads of body fluids pooled and rolled over his golden skin. My poor bed was drenched.

Matt rolled over to face me, semen smeared across his hairy belly, and the sheets stuck to his torso. "Sorry about your bed."

It was great to have a king size bed in the room, but it sucked when there was only one. I pulled up on the sheets. "I guess I'll be sleeping in your room tonight."

Matt laughed as Greg came out of the bathroom drying his beautiful body. He scanned the floor for his shorts and T-shirt. He quickly dressed and handed me a receipt and a pen.

Matt pushed up onto his elbow. "You're going to charge him for that?"

Greg didn't know what to say.

I grabbed the paper and signed it. I added a nice big tip and thanked him.

Greg picked up his butt plug, his oil, and his bag, and left.

As the door closed, I turned to Matt. "I need to shower again, and then we should go to your room for the handcuff key." I held up my wrist. It was sore and red, where the metal had dug in after our sexcapade.

I wore only a pair of shorts to his room, since the handcuffs didn't allow for a shirt. His room was in the next building, connected with a bypass tunnel.

Matt borrowed a pair of my shorts to walk back to his room. Heading back to his room shirtless in dress slacks would appear out of place in this paradise. A towel was draped over our shoulders as we walked arm in arm to his room. I swung my beach bag with my cell phone, lap top, and passport in it. A few other odds and ends were inside, and I set it down on the bed as Matt went to retrieve his key.

"Can you turn your back? I don't want you to see my hiding place." Matt waited.

"It's not as if I'll be back here to use it." I stared at him, refusing to budge.

He opened his shaving kit and unscrewed the shaving cream can. A false bottom held the handcuff keys.

"Ooo, ah, you're so James Bond."

He ignored my comment and unlocked the cuff.

My hand was free, and I rubbed the blood back into my arm. An angry red ring circled my wrist. "Well, it's been fun, but I'm heading back to my cum-soaked bed." I picked up my bag, but Matt blocked my way.

"I can't let you go, until I find what I need." His bare chest heaved with each breath.

I wanted to suck on his copper nipples but bit my lower lip instead. My hand caressed his hairy chest, and I felt the power in the muscles beneath. I tipped my head back and looked into his steel blue eyes. His pouty lips looked so kissable. I could feel my erection start to return. "So what do you want?" I lowered my voice and combed through the fur.

He swallowed hard.

"Tell me, so we can both move on with our vacation."

He didn't say anything. His gaze held me in place.

"Fine. Let me call my brother and see what the hell he has to say." I dug through my beach bag and found my cell phone. I dialed his number and waited. No answer, just his voice mail. "Erik, what kind of shit did you get me into this time? Call me ASAP." I threw the phone back into my bag and stepped toward the door. "I'll let you know when he calls."

Matt pulled a shirt on and slipped into a pair of sandals. He slipped a gun into his shorts, correction, my shorts, and followed me out of the room. "I can't let you be alone."

"Why? Have you fallen madly, deeply in love with me?" I spun around and looked into his eyes. "No? Didn't think so." I headed back to my room.

"Let me take you to dinner. We can talk and see if we can figure this out. Maybe Erik will have called by then."

We passed through the bypass and entered my building, and as I inhaled, there was a scent of smoke in the hallway. I shook my head. Why did they allow smoking in such a nice place? We turned the corner in the hallway, and there was a haze in this hall. I pulled out my room card and slipped it into my door. The smoke seemed worse here. As I pushed the door open, I saw why. My room was on fire. As I opened the door, more oxygen entered and there was a big whoosh.

Matt dove at me and pushed me out of the way and landed on top of me. A wall of fire shot out of the door and singed the opposite wall in the hallway. Fire alarms strobed and the sprinklers went off.

I covered my beach bag and crawled down the hallway to the exit door leading outside. I coughed and choked as my eyes teared from the smoke. "What the hell did you bring to my room?"

Matt followed me out of the burning building. We headed over to the beach bar and watched as my room burned.

"Everything I had was in there," I said more to myself than him.

Matt grabbed my bag and poured its contents out on the bar. The beach bar was a huge aquarium tank in the shape of a horseshoe with a great white shark swimming back and forth in it. The shark sensed the vibration from the items being dumped on the glass, and it swam over to circle the commotion. Its black eye stared at us.

"Hey," I protested, but pulled back as the shark made another graceful pass by me.

"You must still have what they want. Otherwise, they would never have torched your room."

I tossed my cell phone into the bag, followed by my wallet and passport. "Could there be something on my laptop? A secret file? A program?"

"It could, but I doubt that."

"Plans for a weapon?" I asked.

Matt picked up the matchbook and flipped it open. No secret number was written inside. "We'll figure this out."

The bartender approached. "What can I get you guys?"

"Supper and a bottle of wine," Matt said.

"I'll get you a table and be right back, red or white?"

"Red," we said, at the same time.

I picked up my notebook, a paperback, a postcard, and a bottle opener, all cheap dime-store items with no value. Nothing, nothing, nothing. I picked up my keys, and as I was ready to throw it into my bag, I noticed something, the key chain was different. I turned it over in my hand, and a large red crystal caught the bar light and sent sparkles of lights around us.

Matt blinked as he saw the flash of red. "What is that?" He reached across the table and took the key chain from my hand. He looked at the red crystal. "I think we found what we've been looking for."

"What is that?"

Matt held the crystal to the light bulb above us, and a beam of light came through the crystal and set the cocktail napkin on fire. "Oh, no."

From the expression on his face, I realized that if a little light bulb could do that, what could a laser do? This was what they had been looking for. What was Erik thinking? What was he involved in?

Matt handed me a card key to his room. "Before I forget roomie."

"Am I a roomie, since you found the crystal, or am your roomie because my room burned?"

"I want to keep you close to keep you safe."

Before I could say anything else, the bartender returned and took us to our table.

We headed back to Matt's room after three bottles of wine and a wonderful meal. I stopped at the front desk to get a toothbrush before heading to the room, and Matt went ahead. It had been a long day and with all the excitement, I was exhausted and needed some sleep.

The clerk charged the toothbrush to Matt's room, and I figured that was the least he could do for me, since technically, I held him responsible for having my room torched. As I neared the room, I saw Matt standing outside of the door talking loudly to someone.

The man had his back to me, but I recognized his ass. Greg, our masseur, was shaking his hand in Matt's face.

What was going on?

"Where is it? I know you have it," Greg demanded.

I slowed my approached and ducked into an out cove to listen.

Greg grabbed Matt and snapped his handcuff onto Matt's wrist. He pulled the gun out of Matt's shorts and pressed it into his back. "Walk."

I didn't know what to do. I waited until they turned the corner, and I raced back into the room and retrieved the handcuff keys from the shaving cream can. I had no idea where they had gone, but hoped that I could catch them on the beach.

They headed back to the beach bar, and no one was around. The bar was closed and only a few lights lit the shark tank bar, but little else. A dark shadow swam back and forth inside.

"Move over to the bar and stand on top." Greg waved the gun to direct Matt. The handcuff chain dangled from his hand. "I'm going to secure you into the shark tank and let nature take its course."

"You'll never get away with this."

"You're little friend will give me the crystal, and then I'll be on my way."

"After you kill him?"

"What do you care? You'll be long gone by then. Open the tank."

"No." Matt folded his hands across his chest.

Greg pulled down on the handcuff chain and pulled Matt to his knees. He reached over to the latch to open the aquarium.

As the big metal bolt slid open, Matt reached forward and grabbed Greg's wrist, snapping the open handcuff around it. Click. He was trapped, too.

Greg pulled back on the chain and aimed the gun at Matt.

Matt grabbed the chain and jerked.

The gun went off, and the aquarium's lid shattered. Matt fell through the jagged opening and sank into the water, bleeding as he went down.

Greg tried to pull back, but Matt's weight and speed dragged Greg into the dark water. His arm sliced open on a sharp piece of glass.

Matt pulled hard on the chain as he sank.

Greg's body flipped through the opening, his hand ripped open on a shard of glass as he was pulled underwater. His bleeding hand dropped the gun, which sank into the depths after Matt.

I raced to the bar and flipped on the lights. A streak of red floated behind Greg as he was pulled down into the bigger tank under the bar. I couldn't think of anything except Matt, as I dove into the cold water. I swam after them, handcuff key in hand.

Matt pulled Greg further and further. He saw me enter the water, and tried to wave me away.

I held up the key and kicked harder to get to him.

Matt punched Greg, and the men embraced, pulling hard on each other. The water slowed the impact and force of their blows.

I saw a big dangerous shadow turn and head in our direction. I clawed at Matt wrist and found the handcuff. My fingers struggled to insert the metal into the lock. It slipped in, and I twisted hard. A click sounded in the water, and the handcuff opened and sank to the bottom of the tank. I dropped the key and pulled hard on Greg.

He refused to release Matt.

I reached for Greg, but my hand brushed against the handcuff chain. I grabbed it and pulled the sunken open cuff to my hand. I noticed a pipe as my lungs started to burn. I pulled the chain to the pipe and clicked it into place, locking him to the tank.

I motioned to Matt to surface.

Matt continued to fight him. Punching and squeezing.

Blood continued to rise from Greg's arm and hand as he fought.

I pulled on Matt, encouraging him to leave.

The dark shadow of the shark swam closer and headed toward Greg.

I pointed at it and swam away.

Matt nodded as he pushed Greg away from himself and into the path of the man-eater. He turned and followed close behind me. We swam to the opening of the tank as an unearth scream and splashing occurred behind us.

I didn't dare to look back. My head broke the water's surface, and I gasped for air.

Matt popped up next to me a second later.

We looked for a safe place to pull ourselves out of the tank. The water turned a darker red as we flopped onto the beach.

"Thanks," Matt said.

"Anytime," I said as I shook the water from my hair.

Back in the room, the hot shower felt great. It relaxed my bruised body, before I slipped into the clean bed. I felt Matt move over to me. He spooned my back and wrapped his hairy arms around my body. I felt his arousal slip between my butt cheeks and press into me.

"Relax," he breathed into my ear.

"After all we've been through, you think I can relax with you around?"

His hand stroked down my body and found my erection. He grabbed it and caressed slowly up and down.

I spread my legs wider and thrust my cock into his hand. I pushed back against his dick, back and forth, moving slowly.

He entered me, inch by inch, as his hand worked my shaft. It wouldn't be long; he knew all my sensitive spots. He thrust into me faster, and as his cock hit my prostate, my balls released.

I came into his hand and filled his palm with white, hot goo. He continued to jack my tender dick, milking even more cream out of me as his cock filled my ass. Liquid heat flowed into me, sending another wave of cum out of me.

We lay in each other's arms as our breathing turned to normal. A cool breeze entered through the patio door and blew over our sweaty bodies. I could have sworn, the door had opened wider and someone had snuck to our room.

My suspicion was confirmed, when the bed sheet rose up, and the intruder slipped into bed behind Matt.

"What the ..." Matt asked.

A hand across his body and caressed my thigh. "Relax," the intruder breathed into Matt's ear.

I knew that voice. It sounded a lot like mine, and the hand touching me felt all too familiar.

"About time you got here, Erik, to clean up your mess," I said.

"Shhh," he cooed, as he entered Matt. "I have a lot of catching up to do." He thrust deeper as his hand stroked my ass. "And we have a new mission."

Matt moaned, and I felt him grow hard inside me. So much for sleep tonight.

AGENT G: HUGS & SLUGS
By R. W. Clinger

R. W. Clinger resides in Pittsburgh. Sexy, male spies are his weakness. R. W. can be reached by e-mail at kenitorico@verizon.net.

ONE – TIE ME UP

I woke in a fog, tied up to a queen-sized bed, and wearing nothing more than my cowboy hat: a Stetson 4X Buffalo Seneca Pinchfront, which was a gift from the last dude who tied me up. Knotted rope strung me to the four-poster bed. The room was rather nice, I perceived: cream-colored marble floor, French provincial settee, dresser, and reading chair. One window overlooked …

Where was I? God only knew. It smelled like Paris, if you want to know the truth: burned croissants, the stink of the Seine, and the scent of heavy urine. I never liked Paris, and believed I was in the Paris Basin, which was north of the city. French walkers' voices lifted from the street below and floated inside the expansive window opposite me. I estimated being one floor up from street level, without a view of the Eifel Tower, which certainly would have made that uncomfortable moment a little more pleasant.

"The American cowboy wakes," a masculine voice filled the room and echoed off its sky-reaching walls. The voice was thick with a French accent, which I found sexy and alluring. The gentleman's leather heels clicked over the marble, and he stepped in front of the bottom of the bed, between my legs, blocking some of the August sun out. "Bonjour, Agent G," he said and winked at me.

Jacques Cassel, my nemesis in the world of spies, was a very bad boy from Paris who enjoyed selling young boys to older, wealthy men for their undignified pleasures. Jacques

243

stood at six-three, was nail thin, sported an onyx-colored mustache, matching eyes, rugged jaw, and a Parisian-sloped nose. He was dressed in all-black from head to toe, wore gloves, and held a silver-plated Colt .45 in his right hand, which he cocked and aimed at my forehead.

"Jacques, we meet again." I squirmed on the bed like an inchworm. "What will you do with me now?"

He abducted me in Greece next to the Statue of Zeus two years ago and spent three nights with me. Some twelve months later he drugged me in Sydney at a black-tie event and spent another three nights with me. The man always failed to murder me because he enjoyed my American good looks and skin: a six-one frame that weighed 190 pounds, clean-shaven chest rippled with Texas muscle, blond sideburns and matching treasure trail which stretched southward bound from a dented navel into a triangle thatch of always-groomed pubic hair. I knew the man also liked my American cock: nine inches of cut meat with veins and a perfectly capped head between my muscular thighs. I didn't fear him. How could I, since he seemed to seduce me on a regular basis around the world with his rugged and naughty French ways?

He walked around the bed from left to right. Sometimes, he aimed the Colt at me, sometimes he didn't. His footsteps echoed off the marble floor with a consistent beat. "You have the Sendal File hidden here in the city."

I didn't. Not that I was going to share that information with him even if I did. The Sendal File was in Brussels under Louis Bentrider's care, my partner spy working for the US government. Louis was spending the weekend in Brussels with his boyfriend, a muscular violinist named Hector Rumankov. The two lovebirds planned to marry soon, which I was delighted about.

I shook my head and said to Jacques, "The Sendal file is in the United States. You're men are slow armadillos."

"Armadillos?" he questioned with wide eyes, having never heard of the animal before.

I played with him, as usual. "Plated tanks that travel well in the dessert?"

"In Iran and Iraq?"

"Of course."

Jacques shook his head in confusion. "I don't know what you speak of."

"Untie me, and I'll explain it all to you in detail."

"You will never outwit me, G. American spy you is sexy but not smart."

"Sexy gets me places." It wasn't a lie. I thieved the Sendal File – a detailed synopsis of nuclear weapons being traded between Afghanistan and North Korea in the past thirty-sixth months, a zip drive of numbers, facts, and important names that the U.S. Government wanted in their possession – from his sidekick (and lover, according to rumors), Anton Lucas.

"I get you," the international spy said, placed his Colt on a nearby night stand, and climbed on the bed with me, between my legs.

TWO – INTERNAITONAL LUST

I admit, being tied to a bed in Paris with a hot French guy positioned over me, wasn't such a bad thing when it came to spy games. Jacques was steamy-attractive in all the right ways. Still fully dressed, positioned on his hands and knees between my legs, his mouth hung above my semi-hard American cock. He peered up the plane of my chiseled chest and whispered in thick French, *"J'ai faim."* I'm hungry.

"Eat up, Mr. Frenchy. Take what you want from me." I stayed positive for two reasons: one, Jacques could give a pretty potent blowjob compared to Dallas boys; and two, if he decided to eat me up, playing with the nine-inch dick between my legs, that could offer me plenty of time to loosen the rope around my wrists and free myself from the queen-sized bed and his captivity.

The man firmed up my tool with a few licks, which were long and steady. Tongue-swirls occurred to my dick's cap. His right hand grasped the length of my veined and pulsing rod. Jacques had a narrow and tight throat, I determined, as he slipped my pole into his mouth. A grunt surfaced from his lips as he took half of the nine inches into his system. It certainly didn't stop me from bucking my hips upward, into his beautiful face, and continued to have my way with the man, just as he was having his way with me.

How does one who is tied up not bolt their hips up and down, riding a gorgeous Frenchman's throat? This cowboy never said no to a free face-fuck, even when I was tied up to a bed in Paris and being man-handled by my enemy. Honestly, I took my dose of sex-medicine, felt inclined to enjoy Jacques's blowjob, and pumped his right fist and throat with hearty and relentless thrusts.

He gagged above me as his pretty head bobbed north and south. Sometimes his right hand cupped my balls and massaged them with skill. More grunts escaped his European lips. Other times he pulled off and away from my tool and shared thick French phrases with me that I didn't comprehend, suffering from the language barrier.

Yes, my clean-shaven chest bucked up and down during his blowjob. Perspiration formed on my erect nipples, rigid abs, and the treasure trail beneath my concave navel. Haphazardly the Stetson hat upon my head lifted and fell but didn't fall off. As my thighs rose and dropped, the blond and hairy balls between them slapped the foreign mole in his chin, rhythmically.

How long did he lick and suck my throbbing pole? Ten minutes? ... Twenty minutes? ... Thirty minutes? I really wasn't sure. After a long and uninterrupted fuck-gig to his face, I clarified through my gritting teeth, "Shooting, man ... Can't keep it in."

Perhaps upset with me, the professional sniper pulled away from me, panted on his hands and knees, and explained in his broken English, "Not done with you yet."

What exactly did he mean by that? What game did he have up his sleeve next? How was he going to take advantage of my American skin and cowboy niceness? I learned the answers to all of these questions in a matter of seconds when the Frenchman climbed off the bed, retrieved plastic from one of his pockets, stood over me, and said, "First I undress ... Second, you fuck me."

# # # # #

Above me on the bed, facing away from me, the legendary spy with remarkable dexterity lowered himself on the nine-inch flag between my sculpted legs. Two inches of my plastic-coated crank slipped into his crevice and caused a brief and almost-silent groan of initiated satisfaction to float out of his mouth. Two more inches of my dog pried his bottom open with zeal as he fell over them, which prompted the man to let out a few words in French that I didn't understand. Two more inches bucked into his rear because of my forceful hip movement, which was a grunt of excitement. The rider took the final three inches of my cock with ease. He fell rather heedlessly over the swollen mass, connected our balls together, slammed his weight against my weight, rose, and continued his up and down motion in a tirade of sexual enjoyment.

I became exhausted beneath him, but not disinclined to escape my current position of being tied to the queen-sized bed. Instead, I felt the rope against my wrists loosen, which offered enough leeway for my escape. In due time, I was sure to abandon my captivity on the bed, and put my assailant in a not-so-tender sleeper hold, knocking him into a state of unconsciousness. For now, I wanted to explode my spy-juice on his orbs, against his back, or wherever he wanted me to empty my load. Why waste a good fuck when one was offered to you, particularly by a gentlemanly Frenchman with a tight ass?

Truth was the queer rode me silly. North and south motion continued for quite some time, and our bodies slapped together. The bed creaked under our weight and filled the strange bedroom with the noise. My banging to his bottom was intense and rather melodramatic. Behind, and under him, I let out a few American guy woofs, pounded his rump with Texas spy speed, and enjoyed his ride to the fullest.

I decided approximately ten minutes later that it was best that I came first, if I wanted to set my wrists and ankles free from his expected imprisonment on the queen-sized bed. A warning erupted from my mouth as my friction to his asshole only became more stringent, "Blowing, musketeer!" Following my rambunctious alert, I plowed his backside a final time, felt a rushed vibration of international lust ripple throughout my core, and shot my wad of American cream into the plastic that separated the two of us, while howling like a mountain coyote, of course.

The animalistic howling turned the dangerous and French interrogator on. His right hand discovered the meat between his thin legs and started to jack his stick with utter chaos. French phrases escaped his mouth as he continued to ride my shaft. Sweat flung off his back. Within seconds, while gritting his teeth, he cranked his white and sticky cargo out of his dick, which splattered my knees, shins, and feet. A yell of greedy excitement flooded the bedroom and ...

It was time to free myself from that ugly, yet quite pleasurable, situation. That was the time to release my wrists from the loose ropes and devise a prompt headlock on my archenemy. As my captor finished coming, draining his pole of its French ooze, I quietly pulled my wrists out of their knotted rope, sat up, and pinched my assailant in his right shoulder, which immediately caused him to fall unconscious. Other western spies would have surely murdered the man, but I was rather keen for Jacques and his unexpected and sexual antics. Therefore, I simply rolled his sleeping body aside, lost the condom that covered my cock, removed my ankles from their knots, and finally stood from the bed, stretching.

It was a relief to be set free, but there was no time to celebrate such an event. The Crespin-style flat was littered with French bad boys, I knew, which prompted my quick escape. Jacques was a size smaller than my muscled, Texas frame and I couldn't fit into his clothes, but his boxers had to suffice for that untimely moment of escape. After slipping the cotton fabric over my sticky junk, I observed the bed sheets rolled in a ball on the left-hand side of the room. There was no time to fetch such attire to sport in the streets of Paris, though, since a Frenchman wearing a forest green beret and military outfit entered the bedroom carrying what I suspected was a MAC-50.9 mm pistol.

We made eye contact: royal blue American eyes locked with melting chocolate Parisian eyes. Unfortunately, it was not lust at first sight, since the dude popped a shot off at me, which zoomed past my right ear and sunk into the medallion green wallpaper. As panic settled into my system, Mr. Intrusive popped more slugs into the walls around me. Because I was weaponless, I hurriedly dashed for one of the open windows, and my awkward escape.

THREE – LOUIS BENTRIDER … AT YOUR SERVICE

Kismet was on my side as I plummeted into a burgundy canvas canopy, which covered the front patio of a French bakery. The sturdy canopy helped break my fall, but didn't stop me from smashing into one of the bakery's sidewalk tables and two chairs, which crashed under my cowboy weight upon impact. Unharmed, I climbed out of the debris, felt slugs from the crazy Frenchman zoom past my limbs, and bolted away, down the Rue de Bac, among city cafes, hostels, restaurants, and a children's museum.

Semi-naked, I was now being followed by Jacques Cassel's men. Four gunmen chased after me with unfailing deliberation. Slugs careened around my body. Parisian residents screamed and scurried out of my way. Never had they seen an attractive, partially naked, American cowboy in his Stetson make a speedy trek down the Rue de Bac. And I was quite positive that none of them had ever been affiliated with international spying. With skill, I navigated through the alley-like avenues, brushed past terrified civilians, dunked from being shot at, and ...

A coal-black 650i X-drive BMW convertible pulled out of a side street and blocked my way, stopping in front of me. There, smiling from ear to ear, grinning wildly at me, Louis Bentrider, Agent 313, winked at me, and called out, "Need a lift, sexy?"

I jumped into the convertible and Bentrider shifted the vehicle into drive. Within seconds, we zigzagged out of the city, escaping Cassel and his men.

Bentrider was known for his impeccable driving skills. The NYC guy made a living at escaping bad boys. Rarely, if ever, did he end up in such predicaments as I. Perhaps, he was the better spy, but I was sexier. Now, don't get me wrong, Bentrider was extremely good looking with his semi-amber eyes, tight jawline, perfectly coiffed cocoa-brown hair, and his five-eleven build, but I was hotter. The thirty-two year old could melt a cartel of gun-rearing drug dealers or nuclear weapons traders, but not like me. Bentrider lacked a suave nature and sometimes came across as being robustly prickish. Business always came before pleasure regarding his international tasks. Never did I hear about or witness a tale regarding his chiseled and naked body tied up to a bed in a French Basin bedroom.

"No surprise that you're almost naked, Agent G," he shared, calling over to me.

"It was an ugly situation, but enjoyable. Cassel decided to tie me up and take advantage of my skin."

He laughed in an arrogant manner. "That must have been absolutely horrible for you."

I said nothing in return. Sometimes you just had to let Bentrider enjoy his own gig. Instead, I removed the Stetson from my head, admired it, and saw that a bullet had pierced its top, creating quite the hole. I was thwarted with the discovery, realizing the prized hat was forever damaged.

Bentrider laughed at my loss. At the top of his voice, zooming toward the vineyards and villas of France, he called out, "Forget the hat, guy! You could have been killed back there!"

He was right. I could have been easily murdered by Cassel and his men. In celebration of my life, I tossed the Stetson over my right shoulder, outside the coupe, and left it blow away, into the city's narrow street behind us.

"We need to get you some clothes, man." He checked out my cowboy goods with delight: broad shoulders, rippled stomach, and dented navel. "You've been working out."

"Our agency keeps me busy. I haven't lifted weights in months."

"Impressive, my friend."

Bentrider and I had never slept together, but I often wondered if he wanted to. Occasionally, I caught him looking at me in a rather unprofessional and alluring manner. Business was business, though, and it was a line he never crossed. Not once did he graze one of his fingertips over my solid abs or a pointed nipple. Never did he outstretch his tongue to the treasure trail beneath my dented navel.

"What is the plan, chap?" I inquired.

He rattled off, "First, we get you some clothes. I haven't had sex in four weeks and ... you're looking quite irresistible, if you want to know the truth."

It was my turn to laugh. "You're a tease, Bentrider. We both know you're all talk."

He shook his head, shined with an all-white smile, and called out to me, "One of these days, I'll surprise you, man. You'll totally be caught off guard by my advances."

"I highly doubt that, but give it your best try."

# # # # #

Our travels together took us to Villa Rosa in Saint-Denis, which was north of Paris. Agent Bentrider had a personal vendetta to carry out, which was why he had returned to Paris and temporarily ended his sexual adventures with his Brussels lover. It wasn't just to save my ass from Cassel's naughty passion, among other less desirable tactics. Bentrider's task was simple: he wanted revenge on Stefano Marseilles. Long story short: Stefano betrayed Bentrider three months ago in Menorca, the small island off the coast of Spain. The man was to exchange information for money with Bentrider regarding Muhammad Pandel, a high-ranking terrorist leader of the Jihad, a nasty group of hell-raising fundamentalists who practiced Islamic aggression. Bentrider did not get the information he desired and Stefano thieved the money from our agency. Bottom line: Bentrider was not above cutting one's throat and hiding a body. International games were sometimes carried out with barbarian skills, which we both possessed. Stefano was in Bentrider's line of fire and on the man's kill list. Rumor had it that Stefano was temporarily using the Villa Rosa as a hideaway, but not for long, if it was up to my American sidekick.

The French countryside was drenched in summer heat. Not a cloud wafted above our heads. Upon arriving at the villa, I was dressed in a newly purchased pair of chinos, leather sandals, and short-sleeved T-shirt. The shirt was a size too small and defined every inch of crafted muscle on my porn star-like chest. Kudos to me that I looked sexy as hell, almost edible, and certainly fuckable.

Bentrider was incognito, dressed as my big-breasted, pantsuit-sporting bride-to-be. His makeup was heavy and his aroma was overtly floral. Our task was elementary and could easily be executed in my opinion. We were going to play the lost American couple in search of the Eiffel Tower. I would do all the talking and Bentrider (Beatrice Rider as I would call her) would play the quiet, reserved, and introverted fiancé from Chicago. After wooing Stefano's wait staff, finding ourselves inside the villa, I intended to seduce the man (Who didn't love a sexy cowboy from Texas?), leaving Beatrice with the wait staff in the villa's mudroom where he/she could enjoy a glass of afternoon wine from the surrounding vineyards. The rest of the plan was not fully developed between my temples, but I was a spur-of-the-moment kind of spy-guy who worked well under pressure. To sedate Stefano was my intention. I would not murder him, of course. That deed was desired in full by Agent Bentrider, which he would perform quickly and without flaw.

Twenty minutes later, the blueprint of our dangerous task was carried out with efficiency. Queer Stefano immediately took notice of my American sexiness and fell for my Texas build, drawl, and manners. As I lightly flirted with him over a glass of Chablis, he escorted me through the villa, showing off its French paintings and modern furniture. A tour was executed from room to room. In doing so, I consumed his piercing, emerald-colored eyes, gleaming bald head, coiffed goatee, and his broad shoulders. I guessed his weight at 180 pounds and estimated his height at six feet. His meaty shoulders tapered to a narrow waste, tight ass, and thick thighs.

An upstairs stairwell led us to a private patio at the top of the villa. There, we overlooked the French countryside and grape vineyards: pruners, coteaux, and grand cru. The heat was intense but enjoyable and soothing. The patio had a slate floor and was decorated with two lounge chairs with comfortable looking cushions. There, Stefano became forward, faced me, pressed one palm to my cowboy-chest, breathed me in, and explained in his thick French, "I want you, Dallas Rune."

I devised the name with crafty skill, borrowing it from my West Point roommate who just happened to enjoy getting rammed by the nine-inch meat between my legs. "I knew that as soon as you looked at me," I admitted, playing the romantic, knowing that Stefano had every intention of pealing me out of my clothes.

"We have very much in common."

Indeed, we did. More than he knew. Both of us were spies. Both of us were queer with erections. And both of us were sexy as hell with secret objectives. I moved his hand down and over my built chest, allowed it to graze my tight navel, and fall southward, against my private part, which was fully swollen and ready for his use, without my fiancé in the mudroom knowing.

FOUR – AGENT G, UNCLOTHED

A relentless, sexual desire spiked between our bodies and we kissed on the villa's secret patio. The Frenchman's right hand rubbed my inflated cock in a north and south motion, over my chinos. His sexual longing heightened within seconds and he asked in a rather direct manner, "I want you to fuck me."

I played foolish husband-to-be and inquired, "What about my fiancé in the mudroom?"

Stefano pulled my chinos down, discovered that I wasn't wearing underwear, admired the nine inches of upright cock between my hairless thighs, and chanted, "*Ce sera notre petit secret.*" It will be our little secret.

What transpired between us was rather brazenly unexpected. Before I could respond, the Frenchman stripped us out of our clothes. Our mouths connected numerous times. His ten-inch cock kissed my nine-inch one. Our ripped stomachs grazed together, fell apart, and grazed together again. Passion was discovered without limits as I was pulled to one of the lounge chairs. Stefano dropped on the piece of outdoor furniture and yanked me down with him. In a matter of seconds I was parallel to his body, swapping kisses and having our rods and stomachs mingle.

"Fuck me, Dallas," he demanded, spreading his legs for my pounder's access to his hairless asshole. "Ram your American cock inside me."

Truth was I could have knocked him out with a head-butt at that prime moment, and then Bentrider could have done whatever he wanted to accomplish to or with the spy. Instead, I decided to tamp such a fowl action for the time being and discovered a selfish and sexual desire for his nakedness. While climbing off him, I studied his flesh from head to toe and found it unbelievably attractive: hairless chest and cock and balls; sculpted abs; no tattoos; cut shaft between veined thighs. I licked my lips with a certain man-craving for him, greedily grinned to have sex with the bad boy, and inquired, "Do you have a condom?"

"In my shorts, cowboy."

Of course. Why didn't I look there to begin with?

I found the plastic, covered my nine inches with it, and moved up to my target, ready for some heavy duty man-play.

# # # # #

Stefano was on his back and stared up at me with a horny twinkle in his eyes. Positioned on my knees, having all of my nine inches inside his cozy man-hole, I slid in and out of his system. Heat built between our bodies. Moans and groans filled the patio area and beyond. Friction was discovered between his rump and my rod. Together we worked like XXX stars, swinging to and fro in naked bliss, unleashing our sexual desires on each other.

My thick post corrupted his bottom. In doing so, I grasped my hands around his ankles and separated his legs to have access to his puckered asshole. My thrusting to his rump was rapid and uncontrolled. A synchronicity between the two could not be found because I was far too excited to jam my dick inside his core, remove it, and continue that in-and-out process for the next twenty minutes.

Stefano became my toy with such ease. Lust was discovered without conditions. "Grab my cock, Dallas," escaped his mouth, begging to control my swinging body overtop him.

I listened. Why not? What did I have to lose? The man wanted me as much as I wanted him. My hands found the post between his legs and began to maneuver its veined skin in a jerking action. Swift and concurrent strokes ensued. The motion was persistent and exactly what he desired.

"Faster, Dallas. Jack it faster."

Again, I listened. The man was helpless under my touch. As my hips rocked into his center, both of my palms were frisky on his cock and worked its movable skin in an up and down motion. The fists clenched his ten inches of veined dick and wouldn't let the appendage go. Haphazardly wicked movement was processed. Two north and south juts turned into a dozen ... two dozen ... three dozen jerks. The man bucked his weight upward, into my palms. His hips rose and fell with speed. Sweat bubbled on his hairless chest and forehead. A whimper of fulfillment escaped his pursed lips. The man's eyes were closed, and his body began to shiver under my touch. I commanded down at him, "Blow, man. Show me what you've got," knowing that he couldn't keep his cargo pent for another second.

"Soon," escaped his mouth. More lifts occurred to his excess skin with my fists as he fucked my fingers and palms. The bad boy's eyes fluttered open, became wide, and ...

A string of white spew spiraled out of his crank and washed my torso, splatting against my nipples, abs, navel, and the pubic triangle between my legs. His goo clung to my skin, decorating my body's flesh. Spunk hung on my pecs, sticking to their muscular skin.

Bang after heated bang transpired on his tight bottom. My wrists actually stung from holding his ankles. Pump followed by steady pump was carried out. But honestly, it was his explosion that was a total turn-on for me. One of my weaknesses was watching a dude come. There was something erotic about studying a man as he shivered, ready to explode his sap. I was always left breathless, numb, and quite dizzy because of such an event. Add the friction that built between the French spy's ass and my dick and ... I was ready to expel my own load, all over the man.

I huffed and puffed, thrust my weight into him, pulled out, did that a dozen or more times, profusely sweated, bounced my balls off his ass, and eventually called out, "Now!"

One quick jerk backwards released my shaft from his narrow man-hub. The condom was lost on the patio and I wrapped my left hand around my bolt. Then I shifted it east and west a few times for the next ... twenty ... thirty ... forty seconds, until I was ready to shoot my seed all over the plane of his chest.

White and gluey ooze garnished the man's torso. I filled his concave-structured navel, lathered his pecs with the goop, and fired strings of my spunk against his nipples, furry chin, and his left cheek. The man-burst that twirled out of my stick felt infinite. Pinwheels of gunk flew against his abdomen. A vat or more of my cowboy-fluid burst out of the joint between my legs and splattered against his skin, dousing him in my seed.

# # # # #

Spent and breathless, I fell on top of his reclined body. We kissed on the lounge chair, finishing the fiery sex-gig. Tongues twisted together as lips met. The man beneath me moaned with deep satisfaction, enlightened by my touch. Our chests stuck together by our exploded loads. Our still-stiff cocks were aligned with such ease. Relaxed, I lifted my right hand, collapsed it over the man's left shoulder, and tucked its powerful palm and fingers against his neck. A tight and quick squeeze occurred, which offered a hearty pinch, and he fell unconscious with ease, under my hand's spell; something I learned in the military years ago and performed with accuracy each time it was carried out.

Stefano was limp on the lounge chair, naked and in dreamland. His cock flopped between his thighs, deflated and uncut. His arms were spread out on either side of the lounge chair. He looked dead, but he wasn't. I had no reason to murder him; that was up to my friend and world-traveling spy, Bentrider.

My deed was done concerning Stefano, I determined. Bentrider could do what he wanted with the lying and thieving badass. Stefano would be passed out for the next hour, which gave my sidekick spy enough time torture, poison, or off him – whatever Bentrider had in mind to carry out with the man.

Standing over Stefano, I peered at his nakedness, and said, "Thanks for the fuck, pal. It was quick, hard, and sweet. Just how I like my men." Then I found my clothes, started to dress, and ... all hell broke loose in the villa.

FIVE – ON HIS KNEES

Fully dressed, spent and exhausted from my unexpected treat with the French spy, I exited the secret patio, leaving Stefano behind in his unconscious state. Within seconds I found my way downstairs, entered the mudroom, and ...

"Agent G, I'm thrilled you could join our little party," Cassel said in his broken English, grinning from ear to ear in a devious manner. He stood over Bentrider with his Colt .45, aiming the weapon at my partner's forehead. Three French goons stood behind him with their own weapons, ready for a war between nations.

Bentrider was completely unclothed, on his knees, and had his wrists bound in plastic behind his back. The man's feminine makeup was smeared and fear ebbed at the corners of his eyes. A helpless look of surrender floated about his face.

I winked at Bentrider and smiled. My stare told him: Don't worry, buddy. I have everything under control. I can take all four of these thugs with my eyes closed. We'll be out of this jam in a second or two. Leave it up to me. You save my life. I save yours. We make a great couple, don't we?

My attention was then drawn to Cassel. I winked at him, started to plan a speedy and safe escape between my temples for Bentrider and me, and persuasively asked my nemesis, "Cassel, I'm sure you missed me. Don't you want to kiss me?"

AGENT G: HIT IT AND QUIT IT
by R. W. Clinger

ONE – COCKED AND READY

"I do want to kiss you, Agent G," Cassel said, aiming his Colt .45 at my muscled chest. "But first, my men need to release some of their sexual frustrations on your adorable friend here."

I looked down at my spy buddy Bentrider and found him handsomely stunning and eye-awakening, even if his heart was taken by a Russian violinist with the biggest cock. Agent 313's looks had improved over the years, and he was more steamy than ever: thirty-two years old, semi-amber eyes, tight jawline, perfectly coiffed cocoa-brown hair, five-eleven build, and a seven-inch cock that was limp between his legs. His chest was cut with freshly pumped abs and pecs. Above the agent's deflated slab of meat was a nicely trimmed triangular area of pubic hair.

I licked my lips while consuming such details but knew it was for a hopeless cause since he already had a boyfriend. Another wink told him that I wouldn't allow Cassel's three jug heads to hurt his ass, even if they were in the process of unzipping their green military pants and releasing firm tools from their hidden cotton at that very moment.

Cassel (six-three, nail thin, onyx-colored mustache, matching eyes, rugged jaw, and a Parisian-sloped nose) was dressed in all-black from head to toe. He still aimed his gun in my direction and yelled out in French to his three partners, *"Avoir votre chemin avec lou les homes."* Have your way with him, men.

The French trio stepped up to my naked partner. One pretty boy swung his uncut ten-inches from left to right, ready for some out-of-line man-action with Bentrider. A red-headed cutie said something in French that I couldn't interpret. The third assailant, who looked a little bit like an older Zac Efron, pushed my pal's face down to the cobblestone floor, spread Bentrider's legs apart, and decided to slap his nine-inch cock against my friend's bottom.

Bentrider had tears in his eyes, which instinctively told me it was time to react, and fast. My intense stare told the man to hang in there, that I was definitely going to help him. In my back pocket was something called a spew inside a Waterman pen. One click to the pen and a cloud of gas could be released from its slender tube and fill the mud room, which in turn would help us in our escape. Quickly, I reached for the pen, brought it to my center, held it out, clicked its raised tip, and tossed it toward Cassel, his three assailants, and Agent 313.

Within seconds, I bolted across the mud room as it filled with argon and promptly rescued my naked sidekick from the floor. We dashed out of the mud room, into the sunlit driveway, and jumped into Bentrider's coal-black 650i X-drive BMW convertible, which was parked outside the villa. As gunshots fired all around us, I found the vehicle's keys in my rear pocket, produced them, twisted them into the ignition, and sped away from Villa Rosa in Saint-Denis, blowing up a dust storm behind us.

Not a mile later, we were surrounded by the French militia group called Les Guerriers (The Warriors), which I knew was operated by Jacques Cassel. As a dozen or more rifles aimed at us in the BMW, Bentrider and I raised our arms, surrendering to their ambush.

# # # # #

Almost twenty-four hours later, after being abducted by Cassel's rough and tumbled men, slapped and questioned about a flash drive holding valuable information concerning the sales of nuclear arms, I sat in an underground French cell beneath Paris and stared at a massive, big-chested bear with hazel eyes, a white buzz cut, muscular shoulders, chest of steel covered in blond fur, and thighs that resembled tree trunks. Dorian was the man's name, a German thug who worked for Cassel. He eyed me up and down with sexual hunger in his eyes, licked his lips, and said, "You now under my care, Agent G. I highly say you get comfortable."

The cell was comprised of stone and steel bars. Two steel beds were on either side of the ten-by-ten foot room. A sink and toilet sat against the center wall. Water dripped out of the sink's spigot and into a ceramic bowl. To escape such confines, I could have easily found the courage and strength to bash the bad boy's skull against the corner of the steel bed and send him into a state of unconsciousness. Then I could have removed the set of cell keys from one of his pockets, used a key in the cell's lock, and discovered my freedom again. That plan could wait a few minutes, though, since I knew my handsome and alluring captor had something up his foreign sleeve to entertain me. Therefore, I stayed seated, waited for his show to begin, or whatever he had in mind to process with me, and inquired, "My friend … where is he?"

"Upstairs. No harm done to him … yet."

"Where are we?"

"Paris. Deep under The Louvre. Hidden." Dorian grinned from ear to ear. He stood from his bed and showed off his Herculean size. The man's nipples were like saucers and his chest was as large as the front of an Army tank. Dorian sported a snug pair of green shorts, white booty socks, and mountain climbing boots. I determined his height at six-four and his weight at 220 pounds of all beefy muscle.

Honestly, I didn't get off on bears, but he was rather tasty to take in with my perfect vision. The sexy bear was a rock solid piece of mass, all man, and just happened to have an adorable face to go with the rest of his package. I sensed he was horny for my American cowboy looks: six-one frame, 190 pounds, clean shaven cheeks, blond buzz cut hair and matching sideburns, and mega-ripped from working as a U.S. spy for almost a decade. Had I taken my snug shirt off he could have studied my washboard stomach and blond treasure trail, two firm and suntanned nipples on my bronze chest, and my torso's V-cut shape from always staying active. I admit in a rather arrogant manner, I was something to look at. Rarely did a queer guy (and straight men, if the truth be known) turn down my spy-goods for their sexual needs. My magnetism was unyielding and very much like a superhero's. I could down the most powerful and dangerous men on the planet with a mere seductive wink, a glinting smile, or by merely taking off a tight tee. No wonder Dorian was into me. Hell, if I was in a Parisian cell with myself, I'd want to fuck me, too.

But, Dorian didn't want to fuck me, I conceived. He had other things on his mind: a solo act with the massive and throbbing club in his green shorts. Standing across the cell from me with his legs slightly spread and his right palm splayed over the center of his bearish stomach, he said to me in his thick German accent, "You watch."

I was a smartass by nature, particularly when I was being held captive by other international spies and their sexy, bearish men. "I love to be a voyeur."

The hulking beast of a man didn't understand what I said, seemed to ignore me, and continued with his gig. He simply instructed me, "Take shirt off."

I listened, removing the tight tee from my chiseled torso and dropped it to the cell's floor. Why not? I could kick his ass with or without the shirt on. "Now what?"

"You watch, American cowboy."

American cowboy. I loved those two words. Guys around the world seemed to always drop at my feet because of the pair. How many times had they gotten me laid because of their mysterious sexiness? Too many to count. A grin surfaced on my pretty boy face, and I watched Dorian at work in front of me, knowing that he was going to jack his beef for both of our pleasures, since he found my Texas skin likeable, a turn-on for his German desires.

"Let show begin," my captor said, unzipped his green shorts, yielded no underwear, and yanked out his twelve inches of beef from its sleeping triangle of tangled and blond pubic hair.

My mouth fell open with surprise and my eyes widened in shock. The uncut mass in his right palm was over two inches wide. Thick, purple-red veins decorated the tool's length. Its tip was lathered in white pre-ooze, an unexpected and minimal burst that I believed had occurred while I removed my tee and dropped it to the cell's floor. Beneath the man's swollen cock were his balls: blond and hairy sphere-shaped masses that I estimated to be the size of grenades.

I gasped in astonishment. What sane spy wouldn't have at the sight of the German's massively inflated tools? I had taken on many bad boys in my days as a United States spy, creeps with the most powerful weapons used against me, atomic warheads, biological test tubes filled with the nastiest shit, and an arsenal of high-powered guns. Never had I taken on a piece of meat the size of Dorian's cock between his massive thighs. Ten inches? Yes. Eleven? Of course. But twelve inches of masculine tool? Never. Not even close. My ass was tight, and maybe not ready for the massive tool. But what the hell, right? Life was short. Play hard.

Intrigued, startled, and brave, I clearly said to my abductor, "Do your thing. I'm ready."

He did do his thing. Dorian grabbed his dick with two fists, began to stroke the mass up and down, grunted and groaned, and worked the excess skin on the device with some roughness and energetic motion.

I was entranced, mesmerized, and blown away. It was like watching a naughty, Colt DVD at my Dallas ranch. Dorian was incredible to study as he cranked the meat between his legs in a swift and steady north and south motion. Elation surfaced within my middle, pre-ooze leaked out of my own dick, and a buzz of masculine splendidness circled between my temples. In truth, I was turned on by the German's work.

He bucked his fists with his thick hips. He arched his back as he jacked his twelve-inch dick and murmurs escaped the massive man. Sweat flew off the German's forehead and chest as he spanked his pole. His palms and fingers were wicked on the meat between his ripped thighs. One tug followed by a dozen more ensued, and Dorian growled with contentment.

I admit, a chub had formed between my legs. Nine inches came to life and pre-spunk leaked out of its tip and coated my shorts. Elation rippled through my center and ...

Honestly, it was hard not to unzip my shorts, remove the post from its cotton cove, and begin to stroke myself off while watching the German at work. Both of us could be international jack buddies. And both of us could get off while watching each other toy with our meaty tubes. Such nonsense didn't occur, though. If I wanted to escape the cell, it was imperative to have my shorts completely buttoned and my mind on the danger at hand, not on self-pleasure. Consequently, I tapped off the urge to massage the engorged manness between my legs and simply watched the bad boy carry out his sexual act, attempting to reach his bliss.

What a sight it was to witness Dorian in motion, I confess. How drastic his movement was: sharp, electrifying, and nonstop. His hips pumped the pair of fists with unlimited speed. The man's bulky chest rose and fell as he robustly inhaled and exhaled. Perspiration glistened on his shoulders, cheeks, and chin, glazing his German skin. The captor's balls swung between his thighs, smacking against his muscular legs.

"Blow, man," I called out to him, into his gig. Uncomfortably, I sat across from him and admired his diligent work. Hard as steel between my own legs, I only wished to join the badass and his handy work. To no avail, though, I was his prisoner, not his friend, a spy in a spy game that was global, and I needed to escape that ugly, yet dick-rising occasion.

"Coming," he grunted, continuing to buck his hips into his massive fists, getting himself off.

Would Agent 313 believe what was transpiring in the cell somewhere beneath him in his captive room? I imagined so. He knew of the many sexual events that transpired during the past years. Cassel, Michelangelo Totani from Venice, Raaj Dunbi from Dubai, and Carlos Mantiban from Mexico City were just a few of the men that I had shared sexual encounters with throughout the years. Some I had enjoyed to the fullest. Others, not so much. Bentrider was a one man's man and really didn't like to fornicate with such naughty broncos of the expansive world except for his sexy violinist. I, on the other hand, was sort of a spy slut who enjoyed the naked company of guy pals any time I could, no matter what the unpredictable and dangerous situation entailed.

Dorian grew a robust shade of red in his face, huffed and puffed for air, pumped his hips upward, and continued to jack his meat in a swift and concurrent motion. Within seconds he finally burst his load out of his erection and splattered it all over the cement floor between us. Puddles decorated the floor. Gunk pooled between his legs and approximately three feet away from my position. Never had I seen so much goo erupt from a man's tool. How shocking it was to witness such an event as his cream arced out of the dick between his thighs and flooded the floor.

I was feeling drained for him. The sight was exhausting to watch, and quite uncomfortable for me since I was bone-hard between my legs. The moment prompted a horny feeling to skirt throughout my core and to come. I kept my composure together, though. Escape was near; I just had to determine when the right time was available to do so.

The German's sexual labor was complete. He was spent with his hands still wrapped around his tube of protein. A washed-out look surfaced on his sweaty face and mixed with his post-sexed smirk that I considered wildly treacherous. The giant man's chest heaved up and down as he searched for oxygen, exhausted from his work.

"Nice job," I said sarcastically, grinning from ear to ear. "You should jack me off like that."

Dorian shook his head, unsmiling now. "Lick up," he said, removed his left hand from his still-steel post, and pointed at the man-goop on the cement floor between us.

My eyes scanned the semi-limp package that had slowly started to deflate between his legs, then the puddle of his white ooze on the cell's floor. Yes, I enjoyed the occasional spew-meal produced by the sexiest badass. What queer spy didn't? But, I was not about to lick it off the dirty, cement floor in a Parisian prison cell. Removing such sticky splendor from a ripped stomach or swollen pecs was more my speed. Lapping up a sticky mess from a hairy navel was euphoria for me. Dipping my tongue into a pond of man-ooze from a man's torso was total bliss. But to accomplish such a task within a disgusting, foreign jail cell was not something I thought plausible.

Thank God Cassel arrived at the cell before I rejected the German's offered seed on the cement floor. Never had I been so fortunate to see the French spy and his nicely built bod. Cassel unlocked the cell, pointed his Colt .45 at me, entered the small area and ...

His right foot slipped on the German's gunk. The Frenchman's right leg rose from the floor as he lost his balance, plummeting to the cement plane beneath him. In doing so, he accidentally fired off his handgun. One bullet whizzed over the German's head and punctured the cell's cement wall behind Dorian. The second bullet nailed Dorian in his right shoulder, which immediately dropped the massive blond bear to the cell's floor, stunning him. Cassel lost a grip on his handy Colt and the gun spun in three circles across the floor, away from him, and the pool of Dorian's stinky jiz.

Within seconds, noting that both men were down, I did what any American spy would do. I snatched up Cassel's gun, bolted out of the cell, and went in search of my imprisoned spying partner, Bentrider.

TWO – MY SPY-COCK ONLY BELONGS TO YOU

I found my way down a narrow hallway of cement cells, up a flight of steps, two flights, and entered a room with six cells, just like the one I had escaped from minutes before. In the far-left cell numbered SIX, Bentrider was naked, on his knees, and badly beaten. Agent 313 looked like a gay bashing victim. His eyes were a raw black, his upper lip was split and puffed, and his jaw looked crooked. By the deep and bloody notch in his nose, I determined it was broken.

Between the two of us stood a French guard with gray eyes, wide shoulders, and a pumped chest. The guard and I spotted each other at the same time. The man was not pleased to see me and instantly removed a sleek and black 800px Max 50 from his right hip. As shots were fired in my direction, I fell to the floor and rolled. My life flashed before my eyes: returning to Dallas; falling in love with a rodeo champion; marrying the guy; honeymooning in Australia; retiring from my spying games; buying a horse ranch, settling with the rodeo champion, and …

Hurriedly, I came to and popped three shots at the guard by using Cassel's gun. Pop! … Pop! … Pop! The guard dropped to the cement floor. Within seconds, I removed a ring of silver keys from the left pocket of his navy uniform pants. Next, I rushed up to Bentrider's cell, tried a dozen or more keys in the cell's lock, and told Agent 313, "Don't worry, pal … I'll get you out of here."

Bentrider gave me an exhausted look of hurt and slumber, tried to smile, but couldn't because of all his facial bruises. Instead, he simply mumbled, "I was waiting for you. Glad you could make it."

# # # # #

Not even ten minutes later and Bentrider was out of the cell numbered SIX. Thereafter, we scavenged for guard clothes for him to wear: boots, a hat to conceal the damage caused to his face, and a cotton shirt. Before the both of us knew it, we were on a train and heading to Brussels.

The train ride was one hour and twenty minutes long from Paris to Brussels. Once in the capital of Belgium, we took a cab to the Hotel de Ville, checked into two rooms, paid with credit cards, and used our real names. Having that accomplished, we left the hotel, traveled across the city, and ended up in Bentrider's boyfriend's flat that overlooked the Senne River.

Upon our arrival at the flat, Agent 313 passed out from his Cassel bashing, but was caught in Hector Rumankov's arms, Bentrider's Russian violinist and boyfriend. There he was safe, unharmed, and cared for with Hector's help and much affection.

For the next three nights, Bentrider and I stayed with Hector at his flat. There we ate, relaxed, and mended from our dangerous adventures in Paris with Cassel and his brutish team. Undiscovered at the flat, we kept a running tab at the Hotel de Ville for our two bogus rooms. If Cassel or other worldly spies wanted to find us, the fake occupancy at the hotel would deter their laborious searches but only temporarily.

Bentrider was happy to be back in his man's arms. When the two decided to bump and grind together in a naked dance, which occurred often, I left the flat and discreetly toured the Belgium city. My travels took me to the Grand Place with its many exquisite churches and houses; the Place St-Géry with its restaurants and quaint atmosphere; Waterloo, the city's old castles and monasteries; the *Manneken Pis* statue; and the Palace of Justice. I ate *waterzooi* (fish stew), thick waffles, eel and vegetables, and lard balls. At night I visited a queer bar called The Boudin (Pork) Place. Sexy and alluring Belgium men approached me at the bar, but I ignored them. I was simply there to have an alcoholic beverage and enjoy the foreign sights, not to get laid. So many of those horny Brussels men wanted a piece of my American cowboy ass. No less than ten – Lucas, Anan, Rayan, Nathan, Vlinder, Clark, Gabriel, Vos, Wolf, and Blade – insisted that I should return to their flats with them, just so they could have their naked and naughty ways with my Texan good looks.

To no avail, on my third night spent in Brussels, I escaped the queer bar unharmed, found my way through the streets and returned to Hector's flat. Once there, I enjoyed a cup of tea and the flat's silence. But not even seven minutes into my period of relaxation and my new phone buzzed at my hip.

To silence the noise, I immediately grabbed the device, took the call, and listened to a familiar male's voice on the other line say, "Agent G, I saw you tonight at The Boudin Place ... and I want to see more of you."

A horny and robust smile formed on my face as a wave of testosterone circulated through my middle. My sexual longing for the post-midnight caller caused an immediate boner to come to life between my legs. "Toby McDade. The pleasure is all mine."

"Indeed it is, American man. How long are you in Brussels?"

"I cannot disclose that information."

"Of course. My skills as a spy are not as keen as your own."

"They surely are ... or you wouldn't have reached me, Toby." I cleared my throat, nervous to speak with him again. "Now, tell me where you are."

"The Atomium ... waiting for you."

I replied without even thinking, "I'll be there in fifteen minutes. Don't leave."

"Of course not, my friend. My spy-cock only belongs to you."

# # # # #

My history with the Irish spy lacked anything mundane. We were not enemies, but sometimes we acted as such. Approximately two years ago we met in Amsterdam. Our business there was mutual: we were watching Candor Miles, a wicked Brit with loads of money. Candor was a billionaire and lunatic. His pastime was designing lethal bacteria and spreading his concoctions globally. Toby's duty to his country was the same as mine: to off Candor and the slick bastard's high-ranking men, one by one, in the most discreet manners. The job was a deathly game between Toby and me. We fought regularly over one sniper hit and then a dozen ... until we combined our forces and our naked bodies in private. I was Toby's secret lover for six months during our pursuit of Candor and his team of bad boys. When Toby and I were not plinking off the chemical freaks, we were naked and compressed together. Lust had discovered us.

No, I didn't fall in love with the Irishman, and nor did he fall in love with me, but we did enjoy our bare cocks touching, among other unclothed body parts. We were temporary lovers who shared international sex – exactly what queer spies accomplished together in their free time, of course.

I hadn't seen Toby in almost thirteen months and desired the smell of his red hair and freckled skin. There was something about an Irishman that left me weak, dizzy, and wish to be next to his flesh. I longed for the sexy leprechaun's eight-inch, uncut shaft between his pale and muscular thighs. Desire for the man's emerald-colored eyes, pink lips, and five-eleven frame was limitless, I admit. Again, I wanted to be close to his 180 pounds of all muscle, naked, rubbing together, and fully intoxicated by his foreign goods.

Yes, I left the lovebirds (Bentrider and Hector) behind in the flat. A secret and enchanting night with the Irishman was at hand, which was exactly what I needed. Nothing seemed like a better idea. Quietly, I made my way to the Atomium, found myself near one of its base structures, and discreetly stood in the bluish-white streetlight.

Within a matter of minutes, I was put in a headlock by someone positioned behind me. My neck could have easily been twisted, causing an early demise. My left earlobe was grazed by the man's lips and tongue. And his voice filled my left ear canal with: "The pleasure this evening is all mine, Agent G. I can't tell you how much I've missed you." An erotic and spine-numbing kiss was applied to the back off my neck. The man's palms held solid at my sides, unmoving and with much pressure.

"Toby," I whispered into the Brussels night, "I was dying to see you."

"I hope more than that," he said, brushing his lips against the length of my sultry and sweet neck, breathing on its smooth skin.

"I guess you'll just have to spin me around and find out."

That he carried out. Now, face to face with the man, he leaned into my lips with his own, caressed the sets together, shared a light moan of pleasure, and pulled away. "I could have killed you if I wanted."

"You like me far too much to kill me. I prefer if you kiss me instead."

"Your wish is my command, Agent G, as always."

"Where do you intend to fuck me?" I asked, getting to the point, knowing that he had nothing more challenging in mind.

He snagged my right hand within his left one, walked me away from the world-known Atomium above us, and led me astray, into the night ... exactly how I wanted our evening to be carried out.

THREE – TOUCH ME ... I KNOW YOU WANT TO

We walked through a set of hip-brushing hedges, across a cobblestone street lined with a variety of bars and other businesses. The silver-blue moonlight escorted us down a narrow alleyway that was shaded with a Draculan mysteriousness. Beyond the alleyway was a hidden courtyard between sky-reaching residential buildings. The courtyard was a mass of hedges, trees, and flowers which offered much privacy. Wrought-iron benches decorated that secret place like a Lewis Carroll tale. Very little light dove and weaved through the thick foliage; a perfectly secluded place within the city's heart for Toby to have his sexual and rather ungentlemanly way with me.

Facing him, having our chests locked together, I inquired, "You want the Sendal File, don't you?" I breathed the spy's hot scent into my heavy lungs, which caused me to grow hard between my legs, ready for some heated and diligent sexual work between our two naked bodies.

"Of course not. I only want you."

I sensed he was lying. Every man in our business wanted the Sendal file, which was a detailed synopsis of nuclear weapons being traded between Afghanistan and North Korea in the past thirty-sixth months, a zip drive of numbers, facts, and important names that the U.S. Government declared to have in their possession. Bentrider had the file back in Hector's flat. I was not about to expose such valuable (and lethal) information to the Irish spy, even if I adored his chiseled looks and suave nature. Instead, I simply suggested, "Kiss me, Toby," to steer him away from the topic of secret international spy games.

Toby listened; what a very good little sexy bitch of a spy he was. My white dress shirt was untucked from my expensive, Italian chinos. Then he peeled the shirt's buttons open, one by one in a playful and enthralling manner. The Irishman lathered my pecs with long and abrupt kisses. Nipples were fondled by his straying tongue. His hands discovered the abs on my stomach, which rolled their fingertips every so easily and fondly against my skin. The man's breathing was intense and on fire. Obviously he had missed me – and my nicely sculpted flesh – since we had last worked together. The man's hunger for my epidermis was unyielding. Poetically, he licked, lapped, and sucked at my torso, rolling his face along the plane of my chiseled chest.

I deemed his action lustful and unstoppable. Toby's desire for our bodies to mesh together was unfailing. The man moaned with pleasure as he swabbed my lined chest with his hunger. Numerous tongue-tastes occurred to my skin, and "Delicious," romantically spilled out of his mouth as he fell to his knees in the courtyard, discovering the belt buckle and the chino's zipper at my center.

# # # # #

In a matter of seconds the spy had all nine inches of my cut hose down the length of his tight throat. To keep my balance, I held his shoulders with firm palm-grips. Toby's head jostled to and fro as he sucked the tool at my center. My balls slapped against his chin a number of times as we glided in unequal motion. Repeatedly, I banged his face with the swollen meat, plowing into him with zest and a powerful mission. Together we functioned in a non-stop connection: my hips bashed against his face as his throat massaged the cut cock that fulfilled his spy-desire.

No, he did not pull off of my spike for air. Instead, like a bull, he huffed and puffed through his nostrils. Toby's current with his mouth and throat was swift and agreeable. Not once did his east and west blowing seize. The man was infatuated with his work, and my skin. And both of us clearly knew that our tryst within that secret cobblestone-littered courtyard was not about to end until I exploded my seed … everywhere.

When did he stop blowing me in the courtyard, rose from his knees, and found a solid position behind me? I wasn't sure, windblown and intoxicated because of his night's heated appetite. No one would have been sure in my bewildered position, of course.

"I want to jack you," he explained in my left ear, a mere whisper in the night that was as soft as the summer wind.

"I'm yours," I replied. "Do what you want with me."

"Because you're safe with me."

"Of course. Now stop talking and crank away ... before we get caught here."

His action was very much like an XXX star's, willing to get me off. The man's breath was intense against my neck as he jacked my rigid pole up and down with his right palm and fingers. His labor was quite skillful and offered unlimited pleasure for me. Numerous cranks to the sweltering beef between my thighs occurred. Hip-thrusts to the spy's palm were rhythmic and heated. On fire, hitched by his hand and my cock, connected by his tongue to the length of my corded neck, blended by his solid chest against my back, we discovered euphoria together – a man-with-man episode of erotic lust in the European night.

The lumber between his legs, an estimated eight inches covered in Milan fabric, brushed against my bottom. It was impossible not to feel his cock against my rump, snuggled rather impolitely but fully enjoyed between my rear's solid orbs. And how daring he was to glide his material-covered stick against my bottom, turning himself on ... and inevitably turning me on at the same time.

Again and again his right grip allowed friction to build with my nine-inch cut cock. His touch glided the excess skin on my tool in a feisty and north and south motion, which caused me to moan with an eerie but enlightening sound that echoed within the Brussels' night. The spy jockeyed the stick between my legs in a hyper and pleasurable manner. One up and down motion yielded to dozens, which sent me into an inexorable spin of ecstasy.

"Almost," slipped out from between my lips, filling the night's soothing darkness.

"Come," he whispered in his thick Irish accent, brushing his lips against my right earlobe. "Don't keep it pent."

I heaved to and fro one last time. Sparks of erotic fire blazed throughout my core. A grunt escaped my lips and my huffing and puffing intensified. "Coming," was whispered within the night and ...

Spirals of sticky-white seed flew out of my spike and decorated the courtyard's cobblestone. Cream drizzled against his right hand as I emptied my core. The sap continued to twirl out of my solid hose in three long squirts, one after the next, and flew to the ground and our feet.

Limp against his still-clothed chest, I listened to him whisper in my ear, "You're such a good spy."

"You were unstoppable," I chanted in return.

"I was relentlessly desirous for you. It's been too long, Agent G."

As he removed his hand from my joint, I tugged up my chinos, buckled them, and began to button up my shirt.

Toby moved around my upright frame and faced me. With his hands firmly planted on my hips, he kissed me with tongue, plunging the organ down the back of my narrow throat. Once he came off of me for air, he brushed his cream-free palm through my hair, leaned into my left ear, and chanted, "Don't be a stranger in my life, friend. I adore you. You know that. There are so many men who want to take advantage of you, or kill you. Just know that I'm not one of them. You mean too much to me. I consider you my soul mate."

I was floored by his statements. Never had a man presented his heart to me in such a noble and aristocratic manner. Never had my knees wobbled with such passion because of his gentlemanly admission. Never had I ...

Before I could respond to his endearing confession, or kiss him again, Toby McDade had vanished from my side, leaving me alone in the mysterious courtyard with a wide smile on my face, and a pitter-patter of harbored lust within my ab-lined stomach for him ... until the queer gods of night decided to bring us together, again.

FOUR – HIT IT & QUIT IT

Following my sexual adventures with Toby in the secret courtyard near the Atomium, I found my way back to Hector's flat. Something told me it was not going to be a night of healthy sleep, of course. Thoughts of danger lurked within my spying mind, but I really couldn't place a thumb on it detailing why.

From the street, I saw that the flat's lights were out. I assumed Bentrider and his lover had shared some phenomenal queer sex together, became spent, and drifted into sleep, combined in each other's arms. A part of me wanted to leave them to their privacy and find a cheap hostel for the night. An uncanny emotion flushed throughout my body, though. Something was wrong. Peril waited in silence.

Cautiously, I made my way into the building, up the stairs, and entered the flat. Upon my arrival, the sound of a handgun clicked, identifying that it was cocked and ready to be fired. A light flicked on and golden-white illumination filled Hector's living room.

There on the floorboards, tied chest to chest, naked and looking quite petrified was Bentrider and his lover. Both desired my assistance and needed attention.

Standing over the pair was a sneering Cassel, the nasty spy from Paris. He waved a Beretta m9 at Agent 313 and Hector, and said, "Agent G, you just can't hit me and quit me, can you?"

I noticed the flash drive in Cassel's free hand, which he tucked away in one of his shirt's pockets. Again, he was in control, but not for long. A spy such as me always had something up his sleeve, right? I was a professional man that knew I could take him down, without having any blood on my hands.

Cassel winked at me, always attracted to me, and desired no other man in our rough business except for me.

I winked back, unbuttoned my shirt, pulled it off, dropped it to the floor, and displayed off my sculpted chest for his pleasure. Then I unzipped my chinos, pulled out my semi-hard cock for the man's insatiable use, and said in a cocky manner, "It's me you want, Cassel. Let Bentrider and his lover go. Let's handle this like real men. Just the two of us ... naked."

THE EDITOR

ERIC SUMMERS resides in West Palm Beach, Fla., and has been on a secret mission for years.

earing any underwear. "Excuse me," I said, having a hard time loo
linded by that bulge in his crotch, "but don't I know you?" "Mayb
ind of t   bout
with Ray   God,
t loser?   in?"
aid. "Lik   s stror
ce body   e on (
lly, he l   I eve
u up to t   any id
istaking   ne san
n, I coul   ery lo
ood raci   ne sw
ing with   e in s
we go   behir
ill see u   in pu
ed?" he   vent t
rivacy.   grabb
-hard. I
k, traci   t, so
ed it, ha
with m   bing
bbing, I   n coc
he sound of unzipping filled the small space. I don't know who's h
, but before I knew it, I had his rod in my hand, and mine was in h
nt to do?" he asked, his tone challenging. I knew exactly, and sank

www.ingramcontent.com/pod-product-compliance
Lightning Source LLC
Chambersburg PA
CBHW052017020726
47501CB00004B/1103